ACKNOWLEDGEMENTS

My gratitude goes to my mother, Mary, for proofing versions of the book and advising on the use of language. My thanks also to my friends and relatives – including Jacob, Sam, Chris and Simon - for their conversation, comments and encouragement. To David for the push and to Kris for the support and tea. To Mark Wilson and Geoff Walker in particular for their critical insight and feedback.

Thanks also to the many talented and innovative thinkers within the science community who, for little material reward, share their knowledge and perceptive hypotheses with clarity of thought and presentation in order to support the wider goal of broadening our collective understanding of the world around us. They are too numerous to list, but many are, in my opinion, truly inspiring and so influence profoundly my own ideas and writing.

Finally, but not least, thanks to my family for their enduring love and support.

PREFACE

Dual:Races is a thriller about the entangled lives of those with the power to change our future. There is a basic premise underlying the story; an inevitable and radical breakthrough in our understanding of the inter-relationship between quantum mechanics and the physical limitations of the human species will offer mankind the opportunity of avoiding our otherwise certain extinction from the Universe.

Note: There are various musical references – a playlist if you like – embedded in the story. I chose these songs because they somehow seem to encapsulate particular moments, and it might enrich the experience to listen to them as they come up. If you would like a full listing of these, get in touch and I will send a reference link. Contact details can be found at the end of this book.

DUAL: RACES

by **Tipton Froy**

Copyright 2020 Published by Tipton Froy

ISBN: 978-0-9575588-6-1

Cover illustration courtesy of

ESO/M. Kornmesser at:

https://www.eso.org/public/images/eso1328a/

This is a work of fiction. Characters and incidents are products of the author's imagination. Any resemblance to actual events or persons (living or dead) is entirely coincidental.

Contents

CHAPTER 1: NEW LIFE

A golden undulating ocean as far as the eye can see. The intense azure of the expanse nestling above is uniform and flawless. An incarnation of depth worthy of August Macke. Only a gentle breeze for sound. And a heartbeat.

Catherine Jumeau stands in a small clearing scanning the reeds in front of her. They form a somewhat unrelenting wall of slender guards that have closed ranks and point their spears skywards, sometimes swaying and scratching the sky.

No longer is this a place where her body is subject to the pedantic constraint of soporific motion enforced by the mass of syrupy glue rooting her to the ground. This place is now *her* place. The place where she comes daily to speak to Gill, to release her mind from the despair in her world, and to free herself from the limitations of physical form on Earth.

And even though Gill doesn't answer, she senses he is out there. She hopes that he might hear her; that he might gain courage and peace from the sound of her voice. From time to time, she registers a far away sound, a dim light, a change in air pressure, a change in temperature. All on the far side of the field. And she knows that this is another presence.

But at this time, in this place where there can be no time, she has another job to do.

—-

Ava Redmond, Head of Intelligence, is on the phone to Maria Ortega, Head of Homeland Security. The two have been liaising on a secret Intelligence Agency programme at Langley.

"So are we seeing any numbers coming through?" asks Ava.

"Well, she is in there now Ava and we'll know more in about an hour, or whenever she comes out".

"OK. I see Phil has OK'd the trace on the new duallist, is that right?"

"Uh-huh," Maria replies, "if this thing can scale then we'll need more tracers and the ability to bring the new guys over here - wherever they come from."

Ava pauses. "What happens if they are in China? or Russia? What then?"

"Yes, that will be a problem potentially." Ortega is thinking out loud. "We'll need to put them through the counter-intelligence review if they check out. It takes time though, and we'll need to be rigorous."

"Double-agents…" Redmond muses. "What's your assessment? I guess the world is a very different place right now".

"That's true," says Ortega. "Back when in sixty-two they thought the world was going to end and it didn't. There are always winners and losers."

Redmond is weighing up her thoughts. She gets the reference and ploughs on. "OK, Maria. We'll need to keep this level six for now. You'll talk to John?"

"Sure - he's up to date so far, and I think he sees it as strategically important as well as a tactical advantage. He asked me if other countries would be doing this, and I had to be honest; I have no idea."

Ava Redmond thanks Maria again, and the two close the call. In Redmond's office at Langley, she ponders the progress of the recruitment for the Covert Astral Transit (CAT) programme. They will need to ramp up the numbers if this is going to be sustainable, and yet she knows also that the power of just a few duallists may be strategically invaluable in coming weeks and months. She makes a note to call Phil Kirkland, now promoted to be in charge of CAT and Ava's most senior aide in understanding how the knowledge gained from the Garfield revelations can be deployed successfully in the current theatre of war against common, and uncommon, enemies.

—-

Christophe Jumeau walks down the corridor in section H9 of the Kepler Building, a small research annex in the West Area at Langley in Virginia. H9 leads to 'The Pod', a primary NASA/CIA utility that has been commandeered to host a series of twenty padded 'darkrooms' suspended from the ceiling, all equidistant by two metres, and all completely insulated from external sound, light, vibration and extraneous radiation, particulate or other sources of energetic interference. The only interlopers are highly inactive and chargeless neutrinos, which pass through innocuously by the millions every second.

Two air-force security personnel stand guard in front of a sign above one of the units. "Darkroom One' is the only room occupied at this time. The guards seem slim compared with the heavier-set Jumeau. Each is armed with an M16 assault rifle, even though they are inside the compound of one of the most heavily-secured locations in the United States. Jumeau considers what they expect may happen here; a massive influx of super-positioning aliens materialise in one of the units, barge out and run amok in Langley. It doesn't sound likely. His daughter, Catherine, inside Darkroom One gets into trouble when dualling, hits the panic button and needs medical or emotional support. More likely. Either way, the detachment is unlikely to be appropriate.

He approaches and asks in a hushed tone if all is OK. There is a nod. Catherine has been inside for about an hour, but with time somewhat meaningless at the cornfield, there is no telling how long that might be for her. The only reassurance available to anyone while Catherine duals is that her vital signs are visible via display outside the door to Darkroom One. These are fine, so although he is anxious, as always, he thanks the guards and turns towards H8 and then H6, at the end of which is his office.

H6 is a quiet and a little foreboding as corridors go. Exceptionally long and with few doors, implying huge spaces behind each one. At the very end, overseeing all, is a windowed office entrance with a small plaque which reads 'C. Jumeau - Senior Advisor, CAT Program'.

Following the revelations within the upper-echelons of U.S. government security regarding Garfield's identity, purpose and extra-terrestrial nature, a new strand of investigation - and thinking - has emerged within the White House. With Ellis Garfield and Walter Melrose both presumed dead, an entire line of research has potentially been lost. Christophe Jumeau, and his daughter Catherine, are the unlikely keys to understanding more about the nature of enhanced human capacities (EHC's) and the threat from alien lifeforms operating via wormholes.

Both are already exhausted from the weeks and months of questioning and 'information-sharing' which at times has felt more akin to torture. They both realise the importance of their experiences, and Mary Jumeau has moved down to Fairfax county to be with her husband and daughter, where all three now live and all three of whom now have been lucky winners of the Green Card Lottery.

Gone are the carefree University days and fun evenings out among the leafy lanes of Allston for Catherine. Gone are the girls' nights in with Wendy Xiu and friends with flowing wine, takeaway food and a good movie. All that seems like years ago to Catherine, yet it's only a few months. She misses Boston, and although she has visited Wendy and Mal in the meantime, it was different. She was a visitor and not a flatmate, and the whole Garfield kidnapping had changed both Wendy and Mal, both of whom seemed so much more restrained, still suffering from the trauma of the shootings at the warehouse. They were also subject to a gagging order and under surveillance by Homeland Security and Maria Ortega's people.

Gone is Professor Melrose too. Where, nobody knows, although everyone fears the worst. Months on, and no body, no news, no trace. And even if Walter Melrose had done some bad things, he was no monster. Strangely, Catherine, Wendy and Mal all craved for the Professor to come back and for their real lives to return. But this was a new world, and a new beginning for all of them. Each knew that their histories, and their futures would be defined not only by the events surrounding Melrose and Garfield, but by a new threat too.

And gone is Gill. Every day without him hurts for Catherine, and if time is a great healer, then it's not doing its job.

Of course there are the positives; she came through the ordeal with Nuvo and his monstrous entangled twin in one piece. Montgomery is alive and well, and seemingly oblivious to the fact that he *died*. The more she thinks about this side of things, and how much of Montgomery was fighting to overcome his absorption into Nuvo, the more she thinks that President Montgomery must realise, must be in touch with, an alternative truth from which he was spared. She is yet to meet with the President though, due to security concerns. They know now that Catherine is different. Has similar powers to Garfield. And there is a certain edge to the relationship between her and the U.S. government. On balance, her brain tells her that it is understandable. *Logical*. She rationalises that she is, in herself, being used as a tactical military device. Not a weapon, as yet. She has also decided for some very good reasons to keep some information to herself.

However, she wants to meet Montgomery, the man she and Gill fought so hard to save. If nothing else to look into his eyes and be reassured that this man is as human as she senses. She'd also like to ask him about what he can remember, if anything, about what happened in the cornfield. She saw him being released from Nuvo, and that it was Gill's sister Beth that somehow played a part in this. She saw how Garfield couldn't hold John Montgomery down, even after killing him, and how Montgomery's spirit and humanity tempered the wild selfishness of Garfield and Nuvo.

She can't figure which part of her journey is the strangest, but perhaps it is that she has witnessed an alien life form, in the shape of Nuvo. That alien life truly exists, and that they have some unique capabilities, at times incomprehensible by us here on Earth. How Nuvo morphed into Garfield was as disturbing as it was spectacular, and since then she has had nightmares, not just about weird alien lifeforms, but about the unknowns.

So many speculations have been through her mind. Wondering about the dark presence of Nuvo's twin, and the possible fate of Gill. About the wormhole she seems to control, and the possibility that there are others. Other wormholes, other duallists, other aliens, other everything. It can get overwhelming and in any other situation she would probably be on tranquilizers, but of course stoically she maintains a natural intake and exercises as much as she can to keep baby healthy. Not long now.

And this is the comfort, the main positive of all. She's with Gill's child, and will have to have a break soon to give birth. Something which perhaps many mums-to-be might be nervous about, but which for her will be a huge relief and a welcome distraction from CAT. Phase one of the Covert Astral Transit programme is taking up a lot of her time and energy, and after all the interrogation and information gathering by the Intelligence community, her work patterns are pretty hard by any standards for a woman who is 8-months pregnant.

But Dad is here. And Mom just down the road. This helps. Dad's running phase one of CAT operationally and both he and Catherine like Phil Kirkland, government lead for the programme. They have formed a good team, and are implementing plans from the ground up. If it works, then longer term this will be the way to find out the prevalence of dualling, and perhaps the degree of entanglement to be found globally. As far as Christophe Jumeau can make out, there is no logical reason why the wormhole that Catherine and Gill have created, and then found by Nuvo, could not be found by others. The key question is 'which others?'. CAT is a programme that needs people with the capacity to dual to work for the U.S. government in covert ops. For a start, those that can dual might not be suitable for such activity, and even if they can 'find' the wormhole in the first place they might not be able to dual from there accurately.

Catherine can't do much about the first, but she can certainly help those that come to the cornfield. In that environment, Catherine is now boss, and not only that; she can guide anyone who comes there to her own channel back to Langley, such is her command of dualling. Developing this command way more quickly than Gill, her powers at the wormhole seem to be growing. Several times she has elevated and 'drifted' across the field, high enough above to see how vast the expanse is relative to the clearing. At the outer edges of the field the sky darkens and the temperature drops dramatically. She has been close enough to the edge to witness glitches; sudden movement as if the sky is twitching, and then shimmering colours that sometimes form shapes. Shapes that can become bodies, faces, gestures. It's as if all the rules will change if you breach the boundary. While she is in charge inside the field, she suspects she'd be in trouble outside it. But the more her confidence grows, the more risks she takes, partly to find out what she can do, but partly in the knowledge that this is still the only likely route to Gill, wherever he is.

Early on in her visits there she would scream Gill's name so loudly that she felt her lungs would burst. Only once did a far away sound make her think that it could be a response. That broke a continuum of sadness that encapsulated her very being, for most of the time when she returned from dualling she would find she had been crying. But that one time was enough to give her a little glimmer of light in what was turning out to be a very long, and very dark, period of her life, in spite of her condition and being close to family.

Most frustrating in this space is the continual lack of routes out of the reeds opposite. This is worrying, and for months now this has been a constant. Even if she got to a birds-eye level - 'in flight' so to speak - it was clear that there were no pathways visible for either her to use, or for Gill to appear from.

But behind her, things were a bit different. As recorded in the CAT1 journal as 'Correlation 30-#3-000-01', Catherine reported that another gap in the reeds, which was not her own, was clearly visible. At first Catherine got excited by this, thinking that this might be Gill. But in fact, non-one appeared, and when she approached that gap, it closed quickly, as if in response to being observed.

Catherine and Gill had always moved *across* the clearing to the other side from them in order to dual to a new spacetime. And of course she *felt* Gill's sister Beth there, but where Beth had come from she didn't know. But could others come to the cornfield from the same side as Catherine? Well, why not? They would need to find it though. How would they do that? Would some duallists on Earth be able to 'sense' a different wormhole to the one they have used before? Would this be their first time and therefore the only wormhole that they could access? Would their entangled twins also know about the wormhole? Would they be humans? These, and more, questions filled up Christophe and Catherine's journals, as well as plenty of mealtimes, much to the chagrin of Mary Jumeau, who often tried to shift the conversation to more immediate concerns like the state of the local towns under the growing epidemic spreading throughout Europe and now hitting the U.S. This looked to be a nasty one. Nastier than SARS or COVID-19, and hitting indiscriminately wherever it spread.

——-

Fairfax county, and Langley itself, is pretty much cocooned from the outside in many respects. Sure, it is supplied by major autoroutes and trunk roads but in terms of the focus of daily lives in the intelligence community, epidemiology isn't a specialism and so far GARID-7, or GARI, has tended to be a secondary concern. And with the increase in military and NASA-led initiatives in relation to escalating tensions with both China and Russia, Langley, NASA and the U.S. government have their respective hands plenty full right now.

In fact, when Christophe and Catherine first met Phil Kirkland and Ava Redmond, and the latter pair sketched out their ideas for CAT, it was obvious that the purpose was, principally, military and terrestrial. In other words to help the U.S. in its domestic - *earthly* - endeavours with regard to its potential enemies. They didn't really seem to care about Gill at all, although the Nuvo connection and the potential for another Garfield was pretty scary. Not scary enough to warrant diversion of resources away from the immediate here and now though, or the Light Sail and Fusion Propulsion space travel projects. It was only by going along with the majority of the CAT programme, that the Jumeaus could also work on their side plan. This might take a while, but for both it was worth it.

—-

Phil Kirkland, Jacob Lavery and Nelson Olakunde are with Ava Redmond in her office. Phil and Ava have been working closely with the heads of the NASA-private partnership projects 'LS10' and 'Centronus' on so-called 'doomsday' scenarios. Until relatively recently these had been slower-burn projects, at least in terms of government resources and timelines. Great entrepreneurs from the tech revolutions were much keener to get these things moving, and as a result, a number of tensions circulated like a bad smell in most of the project board meetings. A clash of cultures would be putting it mildly, but then again the ensuing creative tension would help drive things forward, even if not by unanimity.

LS10, the U.S.'s furthest advanced inter-planetary travel construction project to date based on using light sails, is also in competition to an extent with the Centronus One project, which is testing nuclear fusion propulsion rockets. The latter have all been unmanned so far due to the potential dangers, and two spectacular accidents have been hushed up to all but the intelligence community and the project personnel themselves.

Nelson Olakunde is genius-level in engineering. His understanding of, and innovation in, atomic engineering is second only perhaps to Oppenheimer and his team back when. More importantly perhaps, he has the capacity to see through division and work out compromises like no other, and as a result has persuaded several billionaires to invest more than they planned in order to expedite testing for Centronus. This means that, although a while away from becoming a reality, fusion space travel is a viable competitor for funding and gaining credibility in comparison to the LS10 project.

Ava has invited the senior figures in to discuss progress in light of world events.

"Are these figures for real, Phil?" asks Redmond.

"'Fraid so," comes the reply.

"It's looking pretty bad, Ava," Lavery, the head of LS10, chips in. "I never thought we'd have to actually think about any of these kinds of numbers after Coronavirus, but here we are."

"So this thing really *is* a global D-Zero…" muses Ava, referring to the U.S. government's denomination of a world-wide doomsday scenario in which all of humankind is at risk from an extinction-level event.

"It's hard to tell, but from some of the modelling that the guys over at CDC have made, the probability levels are rising daily. I guess it's down to the race for a vaccine, and maybe even isolating whole communities. I know that the hospitals can't cope and most now have military checkpoints a half mile all round to stop folks overrunning the place and infection spreading even more," Olakunde informs. "These are certainly worrying times. I can't imagine what it's like to be on the front line. So many nurses and doctors dying."

Redmond gets up and goes over to her window, the clicking of her heels puncturing the silence. It's perfectly still outside. The morning's vibrant winter sun is bouncing off the slanted steel rooftops of the low-lying research labs by the perimeter fence, and she can make out a distant murmuration of travelling birds, majestically and communally creating a theatrical show of shape-shifting dances and moods that defy explanation.

"Are we anywhere near a stage where we could actually create off-earth protectorates?" she asks in a hushed voice, almost afraid to hear the answer.

Lavery takes a deep breath and tries to help out.

"Well, the latest we have is that the light sail at iteration ten is probably good for Mars, but of course we need more than one trip. The trouble is that weight of the craft. It's got to be so light in order to reduce the time to get there, and it's just impossible for us to scale up as much as we'd like; the Astracrane and LS rigs up there are the biggest we can go right now."

"How many trips are we talking and in what timeframe, if we had to do that right now, Jake?" asks Redmond.

Lavery inhales.

"Well, that's hard to say, but my best guess is - provided everything went to plan - we would need about 6 trips to manage the whole thing. You know, the base station, supplies, oxygen and plantation, communications and computing, outbound vehicles and of course the workers and ultimately the inhabitants. Each would be about a month there and the same back."

"So that's the best part of a year if all the trips were back-to-back?" Phil enquires.

"I'd say nearer two, Phil. We can't do back-to-back, just because of the limits on the sail itself. And we need to build in at least a failsafe to get back here of course. And this doesn't take into account any outages or breaks or unknowns. We might have repairs to do, and of course landing anything fragile on Mars is going to be an issue…" Lavery breaks off, musing to himself more than anything.

"And same for you, Nelson?" Redmond continues.

It's Olakunde's turn to get up. he's a big man and sitting in a small chair. It's fairly uncomfortable anyway, and Redmond's question has just made the position untenable in the here and now. The others look on as he goes over to the drinks cabinet and pours himself some fresh orange juice. He takes a slug and almost empties the glass.

"This is very difficult, Ava. I've never found myself being as scared as I am right now. I don't like saying that, but it's true. If this pandemic goes the way we think it's going to go, then conventional wisdom would tell us to pool all our energies with the Chinese, the Russians and the Europeans so we can work out a global solution to a global problem, but we all know that is highly unlikely given current tensions. Heck, President Zhao only yesterday accused us of starting it; of the U.S. actively releasing biowarfare on the planet. And the recent attacks on Taiwan and Korea mean we are not far away from a declaration of war. In my opinion, I mean. I might be wrong."

He pours himself another glass and addresses the group more directly.

"Look, in relation to your question, and in response to Jake's thoughts, I don't think I can offer any magic here. Our programme is ambitious, yes. We have gone so far beyond Tokamak and can harness the kind of power we always wanted, but not in sufficient quantities. This is the problem. Same problem that the positron propulsion guys have, really. We could only generate, and control, enough energy for maybe one trip. A one-way trip. And that's without a proper inter-planetary test programme and roll-out."

Olakunde comes to his conclusion.

"Right now, I wouldn't take the responsibility of asking anyone, or their family, to agree to be a test crew travelling on Centronus. There are just too many risks. And I say that as the lead; someone who, more than anything perhaps, would love to get the go-ahead to get a mission together to test this technology to its capacity. We're looking at a year of intensive testing, further engineering work, and a colossal effort - and investment - to get anywhere near something that we could have confidence in. I mean, if it works, it would get there in two or three days, four max, probably. But it's the control, and the slowing down, and…"

"OK Nelson, I get it," Redmond interrupts. "I think we get the picture, and thanks for being honest. Have you had discussions with John or Bibi in relation to funding?" She cites the President and Vice President of the United States.

"Oh yes," Nelson comes back. "The problem has always been military expenditure on terrestrial armaments and now this Sky-Twin drone programme. They seem to get all the money, and that's why we go private. But Bradley Ford and Lucas Martinez have both pledged more so we can continue the testing. It's just a shame the HL-4M guys won't talk to us right now. That could be a game changer."

"The Chinese guys?" asks Lavery.

"Yeh, we don't know how far on they are and Zhao has cut all comms, so we're flying solo," responds Olakunde.

The group goes silent. It is sinking in that there are very few avenues of hope in the mess that the major superpowers have gotten themselves into. Not to mention the impending cull of the human species that is almost inevitable from GARI. Truly a multivariate problem if there ever was one.

"Maybe GARI will be the game-changer this time," says Kirkland in a rare moment of outward reflection.

"Rapid piloting would certainly be back on the table," muses Redmond, before returning to her chair and sitting upright as if about to meditate. "OK, well here's how I see things," she says. "We have to think *way* outside the box here for worst-case scenarios, and that means that for you guys, unless you can secure up-funding and talk to your opposition counterparts about collaboration, we might not have enough time to get any, how would you call them, 'space settlers' up there. But I'll see if I can swing some funding away from Sky-Twin towards you." She points diagonally upwards towards the sky outside her window. "In the meantime, I'm still exploring the CAT program as you know, and am keen to share any results once they come in. Phil will be your first point of contact on this. I know you'll be busy and it might not be your priority right now, but it could be that we have to pull you in to this if we get any traction."

Lavery raises his eyebrows. "Well, good luck with that, Ava. We looked at the entanglement and wormhole ideas a long time back and, well, as you know they are pretty much disproven in relation to space travel. Unless you know something we don't?" he fishes.

"Not yet, Jake. OK, gentlemen, thank you all for your time. We'll do this again soon."

Redmond closes off the meeting without giving any further information on CAT, but secretly inside she is excited about Christophe Jumeau's reports so far. This *could* be that game-changer.

—-

Three weeks ago, Christophe Jumeau recorded 'Correlation 30-#3-000-09'. Although just a scribble in a journal followed by the digital equivalent, this was a seminal point in human history. Not least because it was the first time that Christophe Jumeau could evidence Melrose's postulate regarding the possibility of more widespread occurrence of the ability to super-position, and of person-to-person entanglement.

While in 'WH1', the Intelligence Agency's exceptionally clever abbreviation for the cornfield, Catherine witnessed, emerging from a gap behind her in the reeds, another young woman. She was clearly struggling, desperately trying to move forward, and obviously not in command of the space at all. But nevertheless it was another human being. Another duallist. Someone who found the wormhole, and therefore someone who could potentially be useful to both the programme, and of course herself. No longer would she be '*the one*' who can dual. Others may come forward as a result.

She didn't get much out of 'Carla' at first, mainly because her young ally was unable to move her mouth, but after a couple more encounters, Carla identified herself and the two then were able to speak 'off-field' as they would call it, meaning speak on secure telecoms lines and encrypted bio-cell chats. It was a revelation, for both. Carla would be known as 'Agent 000002-1-0', or just 'two-one-oh'. Christophe thought that Kirkland and the security community were just veiled geeks who favoured their ID's to be like baseball score cards. Catherine would obviously be agent one, and the '1' and '0' on Carla's number would correspond to the first of potentially two in an entangled pair, and the zero indicating that the second of the pair has not been identified or named. Catherine, or Agent 000001-1-1, could now meet with Carla at will, especially because they could communicate prior to dualling. More difficult was the scaling up of this effort, to try to find out if the other two duallists that briefly emerged from the clearing would come forward to be of service to the U.S. covert ops. Those two didn't even identify themselves and Catherine couldn't sense where they emerged from, or go down those paths. The basic notion that Christophe was following involved his original idea of opening channels between entangled twins, assuming that the prevalence of the capacity to dual was not the same as the super-positioning of objects. In the latter case, Jumeau has postulated that observation need not come from another in super-position, unlike dualling.

Of course, Melrose had been the first to prototype super-positioning of military technology - most commonly drone dualling - where inanimate objects were super-positioned under the control of a human 'pilot', with the only difference from a real drone being that the dualling drone did not have to be physically in the location it was surveilling. This has been of enormous benefit to military intelligence and of course has reduced the complexity and cost. Fewer launching stations and personnel, less maintenance and damage….the list went on. The downside was of course if the drone was observed while super-positioning, but this would have to be by a targeted observation and change of state, like being hit by a laser, or being physically destroyed, in which case the original was also destroyed. Even though it was relatively early in the Sky-Twin programme, the absence of any 'downs' gave the intelligence guys a lot of confidence that the likes of China and Russia hadn't developed a workable equivalent so far, or at least didn't have an active 'observe and destroy' programme. In either case, enemy military would down what they would witness as a real drone, and since the drone itself will not show any signs of being anything other than a drone, very little suspicion would be raised, other than the purely military kind. The main negative here would be the loss of the physical drone at the NASA hanger where it was being 'flown'.

Dualling from entanglement, the Jumeaus believed, was a different beast altogether. The phenomenon they have been working on is just one of a series of extra-human capabilities that can only arise from person-to-person entanglement, and seems to be much stronger but yet at times less controllable for those who possess such talents. Christophe Jumeau had worked out a while back, when looking at the nature of holograms and spatial architectures, that the tendency towards entanglement is greater when objects are closer together, and smaller when objects are further apart, which led him to question the nature of communication between entangled particles. He saw, like a few before him, that spacetime could be something that is not a *given* in our universe. Unlike Einstein's general and special relativities, where spacetime is malleable mainly as a result of gravity, where gravity is assumed as a classical or non-quantum feature of our world, Jumeau figured that it was actually quite different. That the reason 'spooky' action associated with entanglement is such a puzzle to scientists is because the universe is quantum. Features like light, mass, planets and galaxies all emerge from the quantum. He once complained that most explanations of entanglement started with an assumption that true reality - galaxies, earth, people, atoms - is a phenomenon of classical physics - natural forces, gravity, spacetime and so on - whereas for Jumeau this reality emerges from the concealed quantum universe. A world where geometrical structures - crystals, lattices, matrices - resulting from the interaction of quantum fields in different dimensions allow for some amazing possibilities that perhaps most humans cannot perceive.

The key thing about looking at the world from this perspective was that entanglement became both far more plausible because entangled particles *create* spacetime geometry rather than merely existing within it. In that sense, entangled particles seemed to be able to demonstrate 'spooky' communication at a distance by warping spacetime itself.

Of course, the initial entanglement would have been from a single local source, most likely at the edge of a gigantic black hole where literally everything that exists and happens as we know it, that is flatly encoded in two dimensions but experienced in three dimensions by all of us. Moreover, if that encoded 'horizon' of such a black hole was the origin of entangled particles, then reuniting those particles would be like going back to the source code itself, to when they were created - coded - for the first time. The power in this thinking is that, if what we experience in our lives is encoded at some distant event horizon of a black hole, where things are, relative to the perceivable universe, closer together, then the degree of entanglement is obviously likely to be much greater than anyone ever suspected. This was the revelation Christophe had when he first met Garfield, or Nuvo, at the diner back when. That black holes - the universe itself - could be entangled, which fits more readily with his theory that the classical reality we witness day to day is really a result of a holographic display taking place in a two-dimensional, and much smaller, area in our universe.

It also means that seemingly impossible phenomena like 'astral transit', are entirely possible, even probable, as alternative means of space travel because the phenomenon is really about connecting different geometries, rather than having to travel hundreds or thousands of light years in mechanical spacecraft within the confines of classical physics.

Christophe was beginning to believe that Catherine's growing command of the wormhole at the clearing was in fact her growing ability to form and deform spacetime. The associated dark energy in the wormhole environment might allow for some form of anti-gravity and Catherine's ability to overcome the intense condensation of matter there - to *fly*. What seemed mysterious was why, if this ability is conferred as a result of entanglement, Catherine was able to harness this power when her entangled partner Gill was potentially light years away on another planet. That distance *should* weaken the entanglement in some way, yet Catherine seemed to be getting stronger, not weaker. One conclusion could be that Catherine was deforming the spacetime around her so that the wormhole represented by the cornfield was minimising the distance in light years between her and Gill. But it could also be related to some very recent developments in the overall entanglement within the field.

When Catherine reported Correlation 30-#3-000-09, Christophe had a little dance in his office, followed by a large cognac. This was something he would never have dreamt of witnessing in his lifetime and also something that he wishes he could have pursued with Catherine earlier on. However, he was the most excited he has ever been at work, and unlike many older academics, looked to be hitting the peak of his active research in his latter years.

The potential for Catherine to be a siren for other duallists was one thing, but the fact that the new recruits could potentially be deployed themselves as recruiters, was a huge relief for two reasons. First, he has been worried for some time about Catherine's work rate and the seemingly endless demand for her services. Correlation 30-#3-000-09 - Carla - surely meant that she could and should take a break and let others get on with things, even if only for a short time. And then of course there is the small question of Gill and Nuvo.

The Jumeaus' side plan is as much on their minds as the baby and CAT1.

—-

Catherine emerges from Darkroom One. Now heavily pregnant, she descends the fold-down stairs gingerly and with some deliberation, holding onto her belly as if protecting the baby inside.

"Everything OK?" her dad asks.
"Yeh, just tired," she replies.
"I've got the kettle on back at the office. Let's talk in private there."
"OK," she replies, thanking the two guards who have helped her to descend.
Father and daughter walk at Catherine's pace the hundred or so metres to Christophe's office, mulling over the day's events and making small talk. Half way along and checking behind her, she whispers to her dad.

"Big news…"

And with this, Christophe beams a broad smile and gives her a fatherly embrace.
Once at the office, Christophe offers some of Catherine's favourite green tea and pours himself a coffee from the constant-on jug he has had put in the office.

"So, did you see Carla today?" he asks.
"Yeh, she came along as planned. I like her, Dad. She's got real potential and I notice that she's much more comfortable in the space now. Like, she is beginning to explore a little and…"
Christophe can't wait for the new information though, and jumps in.
"And?…" he smiles at her broadly, "Do I get another big journal moment?"
Catherine laughs. "Oh yes you do, Dad. His name is Wes and he's from England. He's pretty cool. I mean, he kinda got it immediately when he came out of the reeds. Wasn't phased or anything; I could see it in his eyes. Still slow in there, though, and will need a bit of help. He was different though, Dad. I mean, in a very good way. He could nod and shake his head so he seems to be quick and I doubt he'll take long to gain a lot of control. But anyway,

I asked him to Yes/No on a whole bunch of stuff. I'll give you all the details, but basically he's been able to dual for quite a while, through a train station. When he gets there he can take a train and travel. But the most promising thing was when he kept nodding when I asked about whether he knew of others. I tried so hard to get more detail but there comes a point when Yes/No gets pretty limited. But the coolest thing about this was that he'd planned the trip."

Her eyes are quite wide at this point, and Christophe is completely enthralled. He has to shake his head a little just to get the next question loosened and ready.

"Yes? I mean, how did he do that? How did you know?" he asks excitedly.

"Well. Like, it sounds bizarre, but he was wearing a lanyard with his badge on it. Maybe he planned it that way. I guess it might have been his work badge or something, but it had his full name, job title and the name of the company, so it means we can contact him. I remember all the details."

She goes on. "Oh, and when I told him a little about myself and what the programme is about, he was super keen. I could tell 'cos his eyes lit up and you could see he was trying to nod more quickly."

"This is fabulous news, my dear! But hey - you followed protocol on how much information you gave out? You know Phil is a stickler for that."

"It's fine, Dad. Seriously know what you mean about Phil! Listen, I know all that is important and we don't want duallists from China and Russia infiltrating the wormhole, but compared to the perfect storm of all the threats around us, I have to go on my sense of the situation, and I swear Wes is the real deal." She pauses for a second, looking out the window on this glorious winter day. "Wesley Wilson-Green," she enunciates in a pseudo-English accent, and smiles broadly. "Welcome to the fold."

"It does have a certain air to it, doesn't it? And Carla? Is she close to being able to communicate the field to others?"

"It will maybe take a another visit or two, but yeh," Catherine replies.

"Hhhmm. We may not *have* two more visits though. This seems to be a race against time."

"That's something we can handle, Dad, don't worry." Catherine sounds quite reassuring. But she is more concerned with something else. Something much more immediate. "Dad, listen, I know the programme is super-important - to everyone - but I was on the phone to Wendy this morning and she says things are getting weird up in Boston. Like, everyone in lockdown and not being allowed out. It's getting really bad, and so far there is no vaccine and not enough testing. It's going to be like that here very soon, and I just worry about you and Mom, and the baby, and Wendy…" she visibly wilts at the thought of her loved ones being at risk from the GARI virus, and this mounting worry tensions the air.

"I understand," Jumeau senior intervenes. "But we'll be fine as long as we take good care, and if there was anywhere in the world I'd rather be, apart from on a beach in Honolulu, it's here. I mean, this is a closed community with the tightest military protocols on earth. Everyone is checked in and out, and all the perimeter guards are wearing masks - look, you can see them from here."

"I guess you're right," says Catherine. "But closed communities are also where infection spreads quickest. Do they have a plan to get relatives into the compound, Dad? You know, if it gets *really* bad?"

"I don't actually know that, Catherine, but let me check. I'm sure they must have. Your mom is only ten minutes down the road, so we can certainly look at that. She is the expert anyways, and you know she'll be the first to take precautions. She gets dressed up like a beekeeper to go to Mrs. Carson across the way!"

They both laugh, feeling the need. Mrs. Carson is the old lady who lives across from the Jumeaus.

"Yes, I saw her stash of masks and gloves in the laundry room the other day. I know she's on top of things."

Christophe changes tack, if nothing else to get away from pandemic talk, which seriously raises his blood pressure.

"So tell me about Wes. We'll need to trace him," he says, and with that, gets out his little black journal and grabs a pen.

—-

Catherine is driving home in her beloved Oldsmobile. One of Gill's many mixtapes is floating through the speakers, 'Through The

Dark' by Alexei Murdoch hauntingly filling the airwaves around her. It's melancholic, yet beautiful in a way that perhaps only she knows.

With some of the money coming in from CAT, she has had the Delta Coupé completely overhauled and faithfully restored. It's a daily reminder of Gill and it has become her pride and joy. Mind you, she'd never have thought that a 4.2 litre gas-guzzler from the 70's would be her thing, and it still takes a whole lot of pride-swallowing to ride in it, just because it's as far from being green as she could imagine.

When Tony, who owned the auto repair shop up in Oakton, asked her what colour to get the bodyshop to spray it, she knew immediately.

"The same colour, Tony - just without all the holes," she replied, at which both of them started to laugh.

Gleaming in the midday sun about two weeks later, there she was. Resplendent, cool, sexy and huge. New alloys, that pecan-russet metallic brown colour now reflecting on glorious days gone by. Maybe the best days. Even inside, the ribbed leather bench seat, the shifter and dash, all restored fantastically well. The first time Catherine drove it she remembered how powerful the beast was. And also how the new disc brakes worked almost too efficiently, coming close to knocking herself out on the steering wheel the first time she braked.

In all this, there was a degree of opulence and history in this car that she just loved. And now that it looked the bomb, every so often she would get it out the garage and take it to work instead of cycling. It was her little indulgence in an otherwise fairly frugal and planet-friendly existence with her parents.

She looks at the dash. The old analog clock - the type that looks as if the manufacturer has literally wedged a sixties special in the fascia - reads ten past six, when Phil Kirkland's call breaks into her thoughts.

"Catherine! Hi. How did it go today?"

"Hi Phil. Yeh, really well," she responds and gives Phil the update on Wes from England.

"Fantastic news, Catherine. Fantastic. Listen, I just wanted to ask you a question about today. Probably nothing, but I got the polygraph, ECG and neural shift readings back and I stumbled across a real spike in all three about an hour in. They read differently to the data relating to your flight mode. It's kinda weird and not like previous visits."

Catherine pauses for a second.

"Catherine?" Phil prompts.

"Hey. Sorry. Isn't that just the 'Wes moment'? I mean I was pretty thrilled to see him."

"Yeh, it could be, but you said that was towards the end that this guy showed up, whereas this was earlier. Well, I mean, in as much time counts for anything in there!"

Catherine attempts an explanation, which is maybe not the best tactic. Phil is pretty shrewd behind that avuncular and slightly frayed exterior.

"Ah, Phil. I don't know really. I mean it could be that others were near to the wormhole but didn't make it to the clearing?"

Phil gets into gear and the conversation begins to take a slight fork.

"Well, yeh, but the data spike is *yours*. I mean, if you weren't aware of that then it wouldn't show up. These are your readings really so unless there is some subconscious activity in there, I would assume it was something you saw or experienced, no?"

Catherine is hesitant, desperately trying not to be shifty.

"Yeh, I see that, Phil. Well, I'm kinda out of ideas then. Did the spike indicate anything that has happened before on the readouts? Like, unless it was quantum vacuum fluctuations I guess. We've had those before, right?"

"Nope," Kirkland replies. "This is brand new. It has to be something that was affecting you at zero plus sixty. Are you absolutely sure nothing happened out of the blue around that time?"

"Not that I can think of, Phil. I'll try to replay events this evening before I go to bed, and if anything strikes me, I'll either text or call. Is that OK?"

Kirkland, slightly frustrated, agrees, continuing "And in any case, you did an amazing job today. We are now on the cusp of getting those numbers in. Thanks again, Catherine, and don't worry about contacting me tonight. Tomorrow is fine."

Kirkland rings off and Catherine, lets out a heavy sigh, and turns on Gill's old mixtape. "Wasting My Young Years' by London Grammar softly fades in.

—-

Some six months ago, Catherine visited Shirley Gill all the way over in Oregon. She had to. It was something that she needed to do for so many reasons. They instinctively liked each other, and Shirley insisted that Catherine stay for the weekend so they could spend some time together and visit Gill's father, Joe, at the Care Home.

A pall of sadness and wonderment encircled Shirley Gill when she talked. This was a woman who had lost both her children without any closure, and her husband to Alzheimer's where closure comes painfully slowly but with an inevitability that is crippling. And through all of this, Shirley Gill fought for her husband, fought for her daughter and was now fighting for her son. All this without any confirmation of death, or bodies, to prove that they were truly gone.

Catherine was mesmerised by the facial resemblance between Gill and his parents; how much the family had a 'look'. At once it made Catherine elated and dejected.

And then there was Beth. Photos of a striking young woman bedeck the walls around the house. A happy person, carefree and ready to explore the world and live a life. And all cut short in Boston some years ago. For Boston police, just another missing person, but for the Gills, devastation and eternal heartbreak.

When Catherine asked about the early experiences with Gill - when he went missing for hours on end - and the role Beth had in those, Shirley told her that Beth was the 'anchor' for Gill. His twin sister was the one who was as solid as a rock while Gill would often be haphazard and get into trouble. That Beth was the shrewd one. The one who would hang back and weigh things up before deciding. Such a contrast to Gill.

But Catherine's knowledge of Gill and what he could do wasn't shared by Shirley. It became obvious to Catherine that the siblings had not revealed their extraordinary capacities to their parents for fear of upsetting or frightening them. On balance, perhaps it hadn't worked, Catherine thought. More importantly, Catherine almost felt a *duty* to tell Shirley that Gill was, at least, alive. That she was carrying Gill's child. But when she tried rehearsing how to tell Shirley this, it all became too bizarre, and, she thought, it might confuse a vulnerable woman even more and have a negative effect. It was for this reason that she offered some platitudes to Shirley, rather than reveal any detail of what she was planning to do to bring Gill back. An incredibly profound, informative, and yet painful, meeting was the result of that long trip. Catherine returned, longing for the day that she could take Gill, and their baby, back to Shirley. To turn up on Shirley's doorstep and make that woman's day.

—-

At zero plus sixty today the strange got plain weird with an encounter unusual even for the cornfield. Not with prospective 'newbie' duallists from London or Milan, but with an altogether more interesting person. Beth.

The light began to change, and it reminded Catherine of the purple in the sky the day that Gill disappeared. Out of the blue, this light began to diffuse into the sky and at the same time the wind began to get up, forcing the reeds behind her to close so that there was no way into, or out of, the clearing. A intensely bright light, like a very near star, seemed to descend and land in the cornfield. At zero plus sixty, this would be a massive spike as Catherine reeled from the impact.

The sensation was warm and exhilarating in equal measure, like riding a big wave into the shore or bumping into an old friend unexpectedly. If endorphins exist in this space, then Catherine's brain was releasing them like fourth of July parade balloons. But she didn't know Beth, other than get a sense of her from the photos on Shirley Gill's walls. But somehow from all that, and Shirley's stories, she sensed that it was her before the encounter.

If there was ever a way for the boyfriend's sister to introduce herself to the new girlfriend, this must have been one of the most leftfield.

'Hey - how did you two meet?' an acquaintance would ask in a theoretical future.

'Ah, it was amazing. We actually bumped into each other in a wormhole. Go figure, huh?'.

Rather more intricate, one might imagine. In fact, as it happened, Catherine didn't recognise Beth immediately, mainly because her presence seemed more sensual than physical. But Catherine, if nothing else, was a pragmatist, and even in a wormhole environment had the presence of mind to shout Beth's name. This seemed to bring proceedings into focus. So much so, that Catherine now noticed that, in contrast to when she had free rein in the clearing to wander and fly and explore, when Beth arrived things regressed into the kind of slow motion environment that she had first encountered there. And this worried her. What could be causing this was undoubtedly, as a first thought, *dangerous*, such was the anxiety associated with both those encumbered initial experiences at the cornfield and the last, torporific, moments when she couldn't save Gill.

No, this was a washing. A simultaneously warm and comforting moment with its equivalent opposites.

Beth eventually emerged in this space through an opening in the reeds opposite her. This immediately made Catherine think that Beth was not coming from any place on Earth. But Beth's appearance wasn't like the others. More like a shimmering, translucent form. Almost a mirage; a holograph of Beth taken from one of the photographs Catherine remembers from the Gill's house back in Oregon. The resemblance to Gill struck her as before, and for a long pause Catherine stared at Beth as if she *was* Gill. And in that moment, of course she immediately loved Beth, for all the love that existed within the Gills and all the love that had been lost. And yet amidst this vision of beauty, of love, of the now, Catherine knew that a vision was all that it could be in this place, and that Beth's presence belied another story, another world, another reality.

And when Catherine asked herself if she was hallucinating, she knew the answer was 'no'. Such was the command Catherine felt in *her* space, *her* clearing, that Beth's appearance had to have happened for a *reason*.

Where is Beth when she is not here? What happened to her? Why is she here now? How did she find this place? Is she in contact with Gill? Does she know about Nuvo and the evil presence that took Gill? *Can she help Catherine find Gill?* Racing, racing round and round her head. Dizzying. What comes first? Disorientating moments in life number nineteen, and counting.

For a brief moment Catherine Jumeau and Beth Gill shared a space in the universe. Remarkable in itself, but not enough for the dogged strangers. So much to ask, so much to share, and only a brief moment in which to do it.

Yet such was the relatively unstable nature of this encounter that there were no questions, and therefore no answers, save for the experience of its very happening. Such a meeting was of the Gods, surely. Of other-worldliness, of fate, of destiny. What chance that this could be by chance? Almost zero, surely. And yet, who can be sure of anything in such an environment exposed to outside hackers and interlopers; those that would usurp the sacrosanct land in the cornfield for malevolent gains, for retribution, kidnapping? For infiltration?

Such was the deep impact of Beth's appearance in the clearing that the revelatory presence of Wesley Wilson-Green ironically seemed to pale into insignificance in the process. Of course, for CAT, Wesley would be a huge leap forward, and Catherine was mindful enough to make this the big news.

It all came down to her and Beth. They would need to meet again, and to work through a whole bunch of stuff. In a way, this comforted Catherine, and in a way it completely zoned her out. All this new information at a time when she needed to take a step back to give birth to Gill's child. It was all too much.

As Catherine let out a sigh on her way back to the Jumeaus' rented house in Fairfax county that day, only Gill's mixtapes on the sound system helped to calm her down. 'Nick Of Time' by Bonnie Raitt came on, a song she was getting to love.

* * * *

CHAPTER 2: KARK

A biting chill sweeps across the huge expanse of desolate lemon-grey rocky landscape, giant boulders peppering the skyline much like some extreme areas of the Mojave desert. Above, the sky is a dusty pale yellow, an angry sandstorm in the distance billowing gigantic swirls of cloud upwards, dancing a menacing waltz around a far outcrop of sharp mountain peaks, bleak and forbidding in their razor-edged profiles.

Through the far clouds shines what looks like a sun, yet struggling to provide any solace to those on the cold surface. Back and to the left lies a smaller, reddish orb that glows much more dimly. Directly above, away from the dust clouds, it is darker, some far stars shining down and sharing their presence freely. This is an unforgiving scene that chills to the bone. But from the nearby hills some heat radiates. Across the jagged, rocky slopes that lie all around this corner of a strange world, warmth and light emanate like candles being lit in some fantastical medieval mountainside. Signs of life.

In one of the caves, Denton Gill takes a deep breath. There is less air here, although the hot spas inside produce liquid oxygen, a proportion of which releases the gaseous equivalent. It means that Gill is trapped in the recesses of the cave, with invisible prison bars nearer the entrance. It's a very physical reminder of his mortality, and of the weird world that is Kark.

Around him nestle a variety of fashioned spaces which are separated by nothing else than an opaque mist in the shape of a curtain. To get move between 'rooms' he has to walk through the mist, whereupon it turns transparent for that moment. For his more human needs one of the areas contains a small opening in the ground, and from a separate tiny porthole trickles a milky form of water in a steady stream which not only seems to agree with his skin but also contains nutrients. After a day without any liquid, one of the guards pointed to the liquid and gestured for Gill to drink. At first

Gill couldn't stomach the idea of putting a strange and disinfecting liquid like that into his body. It seemed to him disgusting. But he had to swallow his pride as well as the nourishing fluid provided by the cave, and soon got used to it.

His 'cell' was spacious enough, and the Karks definitely had a much different command of domestic technologies, all of which seemed so different to those on Earth. Gill's 'bed' was made from a slimy and more solid version of the milky water he used for washing, and in the shape of a bath. Although it was perfectly comfortable, it was pretty strange and for a substantial time he couldn't sleep, such was the level of anxiety and fear. By now he had learned to accept most of the weird nature of things in the cave.

One time he caught a glimpse of the entrance before running out of breath. He could see across to the opposite hillside where another light flickered, dim though it was. Dark and jagged rocks surrounded that cave, and it made for such a schism with the soft form that Karks consisted of, and the unusual postures and shapes they made when moving or communicating with each other.

As it's warm, he needs no clothes, but for some cosmic absurdity his olive cuban shirt, box leather jacket, low-cut jeans and trusty Converse trainers all travelled with him and lie untouched in the far corner of his rocky cell. Such is the depth of human socialisation that Gill still keeps his boxers on. As if any 'one' would care. In the jacket, his old bio-cell has long since run out of battery, or was broken somewhere along the way, as it can't switch on and, as Gill confided in himself, the Karks probably don't have Verizon masts dotted about for his convenience.

No, the Karks seemed to communicate with each other with visual cues and some indescribable noises, some of which sounded like the glitches you'd hear on old vinyl albums.

Somewhere in the kidnapping by Novek, Gill has lost the connection with Catherine, although he can't figure out why. They re-connected in the past and he believes they can again. It's his only hope. And yet somehow Nuvo seems the key. Maybe something in the atmosphere or the rock was stopping Gill from dualling. It was a daily ritual, trying to get to the clearing. At times, Gill would be so anxious to dual that he could feel his concentration was actually stopping him in his tracks. Over-thinking, over-breathing and overwhelmed.

Until the tally of revelations in Gill's forty odd years - enough for any one human being to assimilate - just got bigger.

Gill's only connection here is Nuvo. And as it turns out, Nuvo is a bit of a local hero. The Karkian test pilot, now 'Krotik Astraman', who was the first to test, and successfully utilise, new forms of space travel which did not depend on Karkian propulsion technology. Nuvo the duallist. Nuvo the human assassin. Nuvo the lone Kark on Earth for so many years; the Astraman who Gill invited to use the cornfield to connect with his entangled twin in return for the release of President Montgomery's soul and enactment of an alternative reality on Earth, about which very few people know. Although both Gill and Catherine were doing what they thought was right and had such a positive outcome, from where he is sitting right now, it maybe didn't go exactly to plan. Not least because Nuvo and his Karkian friends accessed a wormhole that connects Kark and Earth, and the small matter of Nuvo's twin, Karosak Novek - 'Sultan' Novek - who Gill, along with many Karkians, dreaded.

It also turns out that Nuvo has a few other tricks up his sleeve, as it were. Like talking. Gill figures this is as a result of Nuvo invading and inhabiting Garfield all those years ago, and his lengthy spell on Earth. Fortunately or unfortunately for Gill, Nuvo transforms into Garfield in order to communicate with him, which is not a little bit unsettling, even for a seasoned duallist.

This is a massive deal for Gill, though; perversely Nuvo has become Gill's confidante.

"You are alone here. Like I was alone for many of your years."

Nuvo, in Ellis Garfield attire, relayed the somewhat obvious to him in one of their early conversations.

"Yes, but you could shape-shift into one of us, like you are doing now," Gill replied. "But I can't do that, so I feel even more alone."

"It is a problem for you, I know. This is as comfortable as it will get for you. You are not suited to this place."

"Then why am I here?" Gill asked.

Nuvo, unable to make familiar expressions as a Karkian, somehow manages in human form, and winces slightly.

"Karosak Novek," came the reply.

Gill knew before he asked who this was; Nuvo's twin and grizzly spectre of dark energy he succumbed to in the clearing that fateful day.

"What does he want with me?" Gill hesitantly enquired.
"You have the key, Detective Gill," Nuvo enlightened.
"Key?" Gill tested the water.
"The Ksaanek. The 'wormhole' as you say. It is a gate through which many Karks will go."

Strange words coming from Nuvo but even stranger through the mouth of Ellis Garfield. Gill's fears were justified. But why is he the key if he can't dual anymore? He can't even *find* the clearing, never mind open it for anyone else. Gill hesitated at this point. He knew he couldn't trust Garfield, and probably it was the same for Nuvo, yet he knew that something in Nuvo seemed human, and that wasn't Garfield's disturbing reappearance in front of Gill.

"But all that is lost. You know that. If I could dual - go to the Kanek or whatever you call it…" Gill says before Garfield's form glitches and cracks for a second. It shocks Gill.

Garfield enunciates very clearly the word Ksaanek, in an annoyed tone.

"K-ss-aahh-n-ik," he mouths.
"OK, 'K-sah-nik' then. It doesn't matter, cos' I can't get there anymore. It's closed - the gate is CLOSED. You get that, right?" Gill counters.

Garfield pauses, and Nuvo decides to darken the environment around them so Garfield's form is momentarily haloed. Now sounding different with a much drier and crackly voice in an even eerier version of himself, he makes a pronouncement.

"It's not that you can't dual. It's that you are prevented from doing so here. This…" he gestures by circling an arm around the cave, illuminating the texture of the inner walls in the process. "This is a controlled environment that allows you to live, but doesn't allow you to travel."

He now points to Gill who feels an intense warmth from the very inside of his torso.

"Your purpose is clear to us. To Karosak Novek. You will take us to the Ksaanek when we are ready."

Gill was rooted to the spot, heavy and almost sleepy. It was almost as if Nuvo was proving his control; proving that it is his decision about Gill's future. And yet in all this, Gill now knew this is why he is not dead.
But the implications of Nuvo's words simultaneously excited and disturbed. Potentially there *is* a way to get back to Catherine. And see his parents. And keep looking for Beth. All the wondrous and earthly pursuits he dreams of getting back to. But in so doing it sounded like the local dictatorial Sultan of Swing, Novek, had malice in mind.

"What if I can't, or won't?" Gill asks Nuvo.
"Oh, you will. One of the advantages I have is that I saw how much you feel for the girl. That she is your twin. How wonderful that must be. To be *in love* with your partner. So I know that you will do this, and I also know that I must do this too."

For a second Gill let this sink in.

"So Novek is your twin?"
Nuvo and Garfield nod.
"And you want to use the 'Sonic' - the wormhole - to go back to Earth? What for?"
"I will show you, but not this day," Nuvo replies. "This day, just be glad that you are alive, Detective Gill. That you have a future, and that I am here to help you."

And with that the outer form that was Garfield seemed to be ingested by Nuvo who then made some form of gesture of departure accompanied by a clicking sound, not unlike the sound dolphins make.

As Gill bathed later, he reflected. That must have been one of the weirdest conversations he could ever have imagined. It rocked his very being, and changed the game.

—-

Although he had no idea of daily cycles on Kark - of sunrise and sunset, or any moons, or indeed any other weather than the seemingly freezing cold outside the cave - Gill had started to try to get a sense of how long he had been in captivity, mainly by his own circadian rhythms, even they were surely all out of kilter now. He slept when he was tired, and that seemed to be a lot in this weird space in which he was confined. But so far, he figured he had notched up maybe two hundred sleeps. Sometimes he would forget and then take a best guess at what the last figure was. Rarely was he more than a few sleeps out, so the one-fifty mark he had some confidence in. That's if any of that actually mattered, now or in the future.

A better way to pass time was to practise the sax in his head, and imagine playing with the band. It was what he used to do, albeit with that ridiculously human form of curved metal. Every key, every mode, every scale, every altered scale - and now even the intensely disquieting Karkian scale that only Gill had thought of. They all helped.

But it was a way to keep sane.

Gill adopted 'Dreams' by Stan Getz as his replay tune when needing to calm himself; almost ten minutes of genius that Gill had memorised a long time ago, still retained in the musical cavern in his head.

The night that Nuvo revealed the future to Gill, he sure needed Stan's earthy tones to ease the journey to sleep.

—-

One of the most unsettling things about Kark was how bleak it seemed to be. Largely reliant on sound and smell rather than vision due to his confinement, Gill had to guess a lot about what happened outside the cave. It wasn't quiet, that much was certain.

The first thing Gill remembered when he woke up in the cave was the smell. Largely what he could remember as methane gas and some malodorous sulphur. Pretty unpleasant at times and only ameliorated by the oxygen emanating from the spring deep in the cave.

From then it was the sound of dripping from the constant supply of the cloudy orange fluid that was mild and seemed to nourish his skin and keep him feeling clean, and of course the clicking and crackling of the guards as they seemingly communicated to each other out of sight up near the entrance to the cave. Beyond them, he could hear the rustle and bellowing of what he imagined were dust storms. At first it was frightening, but after a time he got used to it, even looked forward to it during the long hours of inactivity and nothingness in the cave.

There were never any sounds of aircraft, which made him think that there were no flying machines in the form he would find familiar, and neither were there any mechanical devices on the guards. They were just *there*. Two Karkian lummoxes whose job it was to guard someone who, if they attempted to escape, would probably drop dead before they reached within five yards of them. Easy peasy.

Gill sometimes listened for patterns in the clicking. Any intonation. Any emotion. There were higher and lower pitched clicks, but really the communication seemed to be in patterns akin to morse code or some such. Nothing that Gill could get his head around. On a number of occasions Gill had tried to spark up a conversation with the guards by shouting. They would come nearer but as soon as they realised he wasn't dead or dying, they would flush a little and then hover back to the entrance.

On one occasion Gill made himself retch after drinking his meal - a variant of the orange cloudy liquid, only this time a kind of puce green colour that was enough in itself to make any human want to throw up. He put on a bit of a show of convulsing and struggling to breathe, but the guards just left him again, as if they could tell he was putting on an act. Later he would believe that for some reason Karkians can sense vital signs and the difference between real trauma and fake trauma. So that line of thought got pollarded pretty quickly.

Neither was there any bustle or sounds of horns or huge click swells coming from any nearby collection of Karks. No, these seemed to be hillside craggy spikes with holes in them and very few Karks.

One time, perhaps because the guards had wandered away from their posts, Gill held his breath as he was well practised in by now. He cowered down low at first, then groped his way along the cave wall nearer to the entrance and intersect with the Karkian landscape. For a few brief seconds before his skin began to itch and his eyes began to shed acrid tears, he got a snapshot of the craggy outcrops and ragged slopes that made up this part of Kark. All across there were varying shades of yellow and red light, and for a fleeting moment as he looked further across the bleak terrain, two suns hovered in a cold yellow haze in the distance. The larger sun threw out most light, and due to the particles of dust all around he could see how the rays were filtered and ultimately cooled by the atmosphere. This explained why it was so cold out there. The atmosphere must have been close to zero degrees or lower, although there was no ice so, he surmised, no water, at least in its natural state, on the landscape he glimpsed. Farther in the distance was the smaller, dimmer and redder sun. From his limited knowledge of stars he guessed this might be either a white or red dwarf, and that the solar system he was in had at least two stars. The fractured picture he could get hold of in that moment held so much information.

Although Gill didn't have a photographic memory, his years of policing and dualling made him extremely observant, and he spent time going over and over the snapshot he held in his mind. Kark was indeed an inhospitable place, and one that surely didn't suit the soft-formed and shape-shifting Karks, despite their obvious advantages over Gill in such a location. How did the Karks survive without obvious evidence of animals or plants to eat? What technology would they have used to hunt for food? Did they have towns and cities? Buildings? So acute was this schism in Gill's mind that he surmised that either the planet itself was entirely barren and dangerous to Karks themselves, or that he was being held in the worst part of Kark, and that the Karkian beaches and bars were somewhere over the horizon.

It took all Gill's fortitude to keep from going mad sometimes, or becoming so depressed that he wanted to end it all. The only thing that kept him going was the potential he had to dual again, and to find Catherine and Beth. From the information he had so far, he started to speculate on certain pathways in store for him.

The first thought was a good one. He was going to get back to the clearing. But obviously at a price. Which was what? This was the immediate downer. One thought he had was that there was obviously some need for Nuvo and the Karks to use the clearing, and since that was the route to Earth as far as he was aware, then there must be some strategic use for both him and the 'Sonic' that Nuvo had told him about, and which he couldn't pronounce properly in Karkian. What would be behind this need?

He reasoned that it was clearly an important one. Otherwise he would have been dead long ago. And of course, hovering menacingly in all his postulations was the spectre of Novek, the Karkian lord that had so much frightening power. He really didn't want to have to confront Novek in any way shape or form. For someone who wasn't afraid of much, frequent anxiety attacks became part of his time on Kark.

But of course, he reasoned, because his presence at the clearing was so obviously important to the Karks, the next factor in the equation was what would he be asked to do once there? Was it him they were interested in, or was it Catherine? Or was it the clearing itself? The opportunity it offered Nuvo, or worse, Novek, to dual to Earth? If Nuvo could wreak havoc and wind his way into the higher echelons of world power, what could Novek do? This alarmed Gill. Simultaneously, it made him angry, protective and determined to fight it if necessary. He found it strange saying this to himself, but one amazing positive for him in his isolation on Kark was a realisation that there are bigger pictures than international politics and wars now. There was much more of a sense that the period of history Gill had found himself in was one of the survival of planets. From the green revolution onwards, the whole debate in his mind seemed to be about what would make a better Earth. A better home for humankind, and this sobering thought occupied his mind for some time.

It seemed clear that, although Nuvo was strong and in control of Gill's destiny, he was also in the keep of Karosak Novek, leader of the Karks. Every avenue of thought led inextricably back to Novek. And without much more information, Gill would be in the dark unless he could understand more. This would mean getting inside Nuvo's head.

Gill would remember his initial and revelationary discussion with Nuvo about his situation. Nuvo seemed to be in admiration, if not awe, of the fact that Gill loved Catherine. And this clearly implied that Nuvo did not have that with Novek. No, their relationship must be very different, Gill inferred. If Novek was as scary as Gill sensed, then maybe Nuvo too was afraid of the despotic Sultan of Kark. Was it Nuvo's bad luck to be entangled with Novek, rather than some other Karkian who he could love and spend his life with? The assumption must be that entangled beings don't have to be like him and Catherine. Maybe they were a one-off. Maybe there was something about them that made them different. He would like to think so, but there was nothing to suggest this in terms of power or control, for he had lost all contact and, even by his crude determination of time duration, it was certainly months he had been in this place, even if it isn't months back home.

Gill needed to explore this connection between Nuvo and Novek in more detail, for he could see that this might strengthen his position with Nuvo. So too did he need to get some insight into why the clearing was such a strategic coup for Karkians. What was the purpose of sending Nuvo or Novek back there? Why did they *need* to do this?

—-

Gill opened his eyes as the bright light dictated awakening. It was one of the guards who seemed to glow at some frequency of the spectrum that would wake a dormant sloth.

"Woah," Gill shouted, as he jerked upright and held his hand up to protect himself.

The guard dimmed himself and made a clicking sound while forming into a shape which he knew meant 'come here'. Heart beating at over one-fifty, Gill hesitantly crept towards the guard, now moving to the entrance to the cave. Gill struggled to breathe. In front of him light bounced off some sort of metallic object so that it hit him straight between the eyes.

"Jesus!" Gill exclaimed, trying to accustom his eyes to this different form of brightness. The next utterance he had no control over.

As he neared the shiny golden shape in front of him, he could hardly believe his eyes. It looked like a flute of some sort.

"Wha...?" Gill's vocabulary deserted him for a third time.

As the guard seemed very agitated, he grabbed it and scurried back further into the cave. Sure enough, a rudimentary but pretty well-formed flute. Or a piccolo more accurately.

Tentatively, Gill tried to make a sound. Hoarse and with so little use of either his vocal chords or windpipe, nothing. He would try again many times in that waking period to make a sound, and eventually he did. Recreating simple tunes at first, then trying to build more complex phrases and whole songs. It was obvious that changing between a saxophone and a flute was not straightforward, at least for him, on Kark, in a cave. Nevertheless he was elated, and this became his joy and passion in the days and weeks following. For hours he would practise singing Bobby Garrett's 'I Can't Get Away' and then shifting to piccolo for the little sax solo in there, or remembering Getz' iconic movements on 'Dreams' with the intense concentration that took him to a different place. At least for while.

It meant so much to Gill and he was so preoccupied trying to get musicality from his beloved piccolo that he almost forgot to ask the 'why' question. But it struck him that this must have been from Nuvo, and indeed it later turned out that this was the case. No less of a surprise than any previous event on Kark.

—

And so it came to pass. After a seemingly endless time on the planet, with so little comfort other than some heat, oxygen and a piccolo, Gill finally got his second audience with Nuvo.

This encounter seemed much more like a planning meeting, and it heightened the sense of tension in the air. Nuvo also chose not to transform to Garfield this time. Nuvo's words seemed to float or be transcribed in the air so that Gill just 'knew' what he was saying without having to listen. Almost like the telepathic communication Gill and Catherine fostered in the back of the security van all that time ago.

"You liked the saxophone?" Nuvo opens.

"Yeh, it was kind of you. They call this one a piccolo."

"The diminutive? Like a small saxophone, yes?"

"Sort of," Gill replies. "Different fingering technique to get the sound but I picked it up pretty quickly. Thank you."

"I had it carved. It's what you would call nickel with some, uh, what's the name…rhodium," Nuvo explains.

"Well, it has made my last days on Kark much more…musical," Gill informs.

Nuvo is struck by Gill's use of language. After many years on Earth, Nuvo recognises nuance and the shaping of phrases and sentences to form a particular and subtle variety of meanings, yet himself still struggles with the fine tuning.

"You sense that it is soon time for you and I to go the Ksaanek?" asks Nuvo.

"Yes, I realise that you are under time pressure and that your visit here must mean we have some matters to discuss?"

"Indeed," muses Nuvo. "As the first astraman from Kark that has reached another planet successfully, the great Novek has purposed me with preparing you for your journey. We must travel together to the plain and then to our city where you will open the Ksaanek. This will be possible there."

Becoming uneasy, Gill asks Nuvo to expand.

"Do not worry, Detective Gill. You will be looked after well. We will make all necessary preparations, and you will be able to visit the clearing."

"Will you be coming with me?" Gill asks.

"Yes, I will be travelling with you."

"And will I be able to go back to my homeland from there?"

Nuvo hesitates.

"Not at first, no. Your purpose here is to help us to become more familiar with the Ksaanek and so learn about its uses so that we may replicate one like this and use it for ourselves."

Gill isn't buying Nuvo's story, though. He's had way too much time to think out every possible outcome from the clearing, and so far none of them are ideal.

"But your purpose is to use the clearing to transport Novek to Earth. I am not stupid." Gill reminds Nuvo of his awareness as much as to force more information from Nuvo. He continues his thread when Nuvo does not respond. "So, you see, I need to know what your end game is in all this, otherwise I can't help you. You may as well kill me right here, right now."

Even although Nuvo's form and shape are largely meaningless to Gill, he knows that when Nuvo's colours change it's usually due to a rapid onset of some emotion or change in internal harmony. And Nuvo is flushing vibrantly right now.

"This is not your entitlement, Gill," replies Nuvo.
"It might not be, but unless you tell me, I simply won't play ball," Gill comes back.
"We can make you 'play ball', Detective Gill. It's not a worry from our side. You will open the wormhole for us for some times and we will then let you go back to Earth. That is all we require."

And again, Gill is just too cynical to swallow it.

"Look, I know that you know that I am your key. The person that opens the gate, and potentially opens an avenue for you to go back to Earth, but if you were in my shoes…" Gill looks down at his bare feet. "If you were in my shoes, you'd demand the same. I know that. You got to give me something here, Nuvo. You got to help me decide if this is going to be worth the risk. It's that simple."

Nuvo wavers, and decides to shape-shift into Garfield.

"You humans are strange. You are so bound by your principles and culture. It is at the same time good, and a little bad too. You need to understand that you are here as our guest, but lucky. Lucky to be alive. Do you not value your life?"
"Yes. Yes, I do. But I value the lives of my fellow men and women too. How do I know that you won't use the clearing to send

Novek to Earth to wreak the same havoc and chaos that you did? You escaped back here. What's your problem? Why do you and Novek need to go back, unless it's to do more harm? You aren't going back to help humankind. That is pretty obvious."

And with this, Nuvo is struggling. The limits of his language and culture, from both worlds, are being stretched and it is only the human in him that forces him to concede some information. Knowledge that Denton Gill should not really access.

"I can't tell you details. I am not allowed to. You only need to know that this is for the good of the Karkian people. You will understand this, surely. You will understand that some races in this cosmic space all around us have good times, and some have bad times. We have bad times here. This is all you need to know. Now…" Nuvo, in the familiar human form of Garfield, begins to change.
"Wait!", cries Gill. "Wait. Don't change yet. Listen to me. This is me. Denton Gill, very human and very far away from home. You understand this. I know you do. You understand *me*. Imagine you had been caught or trapped some place on Earth and you had to betray your people so that you could return here? What would you do?"

Garfield's face darkens, just like it used to when the spirit of John Montgomery fought to surface from inside.

"I…I…" Nuvo struggles. "I would not accept that choice. I would find a way to return," comes the voice from Garfield's mouth.

And there it was. The central admission from Nuvo that, in some way, shape or form, Nuvo saw Gill in his own likeness. The wanderer. The adventurer. The person who took all the risks. The test pilot for dualling. The one most likely to end up dead, and paradoxically the one most likely to survive. This was Nuvo's struggle in life. On Kark. And so it was Denton Gill's struggle too. On Kark.

"But remember," continues Nuvo, "This is your hypothetical and not mine. My mission is to ensure you will open the gate. It is for others to walk through."

"You mean 'Sultan Karosak Novek', grand overlord of everything Kark?" Gill asks rhetorically and cynically. "Can you tell me what his plans are? I mean, you said 'others'. You mean he's taking more Karkians through the gate? But how? Do you have duallists here apart from yourself? What is…" and it is at this point in Gill's increasing frenzy of questions, that Garfield disappears and Nuvo returns.

"Enough. You now know more than is necessary. You will rest. And soon I will return and take you to the Kark city. As your people say, 'tomorrow is another day.'"

And with this, Nuvo has some form of interchange with the guards and floats off beyond Gill's horizon.

With every deep breath Gill takes in this space, so too come flooding yet more worrying thoughts.

* * * *

CHAPTER 3: EARTH

Mitch Nicolescu scurries along the corridor of the west wing of the White House. He is late for a critical briefing of the cabinet and security chiefs.

As he enters the Green Room and apologies for his lateness, his colleague Al Mason is the only one to offer any smile or acknowledgement, the others busy reading through a two-page briefing put together by Montgomery's secretaries for Homeland Security, State and Defense, supported in signature by the directors of National Intelligence, FBI and the CIA. He quickly grabs his copy from Al and takes his seat on the remaining soft chair in the large office.

Montgomery, deep in thought at the head of the table, clears his throat and brings the meeting to short order.

"Ladies and Gentlemen. What you have in front of you is a top-level assessment of the current situation in relation to both the military and the pandemic. You'll be aware that this is FYEO and not to be shared beyond this room at this stage. Thank you to Abe, Maria, Bibi here, and Joe for collating and collaborating on this in double-quick time." He looks around the room to gauge the expressions and offer a moment's pause for anyone to raise any immediate issues.

"This is, as most are aware now, formally an emergency cabinet. And will be for some time. I know how hard the last few weeks have been for you and your families and before we begin, I just want you all to know how grateful, and proud, I am to have you here. And I mean *you*, and not any others. Mitch, Al? I include you in this too. Good to have you on board."

At this, both Mitch and Al straighten in their chairs and nod at their President. Mitch is one of the few in the room who are privy to the bizarre series of events surrounding the assassination, and subsequent survival, of John Montgomery. He contemplates that glitch in time which seemed to reset reality and allow John Montgomery to continue in office as the head of their nation. And it is with some relief, in among all the anxiety, that it is Montgomery, and not Ellis Garfield, who is in charge during what is the worst crisis facing humankind since the Black Death.

"Now, as you will see, we already know that President Zhao's military have moved on North Korea but the big kicker is new intelligence emerging that they are actively advancing into the eastern Russian sea lands to the north. Japan will be the big target, and despite amassing a bigger presence in the South Pacific of late, we will not be able to contain any troop movements into those countries without a massive amount of air power being flown into Japan."

Abe Hart shifts in his chair uneasily. "We don't know the extent of the progress into eastern Russia and whether or not it is contested or sanctioned. This is the big danger, as we've highlighted in the briefing note. If Russia is working with the Chinese, probably in consort against us, we think it will be to target the Korean peninsula and Hokkaido, and for those to become strategic bases which could potentially weaken Pacific and Bering lines," he adds.

"Yes, thanks Abe," continues Montgomery. "At this stage our drones are picking up really frenzied activity over there and particular movements which suggest the Chinese will be setting up 'clean lands' that will be both military bases and virus-free zones. 'Highly protected military areas as survival settlements' is what we are picking up on the wires, but we can't be certain that this is the reality." The President looks over at Joe Becker. "Joe, you have an update on our Sky-Twin initiative and recent developments?"

Secretary for State Joseph Becker thanks the President for the invite and hands round a color-coded map his team has produced to show the movements of troops, technology and armaments from various Chinese mainland sites to its periphery over the last month. He takes up the story.

"Thanks to Abe for a lot of this information. So, as you can see, we have a major situation here, and we'll need to consider very carefully the intelligence emerging from the Sky-Twin programme.

Our drones are clearly picking up operations designed to predicate an attack on Hokkaido from the west and the north, as well as potentially from the south in a wide arc around Honshu. Cloaking technologies they have deployed might mean we are missing some major advancements still, and this is worrying. However, data mining and some infiltration shows that the Xo project - that's the one I identified last time for you - is now being implemented across networks in South Asia, and of course that was responsible recently for the hacked intel on our initiatives in Alaska."

"Do we know any more about the outages on Hawaii?" asks Bibi Melnik, Montgomery's new Vice President, and former aide to Abe Hart at Defense.

Joe flips through his folder, puts on his reading glasses and studies a data table so that he can be as accurate as possible.

"So, we're almost certain this is Zhao's MSS who were responsible, Bibi. ISI and MOSSAD also confirmed. We tied it down pretty quickly, but if they have the capacity to do this, then we will need to prioritise Hawaii, and possibly get their infrastructure updated. Won't be easy."

"Well, we can't have any more security lapses like this, that's a given. Do we know what they got, Ava?" Hart intercedes.

"Deep codes were intact. We think it was access sequences to gates, buildings, bunkers. So physical access rather than the arming procedures or any corruption of those. They are separate systems, of course," Ava responds.

"Well that's a relief," Melnik concludes.

"Indeed, Bibi," the President continues. "And thanks all. Now, the question is, 'where does this sit with GARID-7?' - Bill, you got any input here?" Montgomery asks Bill McFarlane, Secretary for Health.

McFarlane's neat frame and somewhat hunched posture belie a strong-willed senator from Georgia who has spent a lifetime championing better living among poorer Americans.

"Sure, John. OK, so belt-up 'cos this is going to be a bumpy ride, folks." And with this he gets up and hands out another map, this time showing the spread of the GARI virus in terms of current and plus-one-month projected rates of infection, hospitalisation and deaths. It makes for grim reading. "You'll see from the chart here that projections are pretty catastrophic for most countries. It's not a surprise that the Chinese and Russians might be looking to create island settlements. They don't want to admit it, but as they are ahead on the curve they are losing tens of thousands each day now. It looks like they've gone from containment and treatment to panic-mode. One of Ava's reports - the Sky-Twin project data - shows that drones were picking up visuals on civil unrest and mass panic. A bit like what we are seeing in New York, L.A. and down in New Mexico and Texas right now."

McFarlane gestures to Redmond signalling to her if she would like to comment, but she declines and waves him on.

"So, the projections mean that unless we can find a vaccine - and actually it might be better to say 'vaccine and cure' as it might be too late for a vaccine if most people have been infected - this is extinction level. There's no other way to say it. The only other possibility is that a lucky few have a natural resistance to the virus, but so far we haven't seen any evidence of this. Nor have we seen any recoveries. And I don't just mean 'not many', I mean 'none'. Nada. The conclusion has to be that what we are doing in Iowa, Alaska, Florida, and Hawaii, and with the Canadian government in British Columbia and North Manitoba, is the only way forward at this stage. As to the military implications, I'll leave that to Abe and Maria to update."

Bill McFarlane looks around the room. The frowning and somewhat beleaguered and bewildered faces of some of the people in the room, including Al Mason and Mitch Nicolescu, don't go unnoticed.

"Folks, these are unprecedented and very scary moments in our lives and the very survival of the American people - perhaps of all people. But we continue to fight tooth and nail to find a vaccine and we are quarantining a population of healthy individuals who, once in our own settlements, will be able to establish new communities, hopefully free of GARID-7." And with that the Health Secretary leans back in his chair and lets out a long sigh.

Montgomery gives his thanks, and looks over to Maria Ortega, who knows the look. She glances at the briefing report and, after seeming to purse her lips slightly, clears her throat before reporting on Homeland Security.

It's been a tough week for Maria. She's had to roll her sleeves up and utilise a hitherto unplanned and unpublicised control centre for Security just off route ninety on Lake Erie. She's been holed up there for the last four days with her senior staff and crew drilling down into intelligence from around the States as to the growing panic over GARID-7 and the flare-ups in New Mexico, Texas, Alabama, Florida, Arkansas and Tennessee, not to mention reports of an exodus from New York city and the subsequent looting across several districts there, and in Los Angeles, San Diego, Minneapolis, Memphis, Chicago and Detroit.

In fact, so close were Detroit and Chicago to Homeland HQ that at one point, Ortega had to decide on staying or heading to Boulder. But Boulder, although at altitude and fairly safe, was too far in both time and space for someone like Ortega to be for any length of time. She brings disturbing new information to the table.

"Thank you, John. I've no doubt you are all aware of what's happening across the country, and I don't want to dwell on any particular state or particular detail here. I need to make you all aware that as far as Homeland Security is concerned, we do *not* think that any of the migrations or civil unrest has been initiated via enemy or terrorist sleeper cells, nor do we believe that there is a belief in the general population that we might be at risk of anything other than GARI. And that is not to minimise in any way the very significant D-zero scenario. So, no invasion conspiracies are taking root apart from in the usual places, which we have covered."

Montgomery is keen to get a handle on possible military implications.

"What about army deployment, Maria? What levels are we at there?" he asks Ortega.

"Right now, we are at level 3, Sir. We can go 4 or 5 at very short notice, but only if we get the R value for the army down significantly. For the time being we gathering data daily, assuming you might need to deploy significant numbers elsewhere."

"We just might, Maria. You and Abe are working on those recommendations, right?"

"Yes, Sir. Abe and myself will have something for you in the next twenty-four hours."

"OK, that's good. Sooner the better. Liaise with Mitch here if you need to interrupt anything. What about you, Joe? What are the Russians saying?"

Montgomery turns to Becker again, who has been listening intently.

"Well, Sir, I had a constructive video call with ambassador Kusnetsov yesterday afternoon, during which he told me that the recent joint field operations with China at Hegang and Khabarovsk were merely joint control logistics to ensure protocols were practised so that both countries could have confidence in the integrity of the border itself. But our drones picked up unusual activity at Vladivostok too, and we're almost certain that they are colluding to annex both Korea and Japan. Now, there are some points here which folks should be aware of. Number one, any plans for annexing either Korea or Japan obviously destabilises the entire region massively. In any other circumstance I'd advise immediate high level talks. Since NATO is no longer an option for us, and we have no direct in with Zhao, it would be trilateral with Putin and Zhao," states Becker.

"Isn't Putin dead? I thought he'd had a stroke in the summer and hasn't been seen since?" asks Hart.

"Our intel suggests he's still taking decisions, Abe. Albeit from his bed, but you know what he's like. He'll probably still be commanding operations from the coffin."

The group let out a collective nervous laugh, almost in concerted relief that some respite in the tense atmosphere is remotely possible. Becker lets the murmuring settle before carrying on.

"The bad news is that we won't get near either. John, you got my memo on this and, well, everyone here should be aware that the way the Chinese and Russians are looking at this is not that different to us. It's a matter of annexing land. And islands seem like the way forward. Or at least land that is either far away from large conurbations or can be cleared of populus, inhabitable, and relatively clean."

"So why doesn't Russia annex its own land up in Ukhta or Murmansk and the Chinese annex Mongolia? I don't get it," pipes in Melnik.

"It's not that simple, Bibi," says Becker. "Mainland areas in both countries that are well served by transport and not well protected by the military are going to be targets for various citizen groups and potentially hard to protect three-sixty and twenty-four seven. It's potentially too dangerous and subject to attack not just from within the country itself but from outside. Russia has already started moving on Dudinka in Siberia, maybe similar to North Manitoba, but they lack the infrastructure and resources. Generally, the Russian lands east of Moscow operate at a relatively low level, whereas with the Canadians we have more advanced infrastructure, and secure and accessible areas identified with the troops available to ensure their protection. We have an advantage there. But coming back to Korea and Japan, I think we are at the point where we have to decide whether or not to abandon our stations in the immediate vicinity. Now although this sounds extremely problematic, the advantage it gives us is that it would take some pressure off our military and allow our own troops to consolidate further up the Pacific. I know this sounds hard, but we are not dealing with anything normal at this point. We must decide whether or not we wish to continue to deploy much of our military resources and personnel in that area when we have so much to do elsewhere. If the Chinese and Russians want to divvy up the islands down there to create their own settlements, then provided they would provide safe passage for the people of Hokkaido and South Korea, I think we would have to accept it. The alternative would be to initiate military action at a point in history when most of the world's population is going to succumb to GARI. This makes no sense. Especially as we don't have the numbers or infrastructure to instigate conscription. And while Abe, John and I have had several differences of opinion in recent weeks, we have concluded that, as this virus spreads its grim reckoning across our planet, it is not the time for international wars."

"What about nuclear arsenals, Joe? Won't they be at risk, or at least more likely to be used if any of the major powers need to secure their futures by getting rid of populations? Why wouldn't China initiate that option?" asks Ava.

"My view is that they wouldn't. I say that because Abe and I have been looking at the chatter. We've seen memos and decoded some video conferencing that shows neither the Russians nor the Chinese, nor in fact India, will want to use this route. And I get that. You don't want to blow up your neighbours with something that will leave the land uninhabitable and risk retaliation. It's too risky, even with GARI chasing you. Of course, everyone will secure their installation, but with no view to utilise. The way forward is to create annexes and hope that you have procedures in place so that we can be sure that each one is clean and remains clean until and unless GARI is stopped, or we can find a vaccine. And since so many health workers and scientists have already succumbed, we need to think carefully about each annex and what they will do. We're looking at about ten in total, with Hawaii and possibly Cuba being the two most problematic. The point I'd like to make here is that we have no time to delay. We've found it difficult to get to this stage in our thinking but in some senses it's already late. We need to move quickly and efficiently and so following this meeting, John, Abe, Bibi and myself will flesh out the detail. Maria, can you make yourself available today? We might need you at short notice," Becker asks.

Maria nods solemnly and as Becker takes a breath, Montgomery comes back in.

"One last thing, Maria. And for you too, Ava. Can we trust in the settlement programme in terms of secrecy? I mean, are the locations and the settlement subjects under tight wrap? If that information went public for any reason, we'd have a major internal security issue and I'd need to pull back all overseas. You know that, right?"

Ava chips in to give Maria a bit of a moment to consider.

"Sir, I believe the encryption and security vetting procedures we've developed are probably the most advanced imaginable. We are using retina, finger, face and embedded nano to ensure we retrodict correctly, filter, track and continually assess all participants. The Chinese or anyone else would need to break through four separate unique identifiers, all of which are bio-medically and neurologically tied to the individual. If there are infiltrators in there, we'll find them though our A.I. programs and pattern-bots."

"Good to know, Ava. Thanks both. Now, we must turn to item 6-11. Can you all please look at the briefing report. I wanted to take a moment to give you my thoughts." Montgomery is soft in tone, and deliberate. He wants to explore one of the more unusual topics raised in the briefing report, on which he has been liaising with Ava Redmond closely.

"For me, as a bit of an old-school type, I have to say that I have enough trouble with my biocell and VR reports. By the way, thanks to the folks over at Langley and Charlotte, we have amazing VR capabilities now. Not just with the combined efforts from Maria and Abe here, but also with Ava's Sky-Twin project which I have now had the opportunity to witness first-hand. I think it's amazing and it makes me think how here in the land of opportunity we can still rely on innovation and brilliance the likes of which we don't see elsewhere."

Bill McFarlane gives Bibi Melnik a look that says 'this is terrific but not getting us anywhere'. But any mention from Montgomery is always uplifting as he is not a man to idly patronise with praise, so Maria, Abe and Ava all follow his eyes and you can see the trust in their faces.

"For example, I was able to remotely visit Luoyang yesterday, and saw for myself the power of our dualling drones. Absolutely amazing, and confirmed my thoughts regarding phase three of the Chinese space programme. We were right all those months ago, so well done all involved. More importantly, with Sky-Twin now deployable more or less anywhere due to lifting of restrictions on bases and fuel, our intelligence is, in my opinion, second to none."

There is a pause while Montgomery reaches for his glass of water, revealing the noble features of the picture of Abraham Lincoln it was obscuring. The light entering the green room seems to brighten, making his glass glisten spectacularly as he raises it, takes a sip, and replaces it.

"But here's the deal. The world right now is like a ball of confusion. Spinning out of control and seemingly in danger of imploding. It's the sort of scenario that none of us thought we'd ever see in our lifetimes, yet we are *living* it. Right now. This is the reality we have. This is *our* world."

There is utter silence in the room, every pair of eyes transfixed on the President.

"And although sometimes I can't grasp what is happening in my conscious, waking days, I know that the decisions we take now, are probably the most important we'll ever take. Forget economics, forget idealism, forget politics. Forget all the stuff that can get in the way. Because we need clarity. Clarity of mind, of vision, of purpose. We need to make the whole greater than the sum of the parts, ladies and gentlemen, and that means we need to free ourselves of some of the fears, prejudices, heck even *logic*, that we tend to hold so close at times. This will mean thinking so far outside the box that you will most likely reject most of what I am about to tell you. But stick with me. Ava, I know you have a special insight into not only intelligence, but also the possible and the impossible. Of what happened to our country, our government, *me*, in another world. Believe me I have spent many sleepless nights mulling over the sometimes weird and always downright fascinating powers of the human species. And now is probably the time we must really put these to the test. And I mean *really*. Not theoretically or possibly or potentially. I mean practically, functioning and *right now*."

Mitch and Al look at each other quizzically. Neither is fully sure where this is going. Montgomery is still the main course.

"So what I want to update you on is the CAT program, which came out of some of the excellent results from CRUSE, if you remember that. CAT - which stands for Covert Astral Transit - has been in development for a few months now, classified six so only some of you will be aware of it. I am quite excited about this programme because it is related to those human capabilities that are so often the stuff of science fiction and comic books, but yet today it seems not so far-fetched."

Montgomery has to take another sip of his water.

"So, Ava and her team, with Phil Kirkland leading the operation, have begun to identify a number of people - from here in America and elsewhere - who have the ability to *dual*. This is a familiar term for what is actually called 'super-positioning' which some of you might know is a technique used in Sky-Twin. The more scientific among you will know that this is when something - usually an object - can be in more than one place at the same time provided it is not observed and so becomes 'trapped' in a particular state of being, or what we might also call a 'reality'. And this is something I have had such a hard time coming to grips with, folks. The idea that there is more than one reality, and more than one world. More than one universe even. That the truth might only be the truth in *our* reality, but that elsewhere it might be different."

While Ava and Maria and Abe are all on board, it is obvious that the rest of the convened group of top government officials are perhaps missing a piece of the jigsaw and are waiting for the punchline. Montgomery takes a quick survey of the room. Most of the team seem pensive, awaiting the next chapter in the history of the world.

"What I mean by all this is that these people can willingly move between different locations in space, much like the drones in the Sky-Twin programme. We've all seen Star Trek, we've all seen a hundred other science fiction films that are all about people who can hop about in space and time. Well, these folks can actually *do* it. Travel using what looks like personal portals - wormholes if you will - in order to relocate or super-position. And this may be incredibly important."

There is a pause amidst which the atonal sound of shuffling and rustling circulates. Montgomery has a conclusion.

"The key here is that we will have a way to help people from around the world with this ability to transit first into remote areas here on Earth and potentially research the viability of terrain and resources for new settlements, but then also to go there and start afresh."

"You mean like astral projection to start new human colonies?" Bibi Melnik enquires.

"We need to careful with the rhetoric here, Bibi. I wouldn't say astral projection really. It seems to be much more than that. These folks can actually interact in the location to which they dual. And I wouldn't say 'colonies'. Let's say 'settlements' and 'settlers', like our forefathers…and foremothers," he says as his glance encompasses the women in the room.

"You said on Earth *first*, John?" prompts McFarlane.

"Yes, Bill. Obviously if some of these people, assuming they are virus-free, can recruit others who are also virus-free, potentially they can locate quickly to other areas. So, imagine that we start a settlement in Kodiak or Clearwater or Maui, but for whatever reason their health barriers are breached and GARI shows up, right? Well, these guys could relocate to another settlement. Don't ask me exactly how they do this - Ava has more on that - but they may be the answer to dodging the virus. There is no reason why, in time, these people could not explore off-worlds. Exo-planets and habitable space. Sure, we can start with the Moon. It's right *there*. But so far we don't see too many restrictions on movement in near space," he continues.

Mitch Nicolescu is on auto-pilot and forgets he is talking to his President.

"So what is 'near space'?" he asks, before adding "Mr. President, Sir."

"Good question, Mitch. Honest answer is I don't know. Ava - do you want to take up the story?"

And with that, Ava Redmond is up at the plate.

"Thank you, Sir. Mitch, John is right. We need to grab this opportunity. It's too important not to. 'Near Space' is what you asked, and honestly I am best-guessing this but I think our solar system would be included in that. Which is amazing."

There is more murmuring round the room before Ava collects herself and strides on.

"We know so far that a few people are 'dualling' - that's the everyday term we will be using for this - across the world. We believe that potentially *many* people might be able to relocate to particular positions across the globe. The question is really how much training and time will be required to get them to a point where they can make a material difference to our present situation. We need a lot more time and contact to work this through, but the main point here is that we have test subjects on the CAT programme who are proving that they can travel through space. And for that reason we think they might be able to travel through time too."

Abe Hart knows a lot of this, but has a big question in his mind.

"Could we potentially go back and prevent the outbreak of GARID-7?" he asks.
"I suspect that would be so complex Abe, not only because no-one knows where it actually started, but because we might not have enough duallists or time to even get near to this, judging by the rates Bill showed on his charts."

Hart nods and then his head drops, in obvious disappointment.

"So who are these people, Ava?" asks Joe Becker. "I mean, can anyone do this, or is it just a lucky few?"
"At the moment we're not sure is the honest answer, Joe. My take on it is that it's to do with something called entanglement, and that in relation to location in spacetime, when things are nearer together they tend to be more entangled."
"So we are more likely to have entangled people because we have such a big population?" Becker comes back.
"Something like that," replies Redmond. "So far we have only identified a few, but the idea is that we domino this so that we get the numbers to at least start a settlement. But the risk is of course that old loyalties might reside in some. That someone from Russia who has learnt to dual will be on a Russian programme set up to do the same thing, and we end up with conflict rather than co-operation. My gut feel is that if you learn how to dual, and can wrap your head

around what that means, you might just see a bigger picture and think *human* rather than Russian. If you see what I mean."

Montgomery is quick to intervene, before the inevitable onslaught of questions comes raining in from all sides.

"Abe. Everyone. Ava's got a point. This is still the most positive news we have had in terms of both off-worlds and terrestrial settlements. From what I know so far, within a month or so we will have some hard data on possible routes and locations. For any off-world journeys, it will be dangerous for those involved, and I suspect that some sacrifices will be made along the way. Like many of our most challenging adventures in the past, this will take the courage and selflessness of those brave test pilots - the duallists - who will boldly explore new environments that may host our future, even if only in the short term until all traces of GARI are absent here on Earth."

Bill McFarlane takes a gentle cue from Montgomery without off-setting too much of his reassurance.

"That won't be for some time, John. As you saw in my memo, this virus is one of the hardiest we've ever experienced, surviving for months, affecting livestock and wildlife as well as ourselves, and seemingly impervious to weather conditions, most alcohols and detergents and the like. So realistically the only way to survive this is by isolating and conducting controlled testing to find ways to kill it. If we can't do that, or find that vaccine, then my fear is that it will wipe out enough animal and plant resource that people will starve before they die of GARI. We have intelligence that shows supply chains around the world are already in chaos, with most countries now looking locally for produce as many of the major ports have become immobilised. No-one wants to admit that their country is falling apart, and so cause panic and unrest, but basically quite a few of the African and Asian countries are already lost causes. I only hope the CAT programme can provide some answers soon. But in the meantime, Maria and myself are working flat out to get the settlements ready and I'll obviously update on any breakthroughs."

"OK, Bill. Our combined thanks go to you and Maria. Thanks Maria," the President responds.

"OK, to wrap up, I need to ask everyone to keep this strictly level six. I only want to hear good news, folks. Tell me what we *can* do, not what we can't. Joe, Abe, Bibi. We'll stay behind. Everyone else - thank you for your time. Let's get to it."

And with that, the group disassemble with Joe Becker, Bibi Melnik, Abe Hart and John Montgomery left to move to the sofas to continue discussions on the sensitive military detail that will affect millions of lives around the world.

—-

Back in Boston, Wendy Xui and Mal Baines scurry quickly across from the main refectory to the Physics building, both wearing surgical gloves, facemarks and lab glasses.

As they get back down to the underground labs where not so long ago they formed a formidable experimental trio with Catherine Jumeau, the two wipe down the packaging on their sandwiches with powerful disinfectant and disrobe, before placing the protective outerwear and their clothes in the blast chiller and hitting the showers. Both emerge and don fresh clothes from their lockers.

Wendy figured a while back that extreme low temperatures might be some form of virus assassin, along with the special chemical reagent they keep in the lab. Her recent focus, along with Mal, has been GARID-7, and as clever as Wendy Xiu is, she is not an epidemiologist or an expert in biomedicine, and so is taking as many educated guesses to protect her and Malcolm as possible. It might not work, but having access to a laboratory has its advantages.

"Mal, are you ready to try again?" she asks Mal after they have eaten their sandwiches and had some hot tea.
"Sure, honey. I'll just wash up and be down in a minute," he responds.

With that, Wendy opens up a heavy, lead-lined, door that leads to another set of steps. After securing the entrance door, down she goes. Once at the bottom, she places her finger on the scanner pad which lights green, and then punches in her specialised security code to Water Melrose's old Lab One, having convinced University management, Boston police, the State senator and the federal government that she was one of three people who could potentially unravel some of the mysteries of Melrose's research.

A second, thicker door opens automatically. Once Mal joins her, and all doors are securely shut, she ushers Mal over to a horizontal padded trolley much like an operating theatre table. Above it hover an array of machines all with various readouts, some graphical, some digital. A mix of devices that will monitor vital signs, electromagnetic radiation, neurological activity, and, critically, electrodes which, when attached to Mal, will relay nervous system activity in one direction and, on Wendy's intervention, a series of impulses to Mal's brain which will cause him to relax and sleep or, if she needs him back, a fairly harsh electrical shock which will break the induced catatonic state.

"Ready?" asks Wendy.
"As I'll ever be," replies Mal.
"OK, here we go. Love you," she says and blows him a kiss.

Mal smiles and as the electrodes begin to do their work, Malcolm Baines' eyes begin to close as he drifts into a deep meditative state. And so, for the fourth time, he attempts to project himself into the cornfield that Catherine so carefully described to him and Wendy when she visited. This was Catherine's way of trying to help both Wendy and Malcolm, both in terms of understanding Catherine's own research which was so important to Melrose's own, and also to try to get to the bottom of Melrose's processes whereby Garfield would use Melrose's lab when dualling.

This was also important as part of the Jumeaus' side plan. Christophe and Catherine knew they were playing the authorities to an extent. That they were more advanced in their thinking and in their practice than they let on. And of course, this made for the best option in their search for Gill.

Originally, the idea was that the end-goal was to get Gill back. And although that was something of gargantuan and cosmic proportions, that would be *it*. Back to some kind or normality. Able to lead normal lives.

But with the emergent and immediate threat of GARI, everything seemed to change. No longer was it a demarcated and time-limited project, something that had a beginning and an end. The time had come to dedicate energies and focus to a much more complex set of problems.

Like not just finding Gill, but making sure that he didn't come back to a world in which highly volatile international tensions were likely to lead to the devastation and destruction of whole countries; to a world where GARI was claiming hundreds of thousands of lives daily; to a world where nothing remained of the relative innocence of early Spring.

Like finding a mechanism for her loved ones to be able to dual if they could. To help Christophe and Mary Jumeau, Wendy Xiu and Malcolm Baines, among many others, to find a way to escape to another reality if they could.

But of course, Catherine's idealism got the better of her, and in her heart she realised that there might not be a magic key to dualling. That some people can just do it and some can't. That some people are entangled and some aren't. Just like some humans are women and some aren't. Like some people have green eyes, and some haven't. And equally this drove Catherine mad with rage. Her father had already worked out that the level of entanglement in a localised area of spacetime was going to be high, or perhaps more accurately that where entanglement levels were high, spacetime emerged under more localised control. As a corollary the decoherence associated with the interaction with the surrounding environment would be less likely to interfere with the super-positioning. This was perhaps why Gill seemed to be able only to dual within relatively short physical distances and timespans. At least initially.

So for Catherine it was just illogical to assume that only a few people were entangled in some way shape or form. Christophe and Catherine wanted to explore the way in which people could access their entanglement. How they could tap into what the Jumeaus believed to be something far more prevalent among the population than first thought. So rather than Catherine or Gill being superhuman, in fact she believed the opposite: that dualling was a basic human ability for many, if not all. Of course the difficulty was going to be the race against time to find a way to help those who hadn't naturally stumbled across this, like Gill from a young age but equally as often like Catherine who seemed to have many dreams while dualling to the wormhole but never beyond until that first magical night with Gill at the motel.

When Catherine visited Wendy and Mal not so long ago, it was supposed to be simple. A happy reunion despite the loss of their esteemed Professor. It turned out very differently. It was there that Catherine started to share her ideas with Wendy and Mal.

Most of the content was, unsurprisingly, around Walter Melrose and his research. And of course Gill. Wendy and Mal had never met the man in Catherine's life, but the way that she would talk about him left them in no doubt as to the fact that he was the *one* and that she had found her match, as had they. The three started to explore avenues for understanding the wider implications of dualling and the prevalence in the population.

It was over a bottle of particularly fine Spanish red, that Mal began to clue into some of the signs that Catherine would list as she tried to create a profile of those who might be considered the 'most likely' to be entangled.

"I think one of my topmost indications would be very real dreams. Maybe dreams about travelling, or dreams about places where you don't know how you got there but you see a path which you follow," Catherine hypothesised.

"I know. Like a train station. You know, where you are on the main concourse and you have, like, ten different platforms you can choose from. That would fit, right?" asked Wendy.

"Exactly!" replied Catherine. "Anything like that. Maybe an airport lounge, or motorway roundabout, or even a boat or yacht, something on the sea or a river," Catherine thought out loud.

"A river?" asked Mal. "I used to have very lucid dreams about being at a river crossing," he said.

"That would work," Catherine responded. "How real were these dreams Mal? Did you cross the river?"

"Yeh, I remember there were different bridges. Three I think, and I could walk along the edge of the river to the one I wanted to use. I'd walk across - sometimes it was scary though, as the river would swell. It seemed big. Wide. You know?" Mal explained.

"What was on the other side, Mal?" asked Catherine.

"Well, I remember I just ended up at home one time. That was odd. I thought I had woken up, but in fact my home was very different. It was decorated like my house, you know, but there were people there I didn't know."

"That's kinda weird. Didn't you think that was odd?" Wendy chipped in.

"Yes, but then you don't have other dreams to compare to really. I mean like what other people dream about. I suppose I thought it was normal. Do you think this means anything?" Mal wonders.

"It could do. I mean, it's on my list so it's worth investigating. When I dual, I seem to go a bit catatonic. It's like I do actually leave my body and I can *feel* that even though you would see me just sitting there or lying there as me. Maybe quiet or with my eyes closed, but that's usually how I do it," Catherine replies.

"That's a bit like how I felt. Mind you, I haven't had the dream for a while. I guess it's not been something I have needed, or maybe I lost that ability somewhere," Mal concludes.

"Well, look, Mal. If you and Wendy are OK with this, why don't we try to recapture that experience. It's got to be worth finding out? I'm lucky to have you as a test subject," Catherine is already thinking ahead. "Did you also have a sense that there was someone else at the crossing? You know, like I've explained about how Gill seemed to be there but I could never quite identify that it was him?"

"Yes. I remember thinking it was my sister, but I kinda knew it wasn't. Maybe it was you, Wendy!" Mal ponders. "Maybe that was you all along." Mal starts to laugh, and Wendy gives him a cuddle.

"Maybe it was," she replies. "It better not have been another woman."

At which point the three then broke into a bout of giggling, if only to delay the inevitable job of planning some seriously intimidating experiments.

* * * *

CHAPTER 4: XARN

It is late morning Saturday in Oakton, and Catherine is on her way to the local supermarket. 'I Got The Fever' by The Prophets is belting out the stereo. It's one of her go-to day-off songs and it's always better high on the volume dial. She parks up to do some shopping for her parents who, much against their will, she has forced to stay at home. Hers is the only car in the parking lot. Normally it would be full.

Oakton is a fairly earthy conservative town nestling in Fairfax County. Settlers here were some of the first in the early days of the country. The streets are clean and the buildings well kept, and folks are nice and friendly. The only problem is, there is hardly anyone around and there is a sense of other-worldliness about the place.

Locals have been watching the news religiously and are now fully aware that, barring a miracle, they are going to get a visit from GARI. And since there is no known protection against this raging foe, there is also a sense of despair. The contrast on this fine sunny winter's day where everything on the surface seems so calm and beautiful, is stark.

More than anything the Jumeaus, as relative newbies to the area, have seen how the community has gone from a vibrant hub of social and recreational harmony, to one of quick dashes around supermarkets by locals in what looks like the kind of outfit you'd wear in an operating theatre; of underlying suspicions of who among them might have the dreaded virus. The lack of accurate testing just serves to heighten tensions, and the resulting air of mistrust and fear is only offset by local community stalwarts' efforts to deliver food and important updates via old-fashioned banners and leaflets telling the vulnerable to tune in to Oakton FM either on the radio or the computer.

Hardy Gillis is waiting at the entrance as Catherine grabs her carrier bags from the car. She's planning on a serious shop.

"No fresh items today, dear," proclaims Gillis from a good forty feet away.

"That's OK, I just need a bunch of basics. OK to scoot round real fast?" Catherine replies, keeping it as friendly as possible.

"OK. You will have to follow the route. Have you got your own gloves and wipes?" he shouts.

"Yes, I have!" Catherine shouts back.

"OK, I'll be in the far corner if there are any problems. Otherwise use the auto-scan and your biocell. Don't touch anything else and disinfect everything when you get home," Gillis informs her.

In a way, Catherine is lucky. No-one else is there so she can have a bit of freedom to get what she wants rather than wait in a queue for an hour and then have to wait for the person in front and the person behind to maintain the shop's distancing rules. In effect, those rules are most likely meaningless, because, if there *is* virus in the store, then it's more than likely that at least one person will be in contact with it.

Tins are the worst. Because they are metallic, and the virus is known to linger on metal for the longest period, then any amount of disinfecting will not guarantee the tin is free of virus if you touch it. As a consequence every shop is a major operation, with each step in the process performed with clinical precision.

Once all is paid, she walks the trolley outside, places the bags in the large trunk of the car, and discards the used wipes and her first pair of gloves in a small incinerator Gillis has had installed outside the store. After a final wipe down on and around the trunk handle, and using her personal disinfectant to clean her hands, she is finally able to fire up the Oldsmobile.

As Catherine returns home and into the wide drive of the Jumeaus' place on Hannah Farm Road, she parks up at the bottom of the drive, gets the hose from the outhouse, fills the bucket with the super-strength disinfectant her dad has bought, and starts to decontaminate the car, then all bags and wrappings. Then she lays everything out in a line, before carefully transferring the inner bags from cardboard boxes or, for tins, the contents, into new, clean containers. Those containers would be kept closed, refrigerated or blast chilled for two days and then decontaminated again with disinfectant before finally being opened with protective surgical gloves. The whole procedure would mean that the contents would only reach someone's mouth by ensuring they would never have any contact with another human or potentially contaminated packaging. It was a complete drag, and Catherine hated it. But if it meant that she was reducing the risk of her parents getting ill, then this was the only way. What would have been an hour-long event had doubled, or on days when others were at the supermarket, it could be quadrupled.

Once Catherine has stored all the food into the large pantry and sealed it, she makes herself a cup of green tea. She feels exhausted. This the one day she doesn't have to be in Langley, and it's her chance to visit the cornfield in relative privacy, free of the confines of the 'Pod'. She tells her parents that she's going to use the spare bedroom as usual, and Mary Jumeau makes sure that the intercom is working between there and the lounge, where she and Christophe will wait for any indication of trouble, and hope that silence ensues until they see her later in the day.

Today's mission is Beth.

As Catherine closes her eyes and focuses on the clearing, it seems to come quickly. More so than the last time. She is developing rapid access to the wormhole and is revelling in this new world; a world of exploration - somewhere to escape the vagaries of visceral incarceration on Earth and where she can soar above the plain.

As she scans the clearing, she is careful to avoid making a sound, and as she drifts upwards, she can see for far and wide to the edges of the field. Realising that she might have a better chance of contacting Beth at the boundary, she makes her way to what seems like the farthest edge up on the left and where there looks to be an extension to the perimeter.

As she approaches, she notices how much darker it is getting. Cornflower blue in the sky turning first to purple, then dark blue, and now almost black. Adrenalin seeps into her stomach and not for the first time she feels the unease of straying from her patch.

However, she must go on. She must push against the barrier in order to communicate much further afield, where this might mean putting her own mission in danger.

A lightning strike lights up the perimeter in front of Catherine, making her jolt and fall. After dropping several feet rapidly, she gathers herself and regains height. Tentatively nearing the fence containing the field, the corn below her is wilted and brown. The black of the sky seems to shiver and shake, with momentary silver ruptures appearing as if this is a mirror about to crack. In this part of the field her abilities wane, and after dropping further the weight in her body begins to become too much to sustain flight. Catherine falls some ten feet and lands with a bump in some soil adjacent to the barbed-wire fence. She is at the very borderline of the pasture.

Sparks fly from the fence wires randomly, illuminating a space beyond which seems to have no floor, no bottom. As if the whole field was floating in a sea of black. As she tries to get up, laden with the increasing mass pinning her down, she begins to mouth the word 'Beth'. It's difficult. Her mouth doesn't want to move. Yet she must assert her presence here if she is to succeed. Determined not to be laid out in this barren corner of her own field, she gives a mighty heave to raise herself onto all fours and then straightens her back so she is sitting up. Control does not come easily, but she begins to form the word again, and this time some sound emanates from her lips.

"Beth?" she calls. And again. And again.

Nothing.

"Beth!" she shouts it this time, using all her energy.

Nothing.

From the other side of the fence, a shimmer of lightly coloured mist appears. It swells so that Catherine can see it coming closer. If this is Beth, she thinks, she better show herself quickly before Catherine wilts, such is the pendulous strain of keeping her torso upright.

As the mist reaches the wires of the fence, the sparks start to coagulate into a series of lines which reveal and form a gap small enough for the mist to penetrate. Catherine feels helpless, and is praying that whatever is in this mist is friendly, as she seems powerless to fend off any unwanted attention from a potential foe such as Nuvo's twin. Fear rages within her, and her instinct is to retreat; to scurry away and hope that she can scramble through the reeds and back to the clearing. This is almost insurmountable, and yet such is Catherine's newfound willpower and strength of purpose, that she knows she must make contact.

Circulating around the fence and breaching the wires towards Catherine's leaden body, the mist glides towards her. She musters the strength to raise her left hand outwards. Barely a few inches off the ground the fingertip of her index finger becomes surrounded in the mist, and suddenly Catherine shivers involuntarily. Now she cannot see her finger, or her hand, and now her arm. As the mist rolls into the field and all around her, it invades her body and her being. Catherine closes her eyes and awaits the worst.

"Open your eyes," comes the voice. And Catherine does.

The disorientation from the change in space is overwhelming and Catherine's head is spinning. Feeling dizzy and sick, she is struggling with what looks to be a new environment. A new reality.

"Are you OK?" comes the voice.

As the spinning wheel inside Catherine's head reforms from a kaleidoscopic mess to become the centre stage of a large, open-air amphitheatre, she fights to make sense of her surroundings. She can hear strange music. All around her, from every direction, emanates Radiohead's 'In Limbo'. She comes to standing on a large wooden floor in front of what looks like thousands of rows of seats, all empty. Twisting her head to see behind her, she can see several stage doors and one emergency exit, lit up in familiar green with the symbol of a person running down some stairs. It is a very human place. And it doesn't seem dangerous. Over the sound system, a woman's voice, quiet and calm, instructs her to go to row nineteen, block D.

Catherine is glaring in the light and, as row nineteen is not too far back, she can make out the figure of someone over to the left. She assumes it's Beth, but can't be sure. Nervously she walks off stage right and down the side-steps to the main auditorium. Gone is the torpor induced by travelling so close to the edge of the field. She moves up the incline of one of the main aisles and reaches her destination.

Beth Gill is sitting quietly three seats in and smiles.

"Catherine," she announces, in a calm and friendly tone.
"Beth?" asks Catherine.
"Good to meet you," says Beth. "I've been waiting for something like this to happen for some time. Are you feeling OK?"
"Yes, thank you. I got a bit dizzy and…where are we?" asks Catherine.
"Oh, this is just my own decor for the wormhole. I love the theatre and always used to dream about being here and meeting the love of my life, and it has a special meaning for me, so I thought it best to recreate it so that it isn't too weird or scary," Beth says. "If you like, we can grab a drink at the bar up there?", pointing to the back of the auditorium which seems miles away.
"Uh, OK," replies Catherine, still too confused to have an opinion in this place.

With a slight turn and wave of Beth's hand, the surroundings morph seamlessly into a large open-plan bar, somewhat Edwardian in its aspect with panelled walls, lush green velvet curtains and thick red carpet. The table in front of Beth has two wide-rimmed goblet glasses filled with a pink liquid, a cherry and a cocktail umbrella. The entirety is opulent to put it mildly, and the seamless transformation surprises Catherine. Clearly Beth has a great deal of command here.

"It's OK," Beth says. "It won't make you drunk or anything."

And with that, Beth lifts a glass as to propose a toast.

"To us," Beth proclaims.

Catherine gingerly lifts her glass and the two clink their drinks and take a sip.

"Oooh. that's good, isn't it?" Beth comments.

"Look…Beth. Can we talk about you, me and Gill? Do you know where he is?" There is a degree of desperation in Catherine's voice.

"I don't, no. I was kinda hoping you might though. Sorry for the charade in here. I realise it must be off-putting and entirely strange. I was just trying to make it less so, but obviously that wasn't working," Beth reflects.

"No. I mean, yes. Oh, please don't misunderstand me, Beth. It is amazing that you are here. That you are OK. It's beyond my wildest dreams to even be here. I honestly never thought this would be possible."

Beth takes another sip of her drink.

"Well, in *here*, I'm queen bee. This is my comfort zone and I've taken the time to make it the way I want it, so if I come across as a bit blasé about things, please forgive me. But let me tell you something. One thing I have learned from my travels? *Anything* is possible. The way our minds are forced to see things back home is just crazy. So many things aren't what they seem."

"I am beginning to understand that," says Catherine. "Was that you in the cornfield back then? Was it you that helped release Montgomery?"

"It was actually me and my twin, Tsera. We had to unite our energies to help you get your guy out of that alien creature. We could see that Montgomery was inside. When you and Gill were struggling against that dark force, we weren't strong enough to stop it though. Whatever that thing is, it is extremely strong and my biggest worry was that they would kill Gill. But my sense tells me he is alive. Is that the same for you?"

Catherine, for the first time since the beginning of this encounter, begins to smile.

"Yes. I feel it. I know he is out there…here…somewhere," she says. "But I think those creatures that took Gill will be back. I could feel them at the edge of the cornfield."

"Yes, the cornfield. It was only with Tsera's help that we were able to cross into it. It was a miracle. After so long being lost in a strange world, and without ever hearing from my family, to feel that

Gill was near was like a balloon bursting next to my ear. Tsera and I used this place all the time to escape some of the hassles we had. We usually had it all to ourselves, although every so often some gatecrashers sit way up at the back - far enough that you can't see them but close enough to make you aware that they're watching. But that day, we were having fun on stage when all of a sudden I could hear a strange sound at first. That one frightened me as it was weird and not human at all. We were going to return to our village when Gill's voice came through the big speakers. It reverberated around the room all muffled at first. Like he was underwater or something, and then it became clear."

Beth takes another sip form her cocktail.

"I think something happens between wormholes. I am not sure what it is. It's like if the frequencies or cosmic positions line up or something then you can port across from one to the other. Or it could be just the strength of the signal, or where it comes from. But for me, unfortunately I can't ever go to any other place than this now," says Beth, and lets out a weary sigh. Her thoughts have taken her to a sad place.

"But why?' asks Catherine. "Was it Gill's kidnapping?"

"I don't think so," mutters Beth, struggling now with her emotions. "Where we are now is not where I live. You probably know that. I wasn't like my brother. I always stepped back from danger, and let him do all the experimenting when we were younger. But I knew I could dual. Denton always told me not to, as it could lead to unpredictable outcomes. And of course he was right. Just look at us!" Beth points out before continuing. "We are all over the place. I am so sad for my mom and dad. I have tried so hard to make contact with them but I've never made it work."

"Where do you live, Beth?" enquires Catherine, almost slurring her words with anxiety and the speed of trying to quicken the conversation.

"Catherine, you know that time doesn't move here, right? I mean, we could talk for a year and we'd both still return to within a very short time of when we left out respective locations, yeh?" Beth informs Catherine.

"Hey, sorry. Yeh, I figured. It's just that even an hour or so might make a difference right now. Back home on Earth there are a ton of problems unfolding fast. But sorry - tell me about your place first."

"My twin was Tsera. A wonderful person. He was the one that I always met here when I first started to dual. He was in human form, which was nice. Tsera was from Xarn. You'll probably find it as one of the planets around multiple sun systems in what you might call the Scorpio constellation. I can see enough in the sky from Xarn to know that we must be in the same galaxy as you. Look up any red dwarf stars and planetary systems with three suns - that's us. And we can breathe too. Yes, there is oxygen there. Only problem is those suns don't give us much heat so we need to stay warm."

Catherine is mesmerised. She can't believe what she is hearing. So instead of asking any particular question, she just nods. Beth carries on.

"The people there are like us. They look kinda weird but they have developed along similar lines. They look like a cross between us and a leopard or cheetah but they stand on two legs like us. It takes a lot of getting used to, let me tell you, but basically they do most things we do. The big danger is the crocs - that's what I call them anyway. Like dinosaurs or something, just not as big. They are scary. Many Xarn folk have been taken and killed by the crocs. They call them Xeti - like 'Sssshhh', you know?

"And do the Xarn folk - the Xarns - do they talk? How do you understand them?"

"They have their own language, but communication is a universal thing, and I used to study languages anyway, so it wasn't too difficult. They make mainly tonal sounds, so I have adapted my voice to make those sounds, and Tsera did the same back, which was amazing." Beth drifts off on the latest mention of Tsera.

"What happened to Tsera, Beth? Is he not on Xarn any more?" asks Catherine, afraid of the answer.

Beth sheds a tear. Which, Catherine briefly thought, couldn't be possible. But here she was. Crying. The tears running down her cheek.

"I'm so sorry, Beth. I didn't mean to…" follows Catherine.

"No, it's OK. It's just always so difficult for me," Beth replies, and wipes her tears away with the back of her hand, which Catherine notices is strangely similar to Gill's, just smaller. "Tsera was taken by one of the Xeti about a year ago. Well, one of Xarn's years which is much shorter than yours. I miss him so much."

Beth continues wiping her tears as she speaks. Catherine is finding it tough to comprehend.

"He was all I had really. My other twin, I guess. The one I could live a life with, however strange. That's why language and looks didn't matter. The bond between us was so strong. I'd never had anything like that in my life, not even with family. And now I never will again."

Beth gathers herself to avoid going into another bout of crying. She obviously hasn't had the chance to recount this to anyone from back home, and Catherine now understands that Beth sought her out because she is so desperate to return and so desperate to be with her family after what sounds like an impossible adventure.

"After Tsera died, I went to stay with his family, who treated me like one of their own. Xarn folk are close knit, and because Xarn is not as advanced as Earth in lots of ways, everyone there has to look out for the Xeti. But it's still primitive living. God, what I'd give for some makeup and a night out…"

Catherine smiles. In any other situation this would be funny, but it is loaded with sadness and regret.

"I brought it on myself, really. I got so depressed in Boston when my boyfriend back then got a job on the finance markets in New York. He just travelled down there and over to London so much that I hardly saw him. I thought I loved him, but I'm not sure he ever loved me. I had moved all that way just to be with him, and it was like he didn't even see me sometimes. I felt like I was going nowhere, and just ended up drinking and taking pills to make the long nights go quicker. I ended up in a real state. Anyway, I got so bad that I took a bunch of pills one night and knocked myself out. They told me I was in a coma for two days. But when I was unconscious I dualled properly for the first time. It was to a place like this. I loved the theatre from when I was a little girl and always made my own theatres in my mind. When I came here the first time, Tsera was on stage. He was magnificent, and I knew. I just *knew*. But then the problem was that we were from different planets. And we needed to make a choice. We'd always intended to try to travel back to Earth once Tsera had had time to learn about Earth. It would be much more difficult for him to adjust to Earth than for me to adjust to Xarn. So we agreed that we'd spend some time there, except it turned out to be such a struggle with the Xeti attacks that we had to hunker down and help Tsera's family. I tried to go back a couple of times, and found that I couldn't. I kinda figured out that the only way to return would be if Tsera and I dualled together, as one. Maybe that's due to the distances involved. I don't know. But now that he's gone, I am trapped on Xarn, and come here as often as possible to keep sane."

Catherine is still mesmerised, but in the pause, tries to relay some positives.

"I'm sure we can figure something out. I mean, we are here together, right? We found each other, didn't we?" she offers.
"That's good of you. I know you are strong. I can feel it. Like Tsera. You and Gill are the only ones that have managed to be close enough to here for me to sense it. You must have been a powerful force too," Beth asserts.
"We didn't get the chance though, Beth. That's the point. We were just starting before he was taken. I have to get him back."

Beth sits up, and after a lot of talking, reaches for the elegant cocktail again.

"Do you think you can get here again, Catherine? Or at least, do you think you can get close enough to send me a message to let me know to come here?" asks Beth.
"I think so. It was tough at the edges of the field. I felt like I weighed a tonne. It was when you breached the fence that things got easier and I don't even remember how I got here. That must have been you," explains Catherine.

"We need to understand more. I can't lose you now. I need to know that we can do this again, or I'll die," says Beth.

"Hey. It's OK, I think the first of anything is probably the most difficult. You obviously control this space almost entirely, and I feel like I am getting there in the cornfield. If we have that, then the key will be to keep the communication between the two open. Let's try to test this as soon as you are back on Xarn. Just try to throw out a signal for me. Something that we both will recognise and no-one else would have a clue about."

"I know," says Beth. "Gill used to practise 'The Girl From Ipanema' on his sax all the time when I was about 14. It used to drive me mad, but I know every note of that damn tune. How about I hum it or sing it as loud as I can on the stage there, and that will be my call. Right?"

"That sounds like a plan. I'll learn it. And I'll try and sing it when I'm near the perimeter of the field - where you found me today. OK?" asks Catherine.

"It will work. I know it," says Beth, and with that the two say their goodbyes, as Catherine takes the emergency exit at the side of the stage and emerges at the outer fence of her cornfield.

—-

Back at the Jumeaus' house, Catherine is lying on her bed listening to her favourite Beatles album. 'Fixing A Hole' gently washes over her and she is humming the tune, taking time to reflect on her latest sojourn beyond the cornfield, when there is a gentle knock on the door.

"Darling?" Mary Jumeau asks in a raised voice to be heard over the music.

Catherine lowers the volume, and sits up.

"I'll be right out, Mom."

"OK, it's just that I've put some dinner on. Be about ten minutes if you want to join us?"

"Great. I'll be down for that!" chirps Catherine, reaching for her biocell to turn the volume up again.

She hears her mother shuffle off along the corridor outside her room, and mulls over what she will say to her parents.

At the dinner table, the Jumeaus tuck into a hearty stew that Mary has concocted out of some winter vegetables she grows in the allotment at the end of the garden, and some beef delivered by Dale Farm, one of the big producers in Fairfax that is offering free delivery around the county for regular customers. As the temperatures outside fall rapidly with the onset of evening, it is now a heightened pleasure to have warmth, good food, and family. Basics that were once thought dull compared to a night out at the diner or restaurant or bar, now the cornerstone of living with all but essential shops and grocers open.

"So, Catherine, tell us," Christophe prompts. "You were going to try to make contact with Gill's sister, you said?" He throws Catherine a couple of raised eyebrows to amplify the request for information.

"Uh, yeh. So, I wanted to follow up on that initial meeting... well, when I think I saw Beth at the clearing. It was a sign that our side project might come off. Mom, this is Gill's sister Beth, if you remember. She was there when Gill was taken, so I knew that somehow she would have at least some way of showing up there again. It was just how that would happen."

Mary Jumeau nods. "Well that's great, honey. You managed to actually communicate with her this time?"

"I did, Mom. But not in the cornfield. It's difficult to describe but after all this time, I had to try something. I had to leave the cornfield," she says.

Christophe stops spooning some more stew onto his plate. "But how would that be possible? Outside the wormhole surely you would be in a different part of the Universe? I mean, the wormhole is bounded by a horizon, sure. But if you cross that you'd just end up in 'normal' spacetime somewhere else, wouldn't you?" he proposes.

"I thought that too, Dad. But recently I have felt more and more like the answers to some of our problems don't lie within the clearing. I can't explain it. It's almost like that is where people that dual would go if they were free to move around, and respond to my broadcasts there. But Gill and Beth are both trapped. They can't come to me in person, I don't think. Seems that I might have to go to them. Today was the first time I have ever gone outside the perimeter of the field. It drew me there. I didn't need any directions. I knew exactly where to go. I could feel it. It was like the early times when I didn't know where I could go in my dreams but I could feel the reeds of corn all around me. I could have battled through those in any direction, and yet the direction I chose took me to the clearing. I don't know how that could be, and I don't know how I knew to go to that far edge of the field. It's so massive that to find the part of the fence where I could move out can't be chance. I think it was Beth's own broadcast or radio signal or whatever you want to call it, but I just knew where to go."

"That's a good sign, honey," Christophe responds. "Now tell us about where you went, yeh?" he asks.

"Sure. Well, I didn't have much control. That's the first thing to say. And I got scared. Things are dark at the edge. You feel like you are more vulnerable and you see glitches in the images around you. Like the sky kept cracking, as if it was just a painting and someone with a sharp knife was cutting into it. It makes you think that there is something weird and nasty outside, clawing to get in. I'm not sure if that's anything to do with Nuvo or his twin, but it frightened me, mainly because I think this is where the field was broken into. It makes me feel like the field might be weakened. I don't know."

Catherine is pondering, her train of thought a little scattered.

"Just stick to the encounter with Beth for now, if you can," Christophe prompts.

"Don't push her too hard, dear," interjects Mary. "Remember her condition!"

"Of course," Christophe responds. "Sorry both. Just trying to get to the main course…"

Catherine smiles at her Dad.

"It's OK, Mom. I want to. It's important," she says, sharing her smile with her mother. "I guess what I'm saying is that I feel more in control at the clearing and need a bit more time to get that in other parts of the field. I do feel strong most of the time, and of course I don't have this bump to worry about there." She points to the large protrusion under her baggy shirt within which lies Alex, the name she will give her baby if it is a girl, or Joe if it is a boy. She doesn't know yet, and doesn't want to know despite all the offers. With the current situation in hospitals across the country completely in lockdown and with the army protecting them, the thought of having to go in fills her with dread, even if GARI hasn't affected Fairfax county as badly as elsewhere.

Catherine takes up the story again.

"So I saw a sort of image of Beth at the perimeter. Well, more like a mist or apparition of her there. Whatever, I knew it was her even though I was so scared of having to leave the field. But then it was like going down the rabbit hole. The shift was really something I can't even explain. I saw a lot from my past - of us in Montreal. And then Gill and when I met him. It all seemed to rush past so quickly, but was real. Like I was re-living it all. I just seemed to lose control when the mist surrounded me. Maybe that was Beth lifting me up and carrying me through the hole in the fence. I mean, she grabbed me and took me right into her own place."

"Go on, dear. Describe it for us," Christophe interrupts, eagerly.

"Well, it was a big theatre. Actually a huge theatre. And when I came to, I was on the stage. She was in the audience. Well, in a seat where the audience would be. We managed to talk. About her story and about mine and Gill's."

Catherine recounts Beth's plight, and how the two have agreed to meet up again as soon as possible.

"OK," Christophe asserts. "There are two big priorities here. First, we've got to work on this wormhole connection and find out where Beth is. She obviously needs our help, and potentially we need hers. If you can practise visiting her - you know, going to the theatre - then find out as much as you can about Xarn. I mean, I am assuming that there will be no-one on Xarn who can dual, but if Tsera could, maybe others could and you don't want to be seen by a duallist and trapped there. That would be catastrophic. Game over."

"Alright!" exclaims Mary. " We know what catastrophic means!" she says, throwing an annoyed look at Christophe, who realises his clumsiness.

"Yes, dear. Of course. Catherine, I just meant…"

"I know, Dad. Don't fret. I kinda figured that out already," Catherine reassures. "But I mean, yeh, I am on the same page. I'll need to go to Xarn at some point, but maybe not right away." She smiles at her Dad, who reciprocates.

"I need to understand more about Xarn too. If we are going to share this at some point - and I suspect we'll have to, I'd like to get a look at where in Scorpius that exoplanet could be. There have to be very few possibles there. I'll do some digging on that. And the other biggie here is this thing you mentioned about Nuvo and his twin. We both know what that means, right?" Christophe looks intensely at Catherine.

"That we need to broadcast at the edge to get the attention of Gill's captors?" Catherine follows. "Well, yeh. I get it. I just don't know how to do that yet. Do you have any idea why they would want Gill, Dad? I mean, I know we've discussed him being alive and being held someplace, but have you thought any more about what they want with him?"

"*That*," Christophe replies, "is the question alright. From what you have told me about Beth and Tsera, and what we know about you, Gill, and Nuvo and his twin, we know that wormholes are where entangled partners can combine in incredibly powerful ways and perhaps travel distances otherwise unheard of - at least in terms of the degrees of entanglement. This must be to do with reuniting entangled entities, like mending something that was broken so that it works again like new, or better. So, for example, Beth told you that the only way she and Tsera could respond to the devastation happening at the cornfield was to travel together to help. But now we know that this was not millions of light years from wherever Xarn is, but rather across the fence from their wormhole to yours. In the same way, I am guessing that Nuvo and his twin will have their own wormhole and maybe they can breach that far fence in the field. But maybe they can only do that if Gill is there. I don't know. As you said a while back, that's got to be how they got in to start with, and also how they got out. But from events in the cornfield that day, you also said that Nuvo was snatched by his twin, in the same way that Gill was; forcibly and seemingly without prior knowledge of what was happening. Now I know that makes this guy, this 'twin Nuvo' character super dangerous and the bogeyman here, but he has to have weaknesses. Some aspects of his relationship with Nuvo, or his own limitations, otherwise he would have laid claim to the cornfield there and then, no? I mean, if he is all powerful, then he presumably could have got what he wanted there and then."

Christophe breaks off, and seems to have a secondary thought.

"What is it, Dad?" asks Catherine, and Mary Jumeau also leans in across the table, knowing the look on her husband's face when he has cottoned on to something.
"I don't know. Something about this entanglement doesn't seem right. Not very 'coherent'. Like Nuvo is very much subjugated to his twin. Obviously these guys are not in love."

Christophe's thoughts only serve to remind Catherine of Gill, and, seeing that in her eyes, he decides to move on.

"Maybe if we imagine a world where these two are holding Gill. Maybe some future civilisation and maybe not too far from here in the Universe, if Nuvo dualled here from wherever their planet is. There could be problems there. They might need Gill because he has something they want. Something they need, which is a human trait, and something they can't get there. Could be his dualling ability of course. It could be something in his blood or in his body that they don't have which saves lives. Or maybe some thing he can do here - like speak a language or understand music - something they need for some reason. But I am just guessing."

Catherine, Mary and Christophe Jumeau sit in silence for twenty seconds or so. It seems like an hour. The sound of the kettle gets steadily louder until the click to stop the current going to heat the water seems like a crack of thunder.

"If they are in trouble, it could be that they have a pandemic too, couldn't it?" says Mary.

Catherine and Christophe look at first bemused, and then more transfixed on Mary, who is pouring the water into a huge teapot.

"That's it. Of course. They need Gill because of the wormhole. There is something about the route that Nuvo took to get here that they must recreate. It might be a pandemic, you are right, dear, and it might be climate change or a war they are fighting. It doesn't matter. The key is that they might be planning some sort of migration. Using the cornfield that Gill will lead them back to," he surmises.

"But why haven't they already come?" questions Catherine. " I mean, it's been months. And why couldn't Gill just dual back when I call?"

"You'd know if Gill was at the clearing for sure?" asks Christophe.

"One hundred percent. I carry that wormhole everywhere I go. I'd know if he was there," she replies.

Christophe nods in deference. "You remember Beth mentioned the distance thing? I think Gill is too far away to get to the cornfield on his own, or maybe they have some way of stopping him dualling. Maybe both. I don't know, but perhaps they are waiting for something."

"Could they be doing the same thing that we are doing? You know, finding duallists like Nuvo and then sending lots of them to invade us?" Catherine asks fearfully.

"It's possible. That's for sure. I dare say Gill would have got back if he could, or at least signalled in some way. His abilities must be severely limited. Maybe they can't access the cornfield unless both you and Gill are there. That's where we come full circle to the trap we need to lay for them. If we are right, it seems the only way to get Gill back is to open the cornfield and expose you and him to more danger," says Christophe.

"Well, that's hardly appropriate right now, dear," Mary interrupts.

"When I broadcast there the people so far have all come from the reeds," Catherine tells them. "From Earth. But if I am broadcasting I have no way of controlling how far that signal goes. I mean, Beth heard it, I am sure. So maybe Gill and Nuvo and his twin all hear it too. Maybe they are just waiting for their moment to come through the reeds," Catherine guesses.

Cristophe pauses again, thinking deeply.

"Is there any way that you can close the wormhole, Catherine? I mean, make it inaccessible to anyone outside. Have you ever tried doing that? You are powerful there, right? You can do almost what you want except at the perimeter, right? Well, how would you go about making it inoperable?"

"Oh, Dad. I've not even thought about that. I have no idea. It's just *there*. I control a lot of the space but…" Catherine tails off.

"It's OK, honey. It's just a thought. And not a very productive one at this stage. We obviously need it to be open so that Gill can access it. You and he don't have any other wormholes, do you?" asks Cristophe in a half-serious way.

Catherine lets out a nervous chuckle.

"One wormhole isn't enough?" she retorts.

"If we're right, honey, maybe it's both one too many and one too few," her dad replies.

* * * *

CHAPTER 5: CHANNELS

Over the horizon lies the Kark city of Kseu. As the small group of hovering gaseous pods speeds across the vast expanse of the Tereskik plain, avoiding the swirling sand above them, Gill's view is partially blocked by Nuvo, who is driving the pod. Over Nuvo's shoulder, Gill can see through the semi-transparent exterior and the unfolding landscape. A series of domes nestle side by side across the breadth of the view. As they grow larger, the Karkian capital comes into full view.

A low, sprawling amalgam of black domes spreads out as far as the eye can see. The edge of the city shimmers despite the lack of heat on the sandy surface. Gill's involuntary shivers are proving hard to control and he is praying that the temperatures ahead are more inviting than inside Nuvo's transport pod, within which he finds himself suspended, seemingly unsupported.

"Kseu," Nuvo exhales, either with excitement or worry.

Much to Gill's relief, the pods start to slow, indicating their imminent arrival. His adrenalin levels spike intensely and he can feel his heart beating hard in his chest. As they enter the gate, he catches a glimpse of more Karkian guards, but these ones have their central limbs extended, holding what looks like spinning shields. As he peers through the pod's shell, the shields appear to be made of some sort of liquid, and he can't imagine how these would be, in any way, classed as weapons, but as he was finding out at every turn today, the Karks seemed to be able to control both themselves and their environment through forms of biological engineering. Nothing seems hard or made of metal, except Nuvo's gift to him. This was beginning to take on a new significance as a result.

Once inside, Nuvo gestures to Gill to come forward so that he is next to him, and begins to speak in recognizable tongue; this time no translation is required.

"This may seem strange to you," Nuvo says. "In order to get you to the high chamber of Kseu, I can no longer use this psuvit we are in. You will be need to be protected from our atmosphere so you will have to be covered. By me."

Gill looks non-plussed. "Is this dangerous?" he asks.

"Not if you stay still and do not panic," Nuvo responds.

"OK."

"This will….feel strange," Nuvo adds, in some way trying to provide a bit of a heads-up to ensure Gill doesn't try to fight what was about to happen. "It will involve me changing shape so that we become one for a short while."

Gill doesn't know what to say, or how to act. 'Strange' is the new normal, so the fact that Nuvo highlights this particular variety of weird isn't exactly comforting. Totally at the mercy of Nuvo, it is too late to do anything other than comply. He takes a deep breath and says "OK, just do it."

On Gill's agreement, Nuvo begins to transform, morphing and spreading his shiny body so that it becomes deformed and more like a large sheet of what looks like white plasma. As this becomes established, a second phase of transformation now moulds this sheet into a circular cloud and as it does so, the mutation from solid to gas frightens Gill, and he starts to panic. Transfixed by events, he feels the gas surround him and as it enters his lungs his manic heartbeat forces a loss of consciousness. In his final waking moment, Gill oscillates between sleep and death. Nuvo has not only anaesthetised Gill but ingested Gill's body within his new state so that they can move as one.

As Gill comes to a little while later, he squints to adjust to the relatively bright environment. Looking around he can see that he is within some form of rock temple under a huge dome, in front of one of five pillars made of some form of liquid. Seemingly free to breathe, he checks himself for damage, and after reassuring himself that he is OK, he attempts to stand up.

A deep and hoarse bellowing sound vibrates so low that he feels the sound deep inside his bones.

"Stay still," the voice says. "And listen."

Gill obeys immediately, frozen to the spot. To his right he can see the figure of a body, bigger than the other Karks he has seen so far, and unusually dark in colour. As the figure hovers over to the centre of the five pillars, it speaks again in Gill's tongue.

"You will speak only when spoken to, and speak the truth. You will not try to escape, for to do so will result in your immediate death. Do you understand? Speak now."

"Yes," replies Gill, unhesitatingly.
"Good. Now, you will know I, Novek, Sultan of all Kark."

Gill swallows hard. He knows they don't want him dead, but this is so much like the end of something rather than the beginning, it chills him to the bone, and he figures that Novek might just hurt him to prove his dominance. As if he had to.

Novek, approaching Gill and descending from the temple stage, metamorphoses his body into a much larger animalistic form, to Gill appearing like a grotesque, slimy centaur, half beast and half man. Suddenly Novek runs straight towards him. Gill flinches, closing his eyes and waiting for the searing pain to hit.

But as the moment lapses, he glances at what is now in front of him and breathing heavily over him. As he looks up, the beast that Novek is channelling stands over him, glowering and snorting, steam and mucus mixing to drip over Gill's face and causing a burning sensation. He raises his hand to try to stop any further physical contact, and in this motion, Novek uses one of his legs to pick Gill up and throw him up onto the temple platform.

Gill is in mid-air and going to land hard. He tries to right himself but it is useless. As he drops from some twenty feet or so in the air, he puts his hands out to try to break his fall. And in the instant that he is about to potentially break one or both of them, he becomes frozen in the air, unable to move and suspended a mere inch or two above the floor. Novek, walks up to him, and in two steps re-establishes himself in Karkian form, completely black now, with only flaring ventricles showing any form of movement, his eye transfixed on Gill.

"You will see that, in this place, I have control. You will understand that you must obey my command, yes?" says Novek, in a sinister and threatening tone.

"Yes," Gill replies, still suspended and looking at Novek from his prone, and horizontal, position in the air. He glances over to Nuvo, who has his head bowed, seemingly in total deference to Novek. Beyond Nuvo, a range of guards circle the entrance. Gill is helpless.

"Good," Novek announces. "Now, we will gather."

Novek gestures to Nuvo, who comes up to the temple platform and holds Gill until Novek releases him from suspension. Nuvo's grasp is slimy and sticky and burns his skin. It is another reminder to Gill of how far from home he is.

As Gill regains his upright position, Nuvo and Novek usher him to a table.

"Sit," Novek commands. "This will be short, so pay attention. In two Kark days, you will travel with us to the field. You will need to travel with Nuvo to ensure you don't die. When we get to the opening in the field, you will also open a path. That path will lead to your planet. Do you understand?"

"No," Gill responds, at which Nuvo starts to flush and Novek's ventricles flare.

"No?" says Novek. "No? There is no 'No'. You do this or you die. This is the truth."

Gill is beginning to see more clearly, and has resigned himself to their ultimate power, so is playing for information.

"I mean I don't know why you are asking this. We do not obey unless there is a reason to. I'd rather die here than let you harm my fellow humans," Gill says. He's bluffing to an extent, but he's guessing that only Nuvo would be able to read human faces with any degree of accuracy, and Gill has played too many poker games to give anything away here, even though he is petrified inside.

Novek turns to Nuvo and various sounds ensue, mainly clicking followed by some very noticeable flushing on Nuvo's part, who eventually turns to Gill.

"Gill. We will speak alone," Nuvo instructs, as Novek waves the two away in an apparent show of disdain. Soon after, Novek retreats and seems to disappear into one of the pillars.

"Detective, you really do not want to question the mighty Novek," Nuvo urges Gill. "He has a plan. A plan we must follow. If you disregard this, you will surely die. Right here." Nuvo is being as direct with the language as he can.

"I'm not playing that game," Gill says, instigating a quizzical look, if one can discern such a thing on a Kark.

"I…I don't understand," Nuvo urges.

"I *mean*, I am not going to help you, which you obviously want, unless I know what is going on. Unless you tell me what your plan is. Come on, Nuvo. You are not stupid. You would be exactly the same if the roles were reversed."

Nuvo still looks quizzical.

"So, I value my life. Yes. I value any life. Heck, I value *your* life. But what I will not do is put millions of lives of my fellow humans at risk, just because some mad dictator like Novek asks me to. Do you understand? Our race has values and integrity, and sometimes we need to make the biggest sacrifice of all. To die for a greater cause. It scares me, yes. And I don't want to die. But if I have to in order to protect my species, my family back home, my loved ones, then I will. Don't tell me you, with all your travels and experience, don't get that." Gill pitches in as few words as he could muster the compromise that he wants from his captor.

Nuvo spends a good thirty seconds or more hovering and flushing, ventricles flapping in varying degrees of frenzy. Karks wear their emotions on their skin, perhaps not unlike humans. Clearly there is something in Gill's plea to Nuvo's sense of honour that has caused a considerable amount of internal conflict. Eventually he breaks the silence.

"I have…I have a respect for you, Detective Gill. I realise this is difficult for you, and that you must feel a little bit of desperation. But this is not a reason to die. You do not have to die. And I do not want you to die," he says.

Gill listens intently, but needs Nuvo to continue his thinking, and decides not to interrupt.

"You see, we are in trouble on Kark, as you know. You can see for yourself. Look around you as you came into the city, or as you travelled across the plain, or saw our sky from the cave. This is not ideal for us. Our planet is dying, and we have no choice but to leave. It has been coming for many hundreds of years, and we have adapted in the best way we can. What you see in our people are many extraordinary abilities which arise from our adaptation to our environment. And we are good at controlling that. But the problem comes from above. The solar winds now batter our hills and plains, and the dark side of our planet is now a frozen wasteland where only monsters can survive. And on the side of the sun, where we are now, the lack of energy is killing many of us every day."

He flushes green and then yellow, before returning to his usual grey-white colour and carrying on.

"Our great leader, Novek, has the vision and the plan to save us. He was the one who sent me many Kark years ago on my mission to explore any viable exorocks that we might inhabit. I was on many missions before landing in the south of your planet."
"The Antarctic," Gill reflects.
"Correct. It was there that I found your soldiers and if it hadn't been for your citizen Garfield, I might not have survived. I was sorry to have to take him, but I had no choice. From there, I knew that while I had to get back here, to my home, I also knew that your Earth was a feasible place for Karkian migration."
"But you can't just invade other planets, Nuvo. Surely, as an astronaut, a duallist, you must realise that this is forbidden, and that you would be in conflict with another planetary race?" asks Gill in a rhetorical tone.

Nuvo doesn't quite get the nuance, and continues.

"It is not a choice for us, Detective Gill. It is our destiny. Look around you here. We have used our brains to control this place, but it is hardly, how you call it, an *oasis*. There was a time when Kark was a good place. A warm place with lush lands that we Karks could harvest for certain foods. That became known as what you might think of as the 'golden era'. But we have found it more and more difficult since our primary star has lost its heat. Almost all of the Karkian people live here, in this one city. The remaining cities are too far from the sun. Some remain as mining communities, necessary to dig for some of the fluids and gases we rely on here."

Gill imagines the scale of the city and the implications.

"How many of you are there left?" he asks.

"Numbers are not important. It is the strength and resolve of those who remain," replies Nuvo, giving Gill the distinct impression that the dwindling Karkian population might be very small indeed.

"And why is Novek so powerful? I presume you don't like the fact that he is your twin?" Gill enquires.

Nuvo pauses slightly, before replying. "You are, how you say, 'fishing', just like a good detective. I understand. But do not mistake our intent. Novek is perhaps a tough leader and someone to be feared, but at this moment in our history we need someone who can lead."

"But he does so by fear, Nuvo. I saw the way the guards treated you at the gates and in the temple. They respect you as someone who has achieved great things. You would be the better leader, wouldn't you?" Gill searches for some insights from the Karkian 'astraman'.

"They also respect Novek. They see his power and this gives them strength. When we get to Earth we will not harm Earth people if we can avoid it. You should not believe that we wish a war with your people. There is enough land for us to occupy."

"You think that you can live on Earth undetected?" asks Gill.

"It is more that we can live among you, like I did as Garfield."

"Ah, I see. You Karks couldn't survive on Earth unless you occupy a human shell, right? That's what the Garfield thing was about."

Gill again asks rhetorically, as if this was fact, but actually prompting Nuvo for the truth. And such is the Karkian mentality that rhetorical questions are harder to identify and react to, so Nuvo misses a trick.

"You worked this out. I see. Well, in many respects it is better for you. You won't have to look at alien forms like us, and we will be able to integrate, eventually setting up our own city," Nuvo responds.

"I think we have enough cities, Nuvo. Besides, it's not as if your entire population can travel like you do. There will only be you and Novek and you will have to remain on Earth. How will you reproduce there without more Karks?" Gill asks.

"Now you are making a guess, Detective. Not a good guess. We have many here who can transit to Earth. You will see when we visit your own wormhole. This is your role, as Novek told you. You will open a channel for our spearhead of pioneers to build our presence on Earth. Once you have completed that mission with us, you will be able to return to Earth, and to be with your twin," Nuvo informs Gill.

"And you expect me to believe that?" prompts Gill in return. "You think I am stupid enough to believe that that thing - Novek - will have the decency to let me go to happy-ever-after-land when I am the only human who knows what you are doing or could trap you on Earth?" Gill is getting angry for the first time with his captor.

Nuvo does not respond, perhaps not knowing how to, and flushes amber. Gill presses on, sensing a weakness in Nuvo.

"And what about you? After Novek decides I am not needed, what is to stop him thinking that you will not be needed? You have much more experience on Earth than he does. You will be stronger there, and he will not be able to demonstrate the same powers trapped inside an ordinary human form. Earth is not going to be Kark. It strikes me that you would be next."

Gill stamps this hypothesis firmly in Nuvo's mind. For a second, Nuvo flushes vibrantly red and seems to start hyperventilating.

"Enough!" Nuvo shouts. This is the first time Gill has seen Nuvo this way. "Do you want me to inform the mighty Novek that you refuse to help us, and so must die right here? You would be foolish to do this. We can still get to your wormhole without you. Novek has done this once before and he can do it again," Nuvo asserts.

This time Gill goes silent. reflecting on that first time he encountered Novek. He knows that he must get back to the clearing, but to do so puts himself and Catherine at great risk. From the previous events in the cornfield he knows that he, and Catherine, would be no match for Novek. Thoughts flash through his mind. Novek never appeared at the clearing itself, instead exerting an enormous pull through the reeds from the edge of the cornfield. In the clearing, Catherine and Gill might be stronger. How could Catherine and Gill prevent Novek and other Karks from swamping them and breaking through to create channels back to Earth? How would anyone on Earth be able to trace dualling Karks? Would Gill and Catherine need to find a way to destroy the wormhole to prevent the Karks using it?

It must be obvious from Gill's eyes that he is having a lightning storm of ideas all at once, for Nuvo senses that Gill is resigning himself to the inevitable. That he will have to help.

"So, you see, Gill. You will have to trust that we do not plan to invade or conquer your planet. No. We just want safe passage. I will protect you, as a return for you helping me. My honour requires that. I give you my word that you will not be harmed on your return to Earth."

This is quite an admission from Nuvo , and if it weren't for the malevolent presence of Novek, he might have more confidence in Nuvo's goodwill. For all that Nuvo is a Kark and serving both Novek and the Karkian people, Gill continues to see human qualities in Nuvo that can only be explained by the years he spent in human form. This vital difference in Nuvo seems to remain Gill's only hope.

—

Catherine's Oldsmobile growls as she hits the gas. The hauntingly beautiful voice of Kate Bush permeates inside. 'The Man With The Child In His Eyes' a particularly appropriate tune for the times. Today she is in a hurry. As she approaches the outer limits of the base at Langley, she slows to a more respectable speed and once her ID is checked at the gate she parks up outside the Kepler building as usual. As she walks in through the security door, she notices Phil Kirkland and Ava Redmond sitting in the lobby.

"Catherine!" hails Kirkland in a very positive tone, and Catherine approaches the two senior government officials tentatively.
"Hi Phil. Hi Ava. You guys OK?" she asks
"Just fine, Catherine," replies Ava. "But you are just the person we need to speak to. Can you come with us?" Ava points towards corridor H1, and Catherine duly follows them into one of Phil's offices. Once seated and pleasantries exchanged, Ava turns to Catherine.
"So, we are very excited by the progress being made, Catherine. It really seems like you have made a couple of significant breakthroughs, right?" comments Ava.
"Thank you. Yes. My father has been keeping the logs. Have you seen those?" asks Catherine.
"Oh yes, Phil shared those. They're proving we are doing the right thing, that's for sure," muses Redmond.
"Catherine, Ava would like to follow up a little on Friday's data if that's OK?" Phil pitches in, and Ava nods. Clearly they have planned the dialogue.
"Sure," Catherine says quietly, revealing a slight hesitancy, as if she is in the headmistress' office waiting to get a telling off.
"It's just that we can't account for some of the data points, and we need your help. Phil says that you didn't report any unusual activity at, let's see where was it, zero plus sixty our time?" Ava questions.
"That's right," says Catherine. "I told you that on Friday, didn't I Phil?" says Catherine, getting a little frustrated that they don't come to the point more quickly. She has a lot to do today and wants to leave early to get back home and do her evening dual to the cornfield.

"Well, what we'd like to do is monitor you on a couple of additional data angles today, and we'd like to pull you from the pod if we see that spike again. We think it's very significant and perhaps you aren't remembering anything because something is cloaking the event after the fact. We really need to know what that spike is," Kirkland explains.

Catherine is trying to figure out what this is all about. The spike was definitely when Beth appeared after she was broadcasting and had visited the outer edges of the cornfield. What Kirkland wants for the CAT1 phase is for Catherine to concentrate solely on getting duallists at the clearing. Even though neither Kirkland nor Redmond can understand fully what happens when Catherine is in the wormhole, they have a good picture of the space and are beginning to work out anomalies between what she, and the data, report. It's a worry, but Catherine still intends to use the broadcast to include Gill and Beth *every* time she goes to the clearing, and once she is in there, no-one can really know what she is getting up to. Or so she thinks.

"If that's what you guys want, then fine. My worry would be that it might be the wrong moment though. You know, what if I was getting a spike because I could feel someone arriving, or about to communicate with a new recruit?" she directs this to Phil.

"Yes, I get that. But why wouldn't we have seen that when Carla first appeared? I guess the thing here is that clearly if you are unaware of the spike then there are other things going on in the wormhole that you're not aware of. And that isn't good. I mean, it *could* be good. It could be that we are missing opportunities. Missing recruits somehow. Or it could mean there may be some danger to you. In your current state, we wouldn't want the spike to indicate, say, a health problem. None of us can afford this right now, and especially not in your condition," Phil answers.

"That's kind of you, thanks Phil," she responds. "But you know I can come out of the field more or less any time I want, right? I mean, I do feel pretty much in control in that space. It's just that it can be exhausting focusing all my senses and powers there into creating channels for other duallists. Most people who do this will use a wormhole for themselves, maybe one other. You are asking me to make the field available to a host of other duallists, some of whom might ask me to help them through."

Ava steps in.

"Catherine, just a question, but have you ever picked up any more negative presences? You know, like the ones when Garfield was taken? Or Nuvo, I mean?"

"Not really, no. I mean, I have heard distant cracks of thunder just once, a while ago, but I figured that could be just a disturbance in the quantum vacuum there. It wouldn't be scientifically unusual," she says.

"OK," Ava continues. "But until or unless we end up with a significant cohort of duallists who we can trust, train and deploy, you are the most valuable asset this programme, and I am beginning to feel increasingly that our *civilisation,* has."

Redmond gets up and goes over to the window. Something she always does prior to concluding meetings.

"Sorry to sound melodramatic, Catherine. Phil and I are just back from Washington. The latest pandemic figures are frightening most governments and we are rapidly approaching the next level in the state of emergency. We will most likely have to lock down this place in the next two weeks, so we need to speed up the progress. I don't want to put further pressure on you, but the sooner we can find more duallists the better chance we've got to deploy them at will to on-world settlement sites. I am sure you will appreciate the urgency."

Catherine is a little taken aback. 'Pressure' is all she has felt in the last few months, and it seems that the only way to keep her family safe will be to get her parents onto the base. If she can get Wes and Carla and the others to start their own broadcasts then they will be able to help identify others who can dual. The risk of course being that more broadcasts mean more chatter on the airwaves for any extra-terrestrials like Nuvo and his evil partner to return, something that she fears must happen anyway in order for her to reunite with Gill.

"What's happening with Carla and Wes?" she asks.

"They are being driven here as we speak. Arriving in about thirty. This is down to you, Catherine. Never forget how grateful we are. We will arrange for a meeting at the Pod before you three begin. We will need to formulate a co-ordinated plan for exponential growth if it's possible," Redmond replies.

"Hopefully they'll take some pressure off you, Catherine. I'm sure you could do with that," Kirkland concludes with a peace offering.

"That would be very welcome," says Catherine, smiling hesitantly at both Phil and Ava.

Ava ushers Catherine to Phil's office door.

"Good luck today, Catherine. Remember, anything out of the ordinary and we'll pull you out. It's in your, and our, best interests. Let's try to get as many new recruits as we can, yes?"

Catherine can't help but respond positively, even with Ava's somewhat patronising tone which makes her want to turn around and tell her boss to 'go jump'. It wasn't that Catherine didn't like Ava. She admired her, but clearly Ava held the power in the relationship and wasn't afraid of manipulating the situation when required. Of course this was for the greater good, but at times Ava's delivery could be a bit clumsy.

—-

After freshening up, she walks over to H9 and another session in the pod, she ponders the constraints she may feel today, and whether or not she might be interrupted from dualling at just the wrong moment. The tension that is building in everyone around her, the pressure she feels to succeed for her fellow men and women, and the overwhelming sense that she is near not only to giving birth but also to that moment when she is reunited with Gill, is almost unbearable.

Chirstophe and Phil Kirkland stand in front of the H9 array of Darkrooms, as Catherine enters.

"Hi Phil. Hi Dad," She says in as chirpy a tone as she can manage.

"Hello, dear," her dad responds, and points over to where a couple of guards stand in front of two of the other pods.

Phil intervenes. "Catherine, do come this way. I'd like you to meet Carla Piccioni and Wesley Wilson-Green!" Phil can hardly contain himself.

"Thanks Phil. Hi!" Catherine greets the two recruits. The pair are obviously anxious and can't quite get Catherine's upbeat introduction given their previous meetings when dualling.

"It's amazing to see you….in real life," Wes responds in a hesitant tone, while Carla is still staring at Catherine as if she's seen a ghost.

"Hey, guys. It's OK, once you get used to dualling, this won't be….*strange*. Are you ready to come with me today and see if we can find the others?"

The two nod sheepishly and Catherine realises that they'll have to settle in real quick if they are going to succeed in the mission. There has obviously been little time to train or vet these guys properly, so she guesses Phil and Ava must be really desperate for time.

Christophe Jumeau addresses the three duallists.

"OK, now what I imagine here is that you will all end up at the clearing, but maybe at different times. I expect you'll be there first, Catherine. The key thing is to make that call. All of you need to understand that the critical factor is to find and trace all the duallists that respond. It's not just Catherine that will try to make that broadcast. Wes, Carla, you need to do that too, so as many possible duallists out there can come find you. Is that clear?"

All three nod, and as they go to their rooms, the only difference between this scene and the Apollo astronauts getting into their spacecraft is the absence of suits.

As she prepares to go into Darkroom One again, Catherine fights back a tear at the thought of how gargantuan all of this seems. For her task is not just the CAT1 test mission today. It's a whole lot more. And standing behind her as she hesitates to ascend the steps, her dad also knows that this is going to be full of risks. A rush of adrenalin races into her stomach, causing her baby to kick violently. Another fighter soon to join the human race.

Approaching the entrance to the pod, she turns around to say goodbye to her dad. As he looks into her eyes, Christophe Jumeau offers hope.

"You are the strongest person there, my dear. Use that strength and passion to help *everyone*," he offers, hoping Phil Kirkland doesn't question such a magnanimous send-off.

—-

Gill's tacit complicity to both Nuvo and Novek allows him a degree of comfort in the following hours in Karkian time prior to the planned trip to their wormhole. Having experienced being within Nuvo's cloak to protect him, Gill figures that this might be how Nuvo plans to get him there in the absence of being able to dual.

The conversations between the pair so far have demonstrated that the two have a degree of respect for each other, despite the vast imbalance of power. Following the freak show in the temple, Gill asked Nuvo if he could at least see more of the Karkian City before they depart, implying the possible grim outcome for himself and that he may as well go out with a taste of another civilisation. At first Nuvo was dismissive, possibly fearing the wrath of Novek. But as time went on it was obvious that Novek had some gnarly problems of his own, as Nuvo reported that the sounds that Gill could hear from the psuvit were from one of the larger domes where Novek was speaking to his commanders and soldiers, possibly having to tell them about the falange preparing to travel to Earth, and therefore leaving behind the many.

So Nuvo and Gill got back in and, much like one of the old sight-seeing hovercraft that Gill remembers from his family holiday to the Everglades, Nuvo slowly manoeuvred through rocky passageways and down towards what looked like a moat running all around the perimeter. As they approached, Gill could smell a change in the atmosphere and quickly realised that it was a fresher and more comfortable mix for him.

"What is that?" he asks Nuvo.

"It's what you know as a fluorocarbon. The reason you feel better nearer here is the same reason you could breathe in the cave. It produces liquid oxygen that evaporates. If I take you close enough you won't need to be in the pod. But be careful. Those guards down at the wall know you are here, and you wouldn't get far, believe me," Nuvo says.

"Hey. Good to know. But I mean, where would I go?"

Nuvo flushes slightly. The colour is one he hasn't seen before and Gill reckons he might just have got Nuvo to smile. A moment later as they get close to flowing fluid, Nuvo instructs Gill to get ready to stand on the ground as the gas cloud that surrounds the pod disperses from Gill, leaving him free from any constraint except the watchful eye of several Karkian guards at the other side.

Gill turns around, emancipated from the somewhat oppressive mist that surrounded the psuvit and obscured much of his view. He takes a deep breath.

In front of Gill are thousands of domes, all of differing shades from black to a reddish brown. Smoke and gas seem to rise all around, and the cacophony of clicking and whooshing play out like what might have been Stockhausen's next piece. It is at first disorienting for Gill, just from the sheer alien imagery and overwhelming realisation of where he *is*. Perhaps because of this, he begins to feel a little weak and takes a step back.

"Be careful," urges Nuvo, showing concern. "You do not want to fall in."

Gill looks round at the seemingly harmless looking flow of liquid that would lull easily with its clarity and resemblance to water.

"You would not last long," Nuvo follows.

Gill nods, steadying himself.

"We should get back," says Nuvo.
"You can't breathe here, Nuvo?" asks Gill.

The scientist and engineer in Nuvo makes him respond.

"The range of gases we can breathe is quite extensive, but oxygen like this is not one of them," Nuvo replies.

"So, I mean, how did you survive on Earth? I don't understand."

"I see. Your mix is mostly nitrogen and a little different to this mix, but we Karks can only survive a short time in such environments."

Gill is fascinated. "Taking Garfield meant you could access his body to function properly on Earth?" Gill probes.

"Something like that. But it was also important to look like a human, for obvious reasons."

Gill nods. He wants to know more, but not sure if he's going to get it. There is an awkward pause, before Nuvo continues.

"Karks are strong. Stronger than you. We have mastered a lot of chemical and biological processes and transformations that you haven't, so we can adapt to many situations. Look around you. This is adaptation, and we do it well."

"True. But not that well. You need heat, and even standing here, I am nearly freezing. You produce heat chemically then?" Gill asks.

"Mostly. We have mining operations that help us get heat from the core, but long-term, as I have told you, we need to move. Now, I can see that you are struggling with the temperature, so I suggest we return so you can heat up and drink your food."

As the pair travelled back in the pod, the sheer scale of the city and his growing knowledge of the Karkian plight gave Gill a better foothold. Perhaps for the first time, Gill was beginning to devise a strategy for his, and Nuvo's travels.

—-

Catherine emerges from the golden corn reeds as part of her mission to recruit new duallists. Standing in the middle of the clearing circle, she surveys all around her. The reassuring brush of gentle wind against her face is something to savor. For it is unlikely that this place will be this way for much longer. The sense of foreboding is growing inside her, and she takes a moment - itself a strange concept here where time seems meaningless.

As she gathers herself, and breathes deeply, all of her dualling power must be focused in order to create the most intense broadcast of the location of the cornfield to others. Summoning her strength from within and building steadily from her core, after a short while Catherine's body begins to shake, almost out of control, before emitting a pulse of energy that radiates outwardly in a gracefully potent wave, so forceful that it flattens the corn reeds in all directions. As she regains composure and looks out and back into the field, her face lights up with a golden glow. Deep into the distance she can see many figures revealed. To Catherine, they mostly look lost, and vulnerable in the reveal. With the flattened reeds so the path to the clearing has become direct and unfettered. A growing sense of triumph overcomes her and she now knows that her command is becoming supercharged in this hallowed ground.

Spinning around to look to the other side of the field, a shadow quickly descends.

Far in the distance she can hear the rumbling of thunder and the spiking sparks of lightning slamming into the field. Something tells her this is a response, but from whom she can't tell. In her dreams she has seen Gill and Beth walk out from the reeds and the three of them hugging and not letting go. What she would give for that dream to come true.

Squinting, she can make out, way in the distance, what she believes is the dark outline of a figure, but it is too far away. The energy in the field feels very different. A sense of panic begins to swell from within her. Rather than give in and turn, instead Catherine decides that she must first deal with her fellow duallists. As the first begin to arrive at the clearing, she moves over to greet them, Somehow her energy pulses dissolve the heavy glue that usually greets her when emerging from the reeds. And so first she sees an older man, somewhat bewildered.

"Who are you?" he says.

Catherine thinks he might believe he has died, or this is one strange form of heaven.

"It's OK, I am Catherine. You are OK. You are dualling. Do you know what that is?" she asks.

After some hesitation, the man responds. "Yes," he says. "I am Sergei. Where is Wesley?"

As Catherine gets more information on Sergei, she is desperately panning around to find Carla and Wes. There are too many emerging duallists for her alone to track, some twenty or thirty dotted around the field and likely to arrive in the clearing next. The extraordinary human capacity to recognise patterns helps her to identify Carla's walk.

'Carla!" she shouts, and Carla's friendly face smiles as she gives Catherine a wave. "Over here!"

Carla moves over towards Catherine, with Wes not far behind. The three of them help Sergei into the clearing and wait for some of the others to arrive.

"Hey!" Wes greets Sergei, who instantly seems relieved. "You made it!"

"Oh, it is so good to see you. Yes, I heard you call, just like you predicted."

"You know each other?" asks Catherine.

"Yeh, Sergei is my mum's friend, and the chap I told your dad about. I *knew* he could do this!"

"Look," says Catherine, trying to stay focused. "I need you to do two things. Help these people as they come out and take all the details so Phil and his team can find them. This is key. And use all your abilities to call for others who might join us. We need to get as many people here as we possibly can. If you sense that someone is strong - like they can move freely and think straight - try to get them to call too. I first started by shouting, but it's more like something that you can do inside your head. It's channeling all your mental energy to broadcast across the field - try to reach the furthest edges if you can. I don't know how long the reeds will stay like this," she says as she glances across behind them.

"What are you going to do? Where are you going?" asks Carla.

"I have to go over there," she says, turning and pointing to the far end opposite them. "I will be back soon."

"What do we do when everyone is here?" Wes asks.

"Once you have got all the details, you must find a way to remember those. If there are too many people, go back to the pod and tell Phil all of the details. If you can, and have enough energy, come back," Catherine says.

"Can these people dual back to the pods?" asks Carla.

"I don't think so. I think they'll need to go back to where they are dualling from. Phil and his team will track them down."

"But what if they don't want to be here, or help us, Catherine?" Carla follows up, panicking slightly.

"You'll need to cross that bridge when you come to it. Listen, if things are not going well here, call me. Shout as loud as you can from here in the clearing. I'll hear you and come back. I won't be long. I promise," she says.

As she leaves Wes and Carla to manage the influx of new duallists to the clearing, Catherine takes to the air. As she begins her ascent and looks back across the field, among those making their way to the clearing she can make out what looks like a familiar large frame. In the heat of the moment she can't quite discern who it is, and has so much racing through her head that she can't waste any time going in for a closer look. Reaching new heights and commanding the space with ease, she begins to race towards the far side.

The field is huge, and seems to be expanding. She looks back for a second to see the scale in all its glory. Spreading far and wide, from here, high in the sky, it reaches out to merge into a distant black ocean.

Her descent towards the far end is smooth as she scans for any parts of the perimeter that break the full circle. She has come to find out who is here. It could be Beth, for Catherine's heralded call across the entire field must surely have connected. But her senses tell her something else. The colder wind now hitting her face carries menace and above her the sky is turning blood red. A bolt of lightning cracks through the expanse and comes close enough to disturb the air around her so that she tumbles out of control only to righten in time not to hit the ground at speed. But hit the ground she does, and it hurts.

Catherine screams in pain. For a space where things seem so fantastical, the shock of the pain takes her by complete surprise.

In her blurred vision as she attempts to get up, vague and ill-defined shapes begin to meander in front of her. Increasingly, they move in an agitated way, as if waiting to crash over the fence. As clarity unfolds, she musters the strength to approach.

—

"Are you ready?" asks Nuvo.

"I have no idea," replies Gill, at which points Nuvo flushes yellow.

"You are making a joke?" Nuvo asks.

"Not really."

"I still don't understand your language as well as I would like."

"Forget it. It's hard to explain."

"But you need to be prepared for what is to come, yes?" asks Nuvo.

"I guess so. Look, why can't I dual by myself?" asks Gill. "I still don't get it. You are an engineer. Can you explain it?"

"It's not so complicated, Detective. Your entanglement is weakened because you are so far from Earth. We are in what you would call the Centaurus A galaxy. It's not that far from your own, but far enough that your abilities are either weak or non-existent without any connection to your Ksaanek."

"So why could you dual when you were on Earth?" asks Gill.

"A good question. I believe I found Garfield because he was dualling. Or perhaps he found me. I don't know. But that's probably why I was trapped on my arrival. I never found out who he was entangled with, but I found I could use that capacity locally."

"Locally, as in on Earth?" asks Gill.

"I could only really dual within short distances, but it was sufficient to allow me to do what was required."

"Like killing our President?"

"That was a mistake. I understand that."

"Well, we managed to change that. We should be thankful. Small mercies, huh…" Gill reflects.

Nuvo starts to click and his ventricles flutter.

"So, you realise now that I will need to carry you to the Ksaanek?"

"Yes. What happens when we get there? Will I be able to see what's going on?" asks Gill.

"Once there, the safety precautions we take to dual will not be needed. You'll see. You've done this before."

"Have I?" asks Gill.

"OK, enough questions. Come with me," instructs Nuvo as he creates the psuvit that will be used to carry Gill to the launch point that will take them to Earth.

—-

Gill senses Catherine in the cornfield. She's some way away but he knows it is her. She is resplendent in a bright green dress which matches her eyes. A bright golden aura is surrounding her, marking her movements out as she moves swiftly and majestically up and towards him. Gill's heart beats so loudly it is calling to her, sending pulse after pulse which reach across the field like stones hitting the water and rippling out to sea.

Catherine descends like a goddess from the sky, veiled in an intense narcotic mist that sends Gill's senses into overdrive. Something is different about her, he can tell. He is about to be reunited with his love, his twin, his partner. And yet he senses another too. So strong is the feeling that he becomes giddy and stumbles backwards as the astral wind that emanates from Catherine hits him straight on. Bowled over, Gill falls to the ground, and loses consciousness.

—

"Get up," comes the voice. It is the formidable yet familiar dark tone and immediately Gill's blood turns cold.

"Get up, now!" commands the voice.

Gill has to come to, realising that he is nowhere near the cornfield. And yet he is free of any psuvit pod, any gas, any burning atmosphere.

"Wha..?" comes his feeble attempt at speaking.

"It's OK, Detective. You know this place," comes the strangely reassuring voice of Nuvo. "You have been asleep."

Gill's eyes begin to focus and sure enough, he does know this place. It is the temple. He must have been dreaming. And now he must adjust. Quickly.

"What *is* this place?" he asks.
"This is the temple. Our staging post," Nuvo responds.

And it dawns on Gill. Of course. This is not Kark, but Nuvo and Novek's wormhole. It explains much.

"You brought me here?" he asks Nuvo.
"Yes. The cloaking mechanism to protect you on Kark works because you become a part of me. If you are a part of me, you can travel with me. Here."

Suddenly the temple shakes violently.
"Enough!" Novek shouts. "Now is the time. There is a calling."

As Gill looks up towards the temple pillars, he can see, behind Novek, perhaps a hundred guards.

"But…" Gill begins.
"Yes. We are many strong, and a channel has opened. You will play your part." Novek looks over to Nuvo and makes a harsh and high-pitched clicking sound that repeats too many times for the human ear. Gill shrinks and covers his ears. Eventually the clicking stops.

Nuvo, flushing anxiously, ushers the guards who grab Gill and bring him up to the temple platform. Weakened by the impact of the razor-like attack from Novek's sonic assault, Gill just about manages to get to his feet. He can see that Nuvo, too, has been chastised in some way, as he wobbles in front of Novek, who calls over several more guards.
Nuvo and Gill are now surrounded. Gill is puzzled, intimidated and feeling a bit like Alice.

"You will be with me," informs Nuvo, but speaking nervously. "They are just here to make sure you don't try anything."

"Like what?" Gill responds.

"Sshh. Now this is important. I will be cloaking you until we get to Earth, so for your safety do not try to break free when we join to your world."

For the sake of getting moving, and finding his way back to Earth, Gill nods. In this split second he realises that Nuvo does not intend to let him loose at the cornfield, under strict instructions from Novek no doubt. No, while Novek is free to wreak havoc in the field, he will be forced to be under Nuvo's 'wing'. Perhaps like Montgomery was inside Nuvo. But that was different, surely. And Gill may miss Catherine altogether. This can't happen. Surely he must have some strength in the cornfield? *His* cornfield.

* * * *

CHAPTER 6: COLLISIONS

Click, click, click, click.

Christophe Jumeau can hear the sound of stilettos. As they approach, he shifts slightly in his chair.

Knock, knock.

"Ava." He welcomes Ava Redmond into his office and offers her a drink.
"Bacardi, please. On the rocks," she says.

Jumeau pours, and, owing to the somewhat tense state of his boss, topples a large Jamieson into a highball glass for himself, and the two settle on the sofa in his ample office.

"What can I do for you?" he enquires.

Ava looks Christophe dead in the eye.

"So, I think we need to level with each other here, Christophe. I mean, you are heading up this amazing programme, and your daughter is doing all she can to help, and you're not even Americans," she quips.
"OK…" Jumeau can't hide his bemusement.
"Here's the thing," Redmond continues. "We both know that Catherine is doing some 'other stuff' in that wormhole. You know it. I know it, and, well, pretty much everyone on CAT knows it. And we have no time - *no* time - for any games right now. You know that, right?" she asks.

Jumeau pauses for a second. He knows that he has choices to make here, and figures that, even if Ava is bluffing, sooner or later he'd have to reveal what Catherine has been achieving at the cornfield. At worst, it's a bit subversive but on-task, and at best it's the only real hope for a solution to the settlement programme that, along with Sky-Twin, Ava has marked herself out with.

"The data surges, you mean?" he says, rhetorically. "Well, I know that she's sensing both danger and opportunity. That spike you got was probably something that happened but she wasn't aware of - like some infarction into the field which for some reason she wasn't - couldn't have been - sensitive to."

"Oh, come now, Professor. I think it's much more than that. When I sat down with Catherine just a week or so ago, I knew that she is in control there. I could see it. If anything is going on in that space, then she'll know it. So..." she trails off, giving Christophe a moment to reconsider.

"Well," he responds. "I do know that part of the equation must be the connection or communication between wormholes. I mean, she thinks that's why Garfield - Nuvo - and Gill were taken. And I am inclined to agree. So the spikes are most likely either Nuvo and crew trying to break in, or some other source that senses the existence of the cornfield."

"'Other source'?"

"Look, Ava. Part of the CAT programme is about finding off-world exoplanets that might host life. It's just not programmed into the CAT1 phase. But what would you say if I told you that there might already be the potential to go off-world?"

Redmond looks across the table to Jumeau, and takes a mighty swig from her glass.

"Go on..." she prompts, as Jumeau mirrors Ava's movements.

"OK, so we don't know what this means, but at the very edges of the wormhole, things...get very strange. It's where the effects of being in a spacetime vacuum and the connection between entropy and gravity become even less predictable; dependent on factors outside the basics of quantum mechanics."

"Like...?" asks Redmond.

"Like…losing control, or being prone to outside influences, time reversal, jumping from one wormhole to another…for example," he offers.

"Outside influences?"

"I mean in terms of what is real and what is not, we need to consider carefully what one would experience at the intersect of two wormholes. Where dimensions of reality can expand and perhaps allow things that we might never have imagined."

"So, you're saying that Catherine might have made contact with others off-world? Others who are not like Nuvo, you mean?" Redmond's voice quietens as, for a moment, she gets lost in her own thoughts.

Jumeau takes up the baton.

"Look, none of this is certain. I feel this because I don't know if one of these strange effects would be having out-of-body experiences or hallucinations. Even seeing a different reality but only in your mind. Without it being *real*."

"But you trust your daughter's recall, don't you?" asks Ava.

"I do. You're right. She's one of the most lucid people I know. I misjudged her once, and I wouldn't do it again. She's incredibly strong, and now I am beginning to believe that she has experienced what most of us never will."

"So these others. There is a world they are from? You have looked into this?" she asks, trying to moderate her excitement.

"I have been digging, yes," he admits, before realising that he is half-way down the rabbit-hole and, with someone as dogged and powerful as Redmond, he's already gone too far to turn back. "OK, so you need to take everything I say with some degree of caution, right?"

Redmond makes no response. She needs him to stop procrastinating, and he senses her urgency.

"Right. So, we think Catherine made contact with someone called Beth. She is Detective Gill's sister. She disappeared some years ago. If you've got his file, you'll have read about this."

Redmond nods, expressing a glimmer of compassion.

"Well, somehow, Beth broadcast some kind of frequency or information wave that reached the cornfield. Or Catherine to be more precise. And when the two coincided, she crossed over. This is what I think happened."

"Wait. Crossed over? I mean, *who* crossed over. Where?"

"Catherine crossed. Into Beth's equivalent of a wormhole. This is what Catherine thinks. In some way, shape or form, the two managed to communicate. I'm assuming from this that Beth must be alive, or at least not dead. I'm having trouble distinguishing these categories now, as I'm sure you are aware."

Ava nods, thinking about Montgomery.

"Well, to cut a long story short, Beth can't dual beyond her own wormhole, and is trapped on a planet in the Scorpius constellation. It's right here in our own Milky Way."

Redmond grabs both their glasses, goes over the drinks cabinet, and pours two large measures before more or less slamming them down on the table.

"Go on…" she urges, taking a considerable gulp of Bacardi.

"Right, well. My best guess is that we are talking about an exoplanet called six-six-seven C-f. It's a planet in the Gliese six-six-seven C planetary system. Six-six-seven is a red dwarf but close to it there is a habitable zone where there are about four of five planets that would support life. 'F' is my best guess. I may be wrong," he says.

"OK, so you said it's near, right? So should I be talking to the likes of Jake and Nelson about this? You know, fusion propulsion is our best candidate so far…"

"I doubt it. Gliese is about twenty-two light years away. Andromeda is about four, and we can't really get out of our own solar system at the moment. I know those guys have made massive progress, especially with the anti-matter accelerator, but realistically in the time-frames we've got left, I can't see it," Jumeau responds.

"Not even if we can buy some time in the settlements, and keep the NASA programme running?" asks Redmond.

"You'd need to ask those guys, Ava," Christophe says. "It's a bit risky. For me, the best contender right now has to be CAT. If we can get a route through to this planet, and Catherine, or Beth, can guide duallists through there, and it's not such a hostile environment, then we might have a chance. But of course, we might not know until we get there."

"There are a lot of 'if's' in there, Christophe. But this is significant. You should have come to me earlier." And with that Redmond turns frosty.

"It's not that I didn't want to share this, Ava. Bear in mind that it's my daughter out there, and that, as a scientist, I'm only interested in fact and evidence. Throwing caution to the wind and sending people to their certain deaths is not something I will be a part of."

Redmond relaxes a little. She gets it.

"Alright. Look, I know there is a lot going on and things seem to be crumbling all around. But we have to work together, Christophe. I know that Catherine must be conflicted. She has so much on her young shoulders, I can hardly imagine. We need to support her, and that's why Phil and I recommended that we pull her out of the pod if there is anything gnarly going on."

"What do you mean?" asks Jumeau.

"I've said to her that we'll pull her out of there if we get another data spike. It's just to protect her."

"But we've just said that this spike is probably Beth. OK, so it could be another more dangerous influence there, but don't pull her out unless you are certain that her signs show she needs to be. Agreed?"

"Agreed," Redmond responds, and gets up to go over to the window. When she gets there, she takes a final swig from her glass. "Who'd think, huh?" she says as she gazes over the sunlit base in all its afternoon glory.

—-

Novek, Sultan of Kark, his large shadowy figure blurring at the edges of his own wormhole, is straining every sinew to claw through to the cornfield. As he struggles in the slow-motion downstream glue that weighs him down and forces him to capitulate to gravity, he

signals Nuvo to push Gill forward to make sure the connection to
Catherine can be established and for the fence to be breached.

As Catherine approaches nearer to the fence, she is acutely
aware that Gill is here, and her heart skips a couple of beats. Almost
in a frenzy of delight, she succumbs to the heavier surroundings and
goes to ground. As her smile wanes, so too does her sense of
optimism. She can see multiple forms all moving agitatedly at the
fence, giving her a sense of foreboding. Over to her left, sparks fly at
the fence which only serve to confuse.

Nuvo realises that he will have to free Gill in some way so that
Catherine can see him and create an opening. This is awkward and
unforeseen and so, as he struggles in the burden of mass that
permeates this edge of the wormhole, he decides he must use Gill to
spearhead the break in the perimeter. Uncloaking Gill is dangerous
and might sabotage the whole mission, yet he seems to have no
choice. He is of course familiar with this area, and has crossed
through before, albeit in a hazy retreat with Novek. This time it
seems different. There is a stumbling block and he can feel it is Gill,
who is becoming difficult to contain. He must let him out, but has to
get as close to the entrance to the field as he possibly can. He signals
to Novek to join him and to push. The two Karks join forces and
with an almighty effort start to destabilise the boundary.

As new sparks fly directly in front of Catherine, she braces
herself for the breach. And then it happens. There, in front of her,
struggling through the hole in the fence is Gill. Straining hard, and in
some anguish, his face contorted in his struggle to get away from the
Karks. And before she can try to call out and move towards him, she
realises that he is attached to a form that she very much recognises.
Nuvo!

"Nnnnooooohh…" trickles slowly out, the sound wave
stuttering at low pitch as it struggles to move through the air in front
of her. And in that moment her eyes meet the eye of Nuvo.

As Nuvo recognises Catherine, so too his concentration seems
to shift, and in this fleeting moment, Nuvo relaxes his hold on Gill
so that he becomes uncloaked. As Gill claws with all his strength
against the sticky floor of the field, half in and half out, Catherine
urgently tries to get to him, but there is nothing urgent possible here,
now. Something is pressing on her, with an almighty mass. As she

senses increasing danger, through the dark she makes out the ominous presence of Nuvo's much larger twin. This is the moment she has been dreading for some months.

Struggling hard to reach the field, Gill claws his way with every ounce of energy he can muster, eyes bulging and desperate to touch Catherine. If he can just reach her, they can reunite; in love, and in strength. For they must have a stronger connection than Nuvo and Novek here, in *their* field. But clambering over Gill and keeping him pinned to the ground is the downward mass of Novek, who uses Gill as a doormat to scramble in through the little glitch where the wormholes meet. Both Gill and Novek struggle to overcome the intense gravitational fluctuations at the join, but Novek has the upper hand.

As the Sultan of Kark traverses worlds, he realises the danger from Catherine and, finding increasing strength and power as he becomes free, mounts an attack. Rushing forward and defying the condensation of the matter all around, he lands an almighty blow to Catherine's head that sends her flying up and back into the reeds. Reeling in mid-air, she gathers herself just in time to avoid a nasty fall. Now a little distance away from the fence, she can see the disappearing cloak covering Gill as he fights to stand upright. Nuvo is behind, and clambering to chase him.

"Gill!" she cries, and Gill looks up, their eyes locking for the first time since he was taken all those months ago. His momentary smile wiped away by a heavy blow from Nuvo who knocks him to the ground.

No sooner has Catherine decided to go and help Gill than she feels a searing pain in her back as Novek again pummels a Karkian fist into her from behind. She lets out an almighty scream as she is sent tumbling to ground again.

But buoyed by seeing Gill, and deeply determined to protect this hallowed ground, she turns in defiance. Looking up into the sky she can see the malicious form of Novek, revealed in detail for the first time. Hovering over her like a dark daemon, his Karkian eye glows red against a large dark body with a long arm morphing to form a hammer shape. As he descends to wreak more violence on her, she focuses on all the positive energy within, and forces Novek's motion to stagger to a freeze frame finale. In the final frame, she transmits a huge pulse of energy that spikes through time, hitting Novek so hard that he tumbles back through the air, spinning helplessly into the distance, the shock of Catherine's power visible in his face as he disappears. But she has sent him towards the clearing, and her intuition tells her that he will recover and gain both strength and further freedom of movement. Should she follow to stop him? All the human duallists are going to be there, including Carla and Wes, and Sergei. And...

In that moment, she suddenly realises that the large frame of Malcolm Baines was who she saw in the reeds.

"Mal!" she cries out. But there is no-one near her to hear, and Mal is way back towards the clearing. In a state of panic, Catherine is losing focus. Should she go to the clearing or go back to the fence to help Gill escape from the strange hold Nuvo had over him? What is more important?

—-

"Christophe! Christophe!" shouts Phil. "Hurry!"

Christophe Jumeau starts to run along corridor H9, his large frame preventing him from gaining too much speed. As his cumbersome figure gradually fills the view as Phil awaits him, the Professor shouts ahead.

"What is it?"
"It's Catherine. She's spiking!"

Out of breath, and heart racing in trepidation as much as the exercise, Jumeau sees that the large LCD display outside Darkroom One has several warning lights flashing along with the sound of computerised alarms.

"We have to get her out!" Kirkland's panic is obvious.
"You're right," agrees Jumeau. "This looks like she is in big trouble. Let's do it. Now!"

As they signal to the guards to let them pass, the two men open the heavy pod door and see that Catherine is clearly in some distress.

Jumeau is the first to act, taking her hand, gently at first, and then wiping away the sweat from Catherine's brow.

"Catherine," he says softly. No response. "Catherine, it's Dad. We need to get you out, so we are going to take the monitoring nodes and medical kit off you. OK?"

There is still no response. An increasingly concerned father gently undoes the blood pressure and temperature monitors from Catherine's arms, and releases the electrodes from Catherine's head, chest, and abdomen. Christophe can see movement indicating that the baby is very distressed. He has to get her to the base hospital, which thankfully is only a short car ride away.

Phil ushers the guards to help carry Catherine out of the pod, and together the four men hurriedly get her onto a nearby trolley and rush up the corridor as if going straight to the emergency department. Half way along the corridor, Phil is shouting to Catherine.

"Catherine! You need to wake up! You are going into labour!"

Catherine's head starts to roll from side to side, obviously distressed.

"Jesus," mutters Christophe, as he grips Catherine's hand tightly. "Hang in there, honey. We'll soon have you ready, just hang in there!"

—-

Feeling the presence of Nuvo behind him and still struggling in the gravitational gloop permeating the perimeter, Gill frees himself first and scrambles into the reeds, hoping to avoid being tracked by his Karkian captor.

Standing upright and wiping some of the droplets of liquified gas from his body, he takes a huge breath. Gill's lungs fill with the swell of sweet fresh air. It's entirely invigorating, and for the very first time in many months Gill feels the power returning to his body and his sense of belonging stronger than ever, looking forward to getting back to Catherine and all the things he holds dear. Catherine, who he just saw *flying* in this space. This gives him much food for thought, but pressing on him is the urgent need to get to the clearing, and from there back to Earth.

There is, however, the small matter of the Karks.

He stops briefly and squints to see if he can see Catherine anywhere up above, but there is no sign. As he scrambles through the reeds, encumbered by the need to clamber his way in between the densely packs stalks while maintaining some form of straight line, he quickly becomes frustrated, and it is only in that moment of exasperation that the old basketball player starts to take jumps to see if he can get high enough to see over the seven-feet tall reeds. Perhaps because of his body's muscle memory from those years of playing, or the increasing space between himself and the edge of the field, with one giant leap he discovers something new; bounce. At first it's a foot or so above the reeds and catching glimpses into the distance. Then it becomes five, then ten feet, like walking on the Moon. Soon Gill is moving in leaps and bounds. In a final flourish from an exponential series of hops, Gill is able to get a sharp view of the clearing. And in that moment, he almost forgets that he has to land. For up ahead he can see many figures, and just one figure. That of Novek.

High above the reeds also come clearer sounds. And Gill can make out screams. Human screams. Panic sets in and he musters all his might to take a huge leap towards the clearing. Maintaining an extraordinary hang-time, the sight of Novek attacking one of the newcomers, signals the need for a superhuman effort to prevent this monster from taking lives and to prevent Nuvo from opening the gates for the Kark army to flood through.

"Catherine!" he cries at the top of his voice and over the reeds towards the clearing. Yet nothing comes back but the sound of pain. Back and to his left, he can hear rustling. Back, and to his right, he can hear the crackling of crisp lightning sparks. As he looks around to see the black sky behind him light up at the far edge, a faint hint of familiarity from his past sweeps over him. Not just familiar... somehow more than that. There is a sound of a saxophone in his head, and it pulls on him to go back and explore. But this makes one too many factors in an impossible equation; one he must resist solving in order to help the men and women he knows are at the mercy of Novek at the clearing. He has to press on, yet it tears at his very essence to ignore the strong calling within him to find out who or what is behind the sights and sounds over in the wilderness.

Instincts in turmoil, Gill makes a dash for the opening in the reeds a short way ahead, and after a gargantuan last stride, finally makes it to the clearing. There, he finds a dozen or so men and women like him, dazed and confused, struggling to understand what is going on. Some move soporifically slowly, others gaining control, and yet others helping others. He can see one of them who looks more in command than most.

"Hey," he greets her. "Are you OK?"

"Yes," comes the reply, in an accent he can tell is Mediterranean.

"What happened here?" he asks.

"There are many of us. We heard the call," she informs him, wiping a tear away. "Who are you?"

"You know Catherine?"

"She is the one we respond to. We were supposed to get as many people here as we could. But she had to go - where *you* came from. And she doesn't come back."

Gill looks behind Carla to where there is a very large opening in the reeds. He inspects it to check for any clues, only finding a name badge lying by the gap, before returning.

"Do you know this man?" Gill asks Carla, showing her the badge.

"Yes. It was so terrible. I saw him being taken. I am so sorry. I couldn't stop this…creature…from taking him. He was big, and powerful. I'm sorry," she says.

"Hey, don't be sorry," Gill reassures her. "I know of this creature, and you have done everything you can. Thank you for caring for these people. What are you going to do with them?"

"We are part of a programme. It is to get as many duallists as we can because of the troubles."

"Troubles?" Gill asks.

"You don't know about the virus?"

"What virus?"

Gill can hardly take it in. He has a billion questions queuing up at every synapse and the traffic jam is beginning to crunch.

"Look, can you finish what you need to to do here? I have to go back there," he points back towards the fence from where he has come. "There are more of those creatures, and I need to stop them."

"But you are too late," Carla replies.

"What do you mean?"

"The big one took Wes, and then more of them - not so big - they come and have taken the others with them. The people here are the ones who survived."

"Who is Wes?" he asks.

Carla points to the badge.

"He is from England. London. He is part of the programme."

"Did they all go through there?" he asks, pointing to the large hole in the reeds.

"Yes."

"Where does that go, do you know?" he asks her.

"I think it's where a man called Sergei came out, or it might be one of the others, but I am not sure. Sergei was new. An older man, from London. He knew Wes. I think he was here because of Wes."

"Where did you dual from? Did you come from Spain? Italy?"

"No. I dualled here from the base. Wes did too. The American base. But I can't see him, or Sergei."

"So the Karks…the creatures…they could have taken one of these routes back to the American base?" he asks, anxiously.

"I suppose, yes."

Gill is speechless. He feels he must get back to Earth, and quickly. After telling Carla who he is, and his connection to Catherine, they agree that Carla will stay to track and trace as many as she can, helping others to find their way back. The decision to go back to find Nuvo or get back down to Earth is yet one more struggle in the never-ending contortion of choice, and one he must follow by heart this time.

Gill tells Carla to get out quickly if she sees Nuvo or any other Karks and thanks her before she shows him to where Wes emerged from the reeds. He takes that route, deciding that it's the only choice in the situation. The damage done, the next step will be to find out who is at the base and any danger there; to find out more about what he has missed in what he would have thought were a few short months, yet he now knows have been filled with game-changing events.

As he moves through the reeds and journeys back to Earth, he wonders what action Nuvo will take, given that it was never Novek's intention to allow either himself or Nuvo access to Earth, instead using both as mules for transporting Karks to the promised land.

—-

Peering through the large glass window to the nurses and midwife attending his daughter, Christophe Jumeau has the look of a very worried father. To his right is Mary Jumeau, who has a vice-like grip on her husband's forearm. To his left, Phil Kirkland is standing awkwardly, tapping his fingers on his jacket lapel. Beads of sweat are forming on his forehead as he ponders the impact of events on the CAT program for which he is directly responsible. It was always going to be risky putting so much pressure on a pregnant woman, but Catherine's dualling schedule has obviously been too much, and Kirkland is feeling as guilty as a boss can feel. Jumeau knows it, but chooses not to challenge, his own guilt for not protecting his daughter preying on this mind. Although she isn't due for another three weeks, Christophe and Mary are hoping against hope that not only will Catherine be alright, but that the stress of events hasn't taken a terrible toll on the baby.

After some time, one of the nurses gives them all a thumbs up sign, indicating that they have got things under control, quickly followed by a 'go away'.

"Let's get some coffee," says Chirstophe.
"I'm staying," says Mary, determined to remain.
"OK, dear. I'll bring back a tea." To which Mary nods.
"Shall we?" Christophe invites Phil to join him.

A minute or so later, the two are in the light and airy hospital canteen on base, sipping some pretty vile coffee. They both wince, before Phil updates Christophe.

"Ava is going to join us."

"Fine. Look, obviously this changes things. She's not going to be able to get back on the programme for a while. What's the situation with Carla and Wes?"

"I'm waiting on a call from Hank, the duty security chief. Carla's signs are agitated but OK, but there is a major problem with Wes."

"'Major problem'?" Christophe asks.

"He's not there."

Christophe is shocked, and struggles for words.

"No sign?"

"None. Do you have any idea what that might have been? Is it a flaw in the dualling process?"

"I don't know. What was going on with his signs before he vanished, do you know?"

"No, just that they went all over the place, and the movements inside the pod were like convulsions," Kirkland comments.

"Jeez. Did you see the actual moment he disappeared? Will we have it on CCTV?"

"We should do. I didn't see anything. I've asked for the entire session stream from all pods to be sent through. I'll look at those when I get back."

"And nothing else? No others?"

"Huh?" asks Kirkland.

"I mean, no-one new. Like, another duallist or any aliens turned up in the pod?" asks Jumeau.

"Hell, no."

"OK. I have a bad feeling about this, Phil. If they have taken Wes, it will be for a reason. Maybe to get somewhere in particular, and they might have already killed him."

"I've got the tracer guys onto that - they're going to contact the parents in London, and we'll see what comes back."

Christophe nods, and the two take a moment to pause for thought.

"So, look, Christophe, I owe you and Catherine a huge apology. We have all been running around like headless chickens on the back of GARI, and, well, things like this make you think. Bringing a child into *this* world isn't something many would envy."

"I feel guilty too. Blinded by science. That's my daughter back there, and I couldn't protect her," Jumeau responds.

"You are a good father, Christophe. With an amazing daughter. She's strong. Even to get where we are has been a miracle. I know she - you - both have a bigger agenda. Ava and I are aware of it, but the primary focus has to be getting these new duallists safe, number one, and trained up, number two."

"You're right, Phil. But I've been doing some thinking," the older man replies.

"Go on…" Kirkland prompts.

"Well, I see it like this. And I'll make this short, as we don't have much time."

Christophe Jumeau takes a deep breath.

"So, I dug a little deeper into Catherine's experiences, what I know from her about Gill, and Nuvo and the dark presence of his twin. There are so many unknowns. 'Rumsfeld time' as they say. But I can speculate. Take this with a pinch of salt, but by my reckoning, we *could* have a way out of the current predicament. I spoke to Ava earlier about the basics of this," he says, as Kirkland stays quiet, preferring to catch every word.

"OK, so Catherine has made contact with Gill's sister, Beth. You know that story, right? It's disturbing and sad, and has been incredibly tough on the Gill family, but she says she has made contact, and I believe her. I also started to think about why this has happened. Why *now*. Why *them*. Fate and destiny versus random chance. All that. I realised that what we are witnessing is the joining of wormholes - the intersection of one form of black hole with another, where the preconditions are that there is a degree of entanglement between the two worlds," he says as he pauses for thought.

"Worlds?" says Phil. "You mean worlds, or people?"

"It might not matter which, Phil. All we know is that these are entangled, and as such the possibility of weird and wonderful deconstruction of spacetime, including interstellar travel, become real, not fantastic. Where, for example, the join between different places in the Universe that would be impossible in terms of separation by light years, becomes possible because of entanglement. In short, it's the entanglement between these worlds - and maybe, yes, the agents within these worlds - that allows this movement."

"OK, I'm with you so far, Professor," Phil remarks. "But where does this take us?"

"That's it, Phil. *That* is the question. I think it takes us away from Earth in a very practical way. Look, those duallists are moving and acting and communicating within a wormhole, for God's sake. We wouldn't have dreamt about this even a year ago, and yet something has changed with Gill and Catherine's connection. You saw how they changed the reality that we are in, right? You saw that it is possible to travel in space and time. The only difference we are talking about here is that this travel can be off-world. So if Catherine has connected with Beth, and Beth lives on another planet, then if the wormholes created by those two connect, then there is no reason why a bridge couldn't be opened to get from one planet to another. It's not on the same level as Star Trek, but it's close. For a start it's a hell of a lot more dangerous. Whatever happened to Catherine in there wasn't a result of an afternoon tea with Beth. No, it was something else. Something that I imagine has to be related to Nuvo, to his twin, and to some need that *they* have to come *here*. And the fact that Wes has disappeared means that, in my opinion, they are probably already here, and that Nuvo might be here too."

"You think Wes has been taken by those aliens?" Phil asks, his voice breaking a little with anxiety. "That's just great. Intercontinental war, pandemic, and now alien invasion. There's a movie in that, if there were a movie industry left," he muses.

"Steady, Phil," replies Chirstophe. "We're not quite at the end yet. What I am saying is that, apart from the settlement programme for the locations we have identified here, the new information I'm putting to you gives me the belief that the next phase of CAT is already here. We really need to work closely with Carla and the remaining duallists that we get out of the field - I mean the wormhole - to grow a community of duallists who will be able to journey to Beth's planet."

"Yeh, you said. So what is the planet? What do we know about it? It's habitable, obviously, right?" Kirkland asks.

"Must be. I mean, she's there, isn't she?" Christophe surmises. "I understand it's more primitive, so they're unlikely to welcome us with coffee and cake. But heck, a shortcut to an exoplanet that can sustain life. Look no further."

"Do we know which planet?"

"I have a fair idea. Look, some reasonably intelligent humans who can dual there will stand a good chance of survival if they keep their wits about them. All I know is that it is lush, and supports life. There are dangers, just as there are here, but they are more likely to be from predatory animals than a crazed gunman. If I am right, and Nuvo has brought his kind back to try to invade, then we may as well look at 'plan D' - that's the one where it's 'None of the above', right? We put a huge effort into supporting our duallists, track any of Nuvo's type and try to eradicate them if we can."

"And duck the ICBMs coming in from China that are going to kill…oh wait, there's no-one left to kill 'cos they all died of GARI," Phil rebuffs.

"If you overthink this situation, Phil, you *will* fail. You know that, right?" Jumeau is becoming more assertive as he lays out what he knows.

Phil Kirkland is about to reply, when they both hear the familiar click of Ava Redmond's heels.

"Gentlemen," she greets them.

"Ava, listen, we have some urgent thinking to do here. We need your help," says Kirkland.

"Sure. Fire away," Redmond replies.

"Well, Christophe here has identified some new developments in CAT that revolve around the off-world potential."

"Yeh, I know. We talked about this earlier, didn't we, Professor?"

Christophe nods, happy for Kirkland to take up the story. It gives him time to think more deeply about the next moves.

After Phil offers the detail, Ava takes her lipstick and small mirror out of her purse, and starts to apply some dark red.

"We have to keep any casualties quiet," she starts. "Dead duallists are not a good advert for CAT. So we keep everything under wraps. The guy, what was his name - Wes - he is traceable?" she asks.

Phil nods.

"Well, my guess is that he might be another Garfield. You know what I mean?" she asks them.

Both men nod, getting the reference.

"So….I think we try to find out what the heck happened in there, and what we've got to work with. And how is Catherine, Professor? Is she OK?"

Christophe jerks slightly, coming out of some deep thought.

"Yes, I think she is fine, but my primary concern is for the child."

"Of course, Professor. Look, I don't want to keep you," Redmond replies. "But latest reports are that rioting and looting are taking hold in various cities and we already know many of our police forces have sick cops or are unable to cope with the levels of unrest. The National Guard can't keep up - there just aren't enough of them, which is ironic. It's the same elsewhere. We are staring into the abyss, gentlemen, and so right now I know that John will be looking for anything - *anything* - that will increase our chances. That means the chances of the American people surviving any or all of the imminent threats. He's even ordered Nelson to trial a mission to Mars. Can you believe that? Anyway, we're all under strict orders to report on what we *can* do, not what we can't. So I need some answers from you two."

Christophe updates on the potential of Xarn.

"Xarn?" quizzes Ava. "Like the conditioner?"

"With an 'x' and an 'a'. It's about twenty light years away, but in our galaxy," replies Christophe, not quite understanding what Ava is talking about.

"OK…?" she says.

"We'll need to plan how this will happen. My daughter can't go back in there for a while. She'll have a young life to support, so it will need to be spearheaded by someone else," Catherine's father asserts.

Ava nods, gets up and goes over to the canteen window, the stilettos clicking against the hard floor. As she looks up towards a darkening sky, she lets out an audible sigh, and turns to Christophe.

"How long is a 'while'?" she asks.

* * * *

CHAPTER 7: KICKER

"Is that you, Wes?" Judy Wilson-Green shouts up the stairs in the direction of the bedrooms, having heard the commotion on the first floor.

There is no response.

She shrugs her shoulders and goes back to the kitchen where the laptop displays the BBC News, transmitting amidst the lockdown of another day of rioting in the provincial capitals, including Manchester and Leeds. News anchor, Nigel Hicks, is reporting.

"In another extraordinary day here in the United Kingdom, there are reports of thousands of protesters and activists attacking council buildings and police stations, as well as attempting to break into supermarkets, many of which are, of course, closed due to current safety concerns. The number reported dead is very approximate, given the situation, but our news drone was above the town hall in Leeds today, which is very near the centre of the city, and you can see from the report coming up that the battleground seems to be centred around the delivery entrance to the city centre Sainsbury's, which we've highlighted here for you. Please note that some of you may find these scenes disturbing."

The screen switches to a birds-eye view above the centre of Leeds which clearly shows a pitched battle between a hundred or more people attempting to break down the back entrance gate to the supermarket store while police and militia move in with water cannons, rubber bullets and stun guns, seemingly firing at will. Within thirty seconds there is clear evidence of carnage. Zoomed high-definition footage shows rioters being electrocuted or hit by water jets. At one point, viewers can see one man catapulted into the air heading towards the spikes of the ten-foot high metal gates.

Before the gory outcome is revealed, the footage is halted before Hicks returns on screen, looking somewhat drained.

Judy, now in her fifties, has seen enough, and closes the laptop lid with a bang. It's a depressing bulletin and yet she feels compelled to watch every one, such is the state of emergency in her once-great country. Out of the kitchen window, its quarter-hatch open to let some fresh air in, she looks up at the rather dull and overcast sky, darkening in the distance. She reflects to herself how things could not be much worse.

No sooner has the thought left her than Mrs. Wilson-Green is speared through the head with the poker used to stoke the fire in her living room. The sharply-pointed, rusted rod of metal enters the base of her skull from the rear and journeys upwards, slicing through the cortex at speed and reappears right at the joint between her hairline and forehead.

She drops immediately to the floor, a soft crumpling sound of her body as it helplessly collapses downwards the only noise. Standing behind her is her son, Wes.

As Novek and some twenty other Karks, all having engulfed their prey and sequestered their human forms, gather downstairs in the semi-detached house on Morgan Street in London's East End, the invasion of Earth is officially underway.

—-

Darkroom Three has a large LCD display outside, flashing red. It has been flashing for about forty minutes, maybe longer. The burly guards in charge of the pods have left their positions and are all looking at the CCTV pictures coming from inside.

Running quickly along the corridor, Phil Kirkland is grappling with his biocell.

"Security? We have a Category ONE. Do you understand?" he shouts into the small device wrapped around his wrist.

"Yes, sir!" the voice responds.

"Lock the base down. Now!"

As he fumbles with the biocell, it too is flashing red, detecting the extraordinarily high anxiety readout coming from the sensors.

But Kirkland is oblivious, determined to run harder down the corridors leading to H9.

As he arrives he sees that the security chief Hank Waters is braced at the door to the pod with a standard issue Colt handgun pointed towards the frame.

"We got an intruder," he reports. "We're gonna go in."

"Wait!" cries Phil, as he looks across to Christophe who is shaking his head and pointing to the CCTV.

"Stand down, Hank!" Phil commands, at which Waters looks puzzled.

"Phil, we need to be careful here. Whoever that is…" Hank says, pointing up to the CCTV camera feeding a live shot of a large form moving in the pod erratically. "…We gotta get him under control."

As Phil looks up at the monitor, a sudden realisation that he is looking at Denton Gill hits him immediately.

"Wait. What?" Kirkland blurts out.

"It's OK, Phil. It's Gill!" Jumeau shouts.

On the CCTV monitor, Kirkland, Jumeau, Waters and assembled guards witness Denton Gill peering into the lens of the CCTV camera, and then trying to open the door to the pod.

"Stand back!" instructs Waters.

There is no more sound, and the monitor shows Gill with his hands in the air, mouthing words which are not coming across the speakers.

"OK, guys, bring him out," commands Waters, coming down from the steps and issuing the command to open the door.

"Hank, it's OK, we know him," Kirkland steps in.

"Alright, Phil, but let's make sure there is nothing…untoward."

As if in a stupor, Gill is manhandled by the guards down the steps, guilty before being proven innocent.

"Easy, guys!" Kirkland raises his voice.

And with that, Denton Gill returns home.

—-

"Mr. President. This way, please," asks Al Mason, joint chief of White House security with Mitch Nicolescu.

John Montgomery scurries along the back wall of the auxiliary annex in the basement of the White House, and after some time he, and several security guards, reach the second helipad which lies back and to the left of the White House garden, where the usual press conferences would normally take place.

As the assembled entourage, including Maria Ortega and Joe Becker, ascend the steps from the secret underground passageway, the force of the swirling wind from the rotor blades slaps them all hard in the face. Any fancy grooming or cute hairstyles vanish in less than a second. Montgomery squints and holds his hand up to try to see ahead of him. Mason ushers him towards Marine Six, a VH-60N White Hawk prepared especially for these sorts of events. With everyone on-board, the helicopter rises quickly to attain several hundred feet. As Montgomery looks down below him, he can see a hoard of armed activists clashing with army and police in a shoot-out right at the gates.

"Jesus," he says.
"We might need him," Becker answers.

Several shots can be heard, and Maria can make out the tracer trail from a near miss.

"Get us out of here!" she screams at the pilot, who banks left and down to try to avoid the bullets, but as Montgomery's side of the helicopter moves to face the ground, he sees more tracer fire coming directly towards him. Strapped in, he can do nothing. He flinches, closing his eyes as if to blot out what is happening.

Skkrinng. A bullet scratches into the glass creating a terrifying screeching noise that rips though the cockpit. The damage is limited but has impacted the shell which now cracks further. More trails shoot by above. As the helicopter ducks and dives in the air, there is a moment of anguish as Ortega and Becker's eyes meet. This could be it.

—

The far side, where nothing really happens, is aflame. Lightning sparks have ignited some of the reeds up and to the left at the very edge of the wormhole. It might be nothing. Or it might not.

Nuvo has been holding the rip in the fence open allowing more dualling Karks through into the field, that end of which is now awash with the hauntingly unsaturated grey of Karkian forms as they make their way to the clearing. But it is taking its toll. With Gill, Catherine and Novek now all gone, the only thing holding the intersect together is him. And he can't hold for much longer.

Up ahead, he can hear the clicks and guttural stops of his people, or at least the chosen ones, in a battle cry where they are picking off earthly duallists and forcing them back to Earth, only to claim their bodies and take on human form. The invisible invaders.

Carla and some of the new duallists help each other and try to battle their way over to where she emerged, avoiding the wrath of the Karks, who seem to be deliberately choosing the younger, and more bewildered, of the emerging men and women. Trying to trace who is who is long forgotten, and in the panic Carla has had to abandon any hope of saving some further away on the outer edges of the clearing. Frightened shouts and screams pervade. But Carla is resolute in her mission. She needs to courier people back to Earth, and the safest place must be the pod at Langley. It's an obvious but dangerous tactic lest she be overrun by the sprawling mass of alien forms now overwhelming the space.

One-by-one, Carla ushers them back through the hole in the reeds from where she emerged, her acute senses allowing her to navigate their return.

As the queue to jump through and back to Earth gets bigger, she spies a nearing Kark. Trembling in fear, unwittingly she throws out her hand as if to put up the 'STOP' signal, straining every one of her mental powers to visualise a ball of light that she aims into the body of the approaching foe. As she does so, and to her utter surprise, the Kark is hit by a force which macerates its body, deforming into a mess of milky fluid that falls into the flattened corn reeds and is absorbed into the ground.

"Huh!" she exclaims, before hastily getting on with the task at hand.

Emilia, a young girl from Venezuela, darts a look at Carla.

"Thank you," she says in her hispanic tone.

After desperately hunting around for any remaining duallists, and seeing the Karks swarming into, and across the clearing, Carla realises that she must return, and close off her duelling channel. She hurries into the gap and starts her return flight, emerging with Emilia and several others in Darkroom Two.

—-

"Watch out!" cries Hank Waters to the guards as he sees a number of arrivals to the pod through the CCTV monitor. "Open the door!" he instructs them, and the big guards duly release the latch on the door, allowing a number of duallists, gasping for breath, out into the hangar space surrounding the pods.

As the survivors from the battleground of the cornfield congregate around the pods, shaken and afraid, Hank Waters is in shock, as are his guards. What they have just witnessed is beyond the limits of their imagination, and the profound sense of the unreal has left them in stunned silence. But Hank has called for backup, and within seconds four more of the Langley security team race through the space to cordon off the survivors. The bedraggled and fearful duallists can't work out if they have been saved or if they are about to be killed. The smell of fear fills the air.

"What to do with these?" asks the squadron leader, directing his question to Waters. But Waters is struggling. His vision is blurry and his heartbeat is way over the uppermost limit for a man his age. Before he can muster any presence of mind to answer, he can hear the hurried clacking sound of someone running down H9. It's Ava.

"My God!" she exclaims as she casts her eyes over a dozen or so people huddling together outside Darkroom Two. Quickly realising that these must be the result of a huge success for Catherine and CAT, she can't help letting out a whoop of excitement, at which point Hank Waters seems to come round.

"OK, everybody!" Ava shouts above the murmuring and chatting. "OK, listen up, yeh?" she continues. "You are all SAFE. You are all OK. Please nod if you understand what I just said."

Several of the group nod, but there are others who seem not to understand.

"OK, listen up!" this time more forcefully, and now using some rudimentary sign language to help the flow. "You have come to AMERICA, OK? You are all SAFE, and we will look after you, right? There is NO REASON TO PANIC. You are SAFE here. Please nod if you understand!" she shouts.

This time most nod, and Ava seems to be sending out at least the beginnings of a comforting welcome.

"We will need to get your NAMES, and where you are FROM. We are your FRIENDS? OK?" At which point, everyone gets the reference and the tension subsides a little.

Carla comes forward and, although shaken by the experience, seems the most lucid of all the duallists.

"Hi. I am Carla, you remember?" she asks Ava.
"Oh yes, of course. Carla! My God, are you OK? What happened?"

Carla offers her take on the events in the cornfield, and although she can see that Ava is happy about so many duallists being in the same place at the same time, recounting the swarming hordes of Karks, quickly wipes any smile from Ava's face.

"OK, Carla, thank you for your update," Redmond says in a more restrained tone. "Please tell everyone that they will be treated well, and in due course we will need to talk to everyone individually."

She turns to Hank Waters.

"Hank, listen up. I need these guys to have access to water, food and a hot shower. Get their clothes cleaned for them at the laundry and take them to Carol over at the recruitment block. Once they are all ID'd and checked in, gather them all in the lecture theatre on H5 and I'll come and join you. Make sure everything is secure. Got that?"

"Yes, Ma'am," Waters replies, glad to have some semblance of order restored.

As the group begins to file out of the hangar and onto auxiliary corridor H8, Ava stops Carla Piccioni.

"I'm so sorry, Carla," she says. "That must have been terrible." Carla nods, not able to offer much else.
"I need to talk to you. Alone. Is that OK?" Ava asks.
"Yes, I understand."
"Good. Follow me," says Ava, and with that she heads up H9 to where Christophe Jumeau and Phil Kirkland are with Denton Gill.

—-

Novek and seven others wait until darkness, the curfew still in place in the nicer part of the Bow district, just west of Stratford. As the troop reconnoitre around the nearby streets, each chooses a particular house to observe over the coming days. In this area there are few police patrols and all the residents are in lockdown, most sheltering indoors.

One by one, each Kark takes careful note of the patterns of behaviour - evening meals, bedtime, and waking time. This will come in handy when the others arrive. With the surveillance coming to an end and the group assembled at the Wilson-Green house, Novek starts to speak, in Kark, to his soldiers.

"Well done to you all. This is a great day for Kark. A *great* day," he clicks. "But this is just the start. The very beginning. And we must get things right. Now you may struggle at first in acclimatising to the shells you have. This is normal, and you may find it takes time to look and feel like these creatures do. Do not panic at this. Nuvo and myself have been through this process and I can reassure you that, as you can see, I have complete command. You will also have complete command, sooner or later. As we bring more soldiers here - soldiers like you, with your abilities - we will also use Nuvo to bring the others who will need new shells. Our job is to collect these shells, to bring them here, to Nuvo, who will uncloak our new settlers. This is how we will grow, and survive here. We are the spearhead; the pioneers. And we are strong!" he proclaims, to much clicking.

Novek switches to speaking English, taking on a more expressive face in the guise of Wesley Wilson-Green.

"And now, we must learn to communicate like this," he says. "It may not come easily to start with, so we need to be careful. Do not get caught out by the trickery of devious humans. Especially in the use of their language. Practise this with each other, and in ordinary situations. But! Do not underestimate our enemy."

This time, there is muttering among the humanoid forms gathered, and the hollow sounds of low-level acknowledgement circulating in the large living room. A collection of ordinary people, it appears, having a meeting.

"There will be many more coming, so we need to prepare the ground. Seek out the young and healthy. These will be the shells that will last longest, and give us the opportunity to develop our own technology to survive without them. Return here. This will be our base for operations. Clear?"

A quietening of all sounds indicates consensual understanding.

"One last thing. You need to be focused. My return to the humans' ksaanek is required. Remember that you are the chosen ones. The supremely gifted ones chosen to lead this mission. There will be many rewards. Many. Look forward to those rewards by giving everything you have to the cause. Our cause, and the future of our kind."

—-

Back in Boston, Wendy Xiu is wiping the forehead of her boyfriend Mal, lying prostrate on the soft lab table.

"I got a bit lost," he whispers, still coming round after passing out on his return from dualling.
"I've got you, Mal. And I'm not letting you go," she replies. "Here, have a sip of this." She offers him a warm cup of herbal tea from the flask. She knows he's not a fan, but it's the nearest thing to hand and inside she is incredibly anxious. "Your readings went haywire about 3 minutes in. What the hell happened?"
"It's mad, Wen. I seemed to be suspended in time. I thought I was away for hours. I saw Catherine!" he exclaims, unable to order his thoughts but suddenly remembering snapshots of what happened at the clearing. "I knew I would. She can call out - like a siren or radio broadcast or something. You just follow the sound. When I got to the cornfield, all the reeds were flattened for a while, so I could see that there were many others who heard too. But that's where it got weird." The big frame of Mal Baines starts to judder as he coughs and splutters as he tries to get up.
"Woah! Not so fast. Take it easy!" barks Wendy. "Take your time. Tell me exactly what happened, Mal."
"Well the reeds started to straighten up so you needed to remember the way to the clearing. I heard a lot of rustling at first but it just confused me, so I had to kind of guess where to go, but after a lot of wandering around I eventually got to the opening. It's like a massive crop circle. That was mad. Like watching 'Signs' or something."
"Go on…" she urges him.
"OK, well, there were about a dozen or so people all staggering about. It's hard to move at the opening. I don't know why. I managed OK, but I could see others struggling to scramble their way out. The route you take might be important. I don't know, but you have to go back through one of the gaps in the reeds. I saw others doing that. The best thing to do is leave something at the gap you came out

from, so you remember which route to get back. At least I think that's how it works."

"Yes, yes, but what about Catherine?"

"Well I only saw her for a few moments. Wen, she was in the *sky*. Like, I mean, *flying*. Man, I thought I was trippin'."

"Mal, get to the point. Why did you have a meltdown? And where is Catherine now?"

"Sorry. It's just all so weird," he says as he squeezes Wendy's hand. "I think she flew off to find Gill, or try to stop those creatures from breaking through."

"Creatures? You mean like the ones Catherine told us about?"

"Yes. But I *saw* them, Wen. They are *real*. They started to attack and take hold of some of the guys in the opening and force them back through the holes in the reeds. What does that mean?"

"It means that we have a bunch of aliens who have taken a bunch of us hostage, that's what it means, Mal. Did they come for you?"

"I saw one approaching me, but rather than wait around, I got scared and ran back into the reeds. I shouldn't have, though. I feel so guilty."

"Hey, honey, you did the right thing. We need you…*I* need you here with me. You couldn't have done anything anyway, by the sounds of it."

"I suppose. Thing is, I left while there were still many there. The place could still be overrun. I could go back," he concludes.

"No! You are not going anywhere!" Wendy commands, as Mal eventually sits up with her help. "We need to work together to understand this better before you go anywhere else. And we need to call Catherine to make sure she is OK."

"I feel certain she is. I mean, she has amazing abilities in there. Like something out of DC mags. Just mad," he tails off, reflecting on the strangest experience of his life.

—

Click, click, click, click.

Novek has returned to the perimeter in the guise of Wesley Wilson-Green before morphing into his more familiar Kark form. He signals to Nuvo, his weaker half, to move aside while he journeys back to the temple on the other side. Nuvo appears worn out, flushing slowly in an off-yellow colour, seemingly drained of all energy.

"You are doing Kark proud," grins Novek. "Where is the human?"

"And you?" Nuvo asks.

"What?"

"Are you doing Kark proud?" comes the acrid reply. "You are killing many humans, yes? And you will be leaving many poor Karks behind. What are they to do, while you and the 'chosen ones' settle on Earth?"

"Silence!" shouts Novek. "I will not have such insolence. First and foremost you are an astraman, and part of the Kark federation. Do not let your elite status and special abilities mask the fact that you are a servant of the Kark people. You will do your duty. You will help to save our species from certain extinction, and you will have the honour and dignity to do this as I do. We all have our part to play. This is yours," Novek clicks, with increasingly high pitch, causing Nuvo to wince.

But Nuvo is not letting go.

"And what, then, of us. Of you and me, once we are on Earth? What plans then, and what part do I play?" he questions.

Novek swiftly approaches Nuvo and, extending his limb, batters him square on the head, causing Nuvo to deflate and effuse clouds of deep amber gas from his ventricles. Nuvo's arm separates from his body as he starts to flush bright red. As the gap in the fence begins to start sparking and glitching, Nuvo attempts to land a blow on the imposing Novek, but the Sultan of Kark is too fast, and too strong, ducking the blow and again attacking Nuvo, this time to the torso, causing a deformity in his entire body, which only slowly begins to reshape.

Novek approaches Nuvo, his dark sceptre form clicking and clucking with such high frequency that Nuvo's head feels like it is going to explode. Novek then shoves his face into Nuvo's.

"Mark my signals, Nuvo. Your place is on Kark when you are not here. You can tend to your little flock of admirers in Kseu. Oh, I know who they are. They won't survive, and neither will you. Because you are weak. Weak of mind, and weak of body. A freak in all but one respect - you happen to be my twin. Well, I never wanted you, and soon I won't need you. It is only the elite that can prevail, and your job is to carry the chosen ones here. That is all. Soon you will be done, and I will allow you to go home. So you can have Kark all to yourself and enjoy the adulation of the crowds while it lasts. Give yourself the privileges you so clearly envy. Form a democracy. I don't care," he exclaims as he starts clicking again.

"Stop!" cries Nuvo, and for a second Novek flushes bright yellow. "Now you have proven how much of a traitor to the people of Kark you really are. When this is over, I will tell the real story of the 'great Sultan'. Tell of the countless murders of innocent Karks in the dungeons of Kseu, of the bodies you dissolved in the moat, and of the crimes against Kark. I will tell of the wealth and luxury you secretly amassed through the slavery and exploitation of the Kark miners, and how you wrecked the chances of ordinary Karks to have a decent life. Of how you and your elite guard built your power through intimidation and fear."

Novek hovers over Nuvo menacingly, and in that moment the brilliant pulsing sparkle of Novek's red eye forces Nuvo to expect a killing blow, right here. But at the back of his mind, he knows Novek can't kill him. For to do so would be to endanger the entanglement between them and stop Novek from ensuring the safe passage of the remaining Kark duallists, of whom there are so many still to come.

"You have come very close. I pity you. You even lost the human. For this you have to stay here. You see what your inept weakness brings? When I do not need you any more, I will deal with you here. Mark my signals," Novek spits out in disdain.

—-

"I need to see her *now!*" Gill is shouting. Kirkland and Jumeau are contemplating how to deal with the traumatised detective.

"Calm down. Just calm down. She's fine and we will take you over as soon as we debrief," reassures Phil Kirkland.

"Really, Gill, she's been well looked after," Christophe Jumeau adds.

Gill is struggling with the news. He's going to be a father. The world is at the mercy of a vicious pandemic. Rioting and looting are taking place across every country affected by GARI. And Chinese and Russian troops are massing around Japan and the Korean Peninsula, effectively ignoring any international peacetime agreements and ensuring the destabilisation of the entire planet. So far, it's not the sort of homecoming he had had in mind.

Ava Redmond enters, her rather imposing presence quietening the room. Behind is a rather sheepish Carla Piccioni, who tentatively follows her in.

"Ah, you must be Detective Gill. My name is Ava Redmond. You all know Carla by now. Phil, has Detective Gill had all necessary medical checks?"

Phil nods.

"Good. Gill, I head up our intelligence agency, and work closely with the NASA guys on covert initiatives. Every word spoken in this room is subject to level six United States government intelligence classification, which means that nothing goes beyond these walls, or us. This is a rule, and cannot be broken. I'm sure Phil has already briefed you on this. I personally wanted to conduct our conversation as I understand that you have had quite an interesting few months off-world," she says with a wry smile. "Now, I realise that your good lady is expecting. So congratulations on that. But before you can see her, we absolutely need to get some details, as I'm sure you, of all people, will understand," Redmond asserts, rhetorically.

Gill takes a deep breath. "I need to see her today, not tomorrow or the day after."

"Well, if we can move things along, I'm sure that will be feasible," Redmond comes back, and diplomatically ushers Gill over to the sofas in Christophe's office. "What's your poison?" she asks.

"No, I'm fine," Gill responds, to which Ava doesn't react, other than to pour herself, and Carla, large Bacardi's and ice.

"In that case, can we get down to business?"

The group settle into the sofas and Gill gives a relatively lucid account of his kidnapping, time as a hostage on Kark, and his understanding of the Karkian plan to invade Earth. By the end, there is a stunned silence. Even the normally assured and composed Redmond seems to be far away in thought, desperately trying to juggle her reaction and how she will be presenting such an explosive piece of news to her senior colleagues.

As the oldest person in the room, and perhaps the most knowledgeable in the science behind wormholes, Christophe is the first to dive in.

"So, from what you saw, you believe that Nuvo and the other Karks can dual automatically - as in, they have that as a natural ability?" he asks Gill.

"I'm not convinced of that. I do know that their leader and Nuvo are entangled, and that I saw a whole bunch of Kark soldiers in the temple, which acts as their wormhole just as the cornfield is ours," Gill replies.

"OK, so if I am trying to get a handle on how many of these Karks are now here, what should I be thinking?" asks Redmond.

Gill tries to be as accurate as he can, knowing that this will be important. "I would estimate between fifty and a hundred, maybe more. I don't know if they have a programme that trains people to dual, or if the ability is prevalent in the population as a whole. But my intuition from my discussions with Nuvo is that it's not inherent. But as you know they can shape-shift, and they were grabbing our guys in the clearing. Carla here will tell you. I don't know what else they might be able to do."

Carla is nodding.

"So where are they?" asks Phil.

"I honestly don't know," replies Gill. "But my guess is that every person that emerged on our side of the clearing will have left a gap to return. So they would have gone down there. Since we don't know where these guys were coming from, my guess is that they might have used all of those, or maybe just one or two. You said you saw a few disappearing into one particular gap, Carla?"

"I saw many there, yes, and I could remember much detail, but I couldn't be sure who came out of that one. Maybe Sergei, but I can't be certain, I am sorry," Carla updates anxiously.

In normal circumstances, she and Gill would go through a forensic, military, microscopic debrief in separate rooms with different Langley staff interviewing them. But there is nothing normal about this situation.

"Sergei? You mean some of the duallists were from Russia?" Redmond enquires
"He was a friend of Wes. From London though…"

Ava is nodding, thinking through what matters most in all this.

"Let me just take a step back here. Are any of you of the opinion that these Karks will be more dangerous than GARI? I mean, it's the big question, yes? If they are setting up in some hideout somewhere, and taking human hostages or worse, how long would it be until there were enough of them to actually pose a risk greater than any other risk that we are dealing with right now?" she asks.
"Ava, can I jump in there?" asks Christophe.
"Sure. Fire away," she replies.
"Well, I am no military man. I deal with the scientific evidence. But what we know so far is certainly a huge cause for concern. If we weren't facing the wall with GARI and international war, we'd class this as some form of invasion, and one way or the other we'd have to assert a response, purely based on the fact that an alien species has found a way to reach Earth. So, say we get that vaccine and the Earth survives beyond GARI, we'd need to have some way of determining how to find these guys, and potentially negotiate with them some form of land deal, at least if no-one tried to annihilate them. We'd need to understand their biology, their technology, social structures and so on."
"But these creatures can take on human form, like Nuvo did with Garfield, so very shortly they might be living among us without being detected," Gill adds.
"Unless they are observed," interjects Jumeau.

"Yes, we could try to get our duallists to detect them, assuming that they are still dualling…" Kirkland suggests.

"Or their super-positioning may be time-limited," the Professor replies.

"How's that?" asks Redmond.

"Super-positioning things interact with their environment. In the process, they can be forced to adopt one or other of the super-positions, mainly because they become entangled with the things around them."

"I understood about three of those words, Professor," Ava castigates Jumeau.

"Sorry. To put it another way, most duallists can't super-position for too long because, over time, they also become partially entangled with their local environment *anyway*. You know, electrons and photons and atoms that bombard them all the time in their new surroundings. So they *can* get trapped in just one of the realities if they stay for too long. It's just that if time is critical, as it was with Garfield and Montgomery for example, other duallists could bring forward the entrapment by consciously measuring, or breaking up, the super-positioning."

Gill has a sudden revelation, and the others sense he needs the floor.

"Of course. That's it. There was something at the back of my mind in all this. The way that Novek dealt with Nuvo, and how Kark is such a bleak and forbidding planet," he says.

"What do you mean?" asks Ava.

Gill sits up. They all look up to him, expectantly.

"Well," he replies. "It's just that, if you think about it, the Karks don't need to go back. This is not an invasion. I mean, it *is* an invasion to us. But for them, it's an emigration, and exodus. They might not *need* to super-position, at least not back to Kark, if they settle and can survive here."

"That makes sense," announces Christophe. "Except for one thing."

"And what's that?" Ava enquires.

"GARI," the Professor responds.

"You mean, they will die from GARI just like us?" she comes back.

"Well, that's the possibility, isn't it? That if they can't breathe our atmosphere like Gill says, and so need to occupy human forms, like Garfield, then what happens if the human that they occupy gets GARI. The Kark would presumably die too, no?"

"I see. Yes, good point, Professor," Ava thinks out loud.

"Ava, you asked if the Kark invasion is an immediate threat to the Earth. I'd say we can't separate this from what is happening to our world, and whether or not there will be any of us left to resist. I mean, if this thing is as bad as you say it is, we're all in a great amount of danger, and the first priority will be to ensure our own survival, rather than fighting with some cosmic enemy, even if they are on our doorstep," says Gill.

"Think they're already inside the house, Gill," Kirkland corrects.

Carla has been sitting quietly, but now grabs her glass and takes a swig of high quality Caribbean rum which electrifies her into action.

"I killed one," she announces, and looks at Gill.

"You did?" asks Ava.

"Yes, I am not sure how, but I focused some energy into a rock I imagined I had in my hand, and threw it at one of them. It was like I could pick up and throw something very heavy, but not heavy. I can't explain it. The rock made them…burst," she says, tailing off in a strangely matter-of-fact voice.

Christophe and Gill look surprised, while Phil makes a little note on his biocell.

"Gill, if you died in the wormhole, you would die in real life, yes?" asks Phil.

"That's how I see it."

"So, maybe the key is to stop them coming through the cornfield. Do we know the situation in there, like, right now?" he follows up.

"I'm guessing Nuvo is helping more to breach the join between the two wormholes. Without my connection to help, I imagine it will be slow for them, but they'll occupy the cornfield and wait for more of us to show up," Gill supposes.

"So the cornfield is an open channel for them? You can't close it down?" asks Ava.

Gill is restless, thinking about Catherine again. He gets up and this time he pours himself a large glass of water. By habit, he'd have a Scotch, but after eight months without alcohol and in his current state, he'd probably fall over.

"I thought about that, you know. But you told me that the reason so many new duallists turned up was the strength of the call from Catherine, right? Well, it seems to me that an open broadcast like that, and the rather public location, will mean it's just too easy to find, not just among our own duallists, but the likes of Nuvo and Novek and their Kark guards. They found it through Garfield and us back when, and they used me to find it again. The only way to shut it down might be to get everyone out of there and then torch it."

"Huh?" Kirkland is squinting up at Gill.

"Metaphorically."

Christophe Jumeau is feeling increasingly uneasy, and feels that everyone is missing some central information.

"But we *can't* close it down," he asserts. "It's too important. The CAT programme has come too far, and we need the cornfield as the jump-off point."

"I don't understand," says Gill.

"I'll come to that in a moment, Gill. Let me try to explain where our thinking is, and see if we can work out what our next move is going to be. That's what you need, Ava, right?"

Redmond nods again. "Remember. We need a plan for CAT, and it needs to be based on what we can do, not what we can't,' she asserts.

"Understood," replies the Professor, taking a tissue from his jacket pocket and wiping his brow.

"I've been trying to put everything together, and basically it seems to come down to entanglement. It is this phenomenon that forms the threads that stitch space and time together. 'Spacetime' is therefore not a fundamental of our universe but rather *emerges* from entanglement and not the other way around. That's why faster than light information exchange and time travel aren't spooky any more," he begins.

"In plain English, Professor, if you don't mind?" Ava retorts.

"Sorry," Christophe replies. "In a nutshell, this all started with Gill and my daughter discovering that they were entangled - that their bodies consist of an unusual amount of matter which was originally created in one place, or from one event, like a comet or an exploding star, for example. In most places in the Universe that matter has flown apart and might never recombine. But for some people here on Earth, and from what we know from Gill and some Karks, bits of this matter must have formed into rocks, planets, perhaps recombining over millennia, over and over again and in different combinations until, in the most sophisticated animals like us where concentrations of these particles can accumulate in sufficient amounts, the most profound connection between entangled people goes beyond DNA, and goes beyond family per se."

Jumeau wipes his brow again, shuffling on the sofa to get up. He goes over to his desk and grabs the large glass of water there.

"I think we all get this, Professor. Did you have a particular insight in terms of what this means for us?" asks Kirkland.

"I'm getting there, Phil. Bear with me," says Christophe as he leans against the edge of his desk, his large frame partially blocking the sunlight coming through the window behind him.

"So, OK. We have Gill and Catherine entangled. Carla, you are entangled, right? You know that there is someone out there that is a kind of twin of yours, just not in the sense of family, yes?" he prompts Carla.

"Yes. For some years I have seen this picture of myself with another girl. We are at a train station, saying hello, or goodbye. I never see her face. It makes me sad sometimes," Carla explains.

"Right, so your sensitivity to these communication channels is heightened, and you heard Catherine calling when you were at the railway station, right?" he asks.

Carla nods. "Yes!"

"And how did you get to the clearing. Did you take a train?"

"I…I m not sure. I remember, yes, seeing the sign, and going to the platform. After that, it's a bit…blurry."

Christophe turns to the wider group. "Good. So, basically, my point is that entangled people when they dual, or super-position - whatever you want to call it - can connect from their own particular wormhole through to other wormholes. It might not be everyone who can do this, but the ones that came through into the field, all got there because they heard Catherine's call. That make sense, Gill?"

Gill is nodding in agreement.

"Taking that one step further, this also means that Catherine's call could potentially be heard by Karks. And maybe even other races - alien races - that can tune in. I don't know how this happens, or why necessarily, but, for example, there is nothing to stop a particular region in spacetime having multiple wormholes in it," Christophe adds.

"So, Nuvo and Novek were able to gatecrash our field because they are entangled and the wormhole they use can connect to ours because of the overall degree of entanglement?" asks Gill.

"Sort of," says Christophe. "My best guess is that the wormholes work like black holes and that their horizons can be susceptible to entanglement, especially if they are near neighbours. The bridge between these wouldn't be unusual, just hard to survive in. My own view is that the bridge itself is only possible as a result of the entanglement on both sides. I won't harp on about my grand theory, but suffice it so say that, if we live in a holographic universe, it's entirely possible that the level of entanglement within, and possibly between worlds, is way more than we realise, precisely because they are encoded in two dimensions. With one less dimension in space, and with one less dimension in time due to time dilation, it sort of makes sense that everything is a lot closer together than convention would have us believe. The bigger you think about these things, the less crazy wormholes and super-positioning through them becomes."

"So where is this all going, Professor? You are saying that our action plan is already coded and ready to go?" Ava barks, clearly not enjoying the Professor's meandering, if eloquent, proposition.

Jumeau, still not used to doing anything in a hurry, seems irritated enough by Redmond's comments to wind things up, at least for the time being.

"Look, given that a wormhole warps space and time, creating a world in which things are very different - where Catherine can somehow be released from normal gravitational forces and Carla here can harness powerful pockets of energy which can potentially destroy another person in the wormhole - these are at the same time dangerous and liberating. Dangerous because others that come in through the connection might be able to do the same. And liberating because such phenomena might allow some of us a route out. Right now, I wouldn't be looking to close anything down."

"Xarn," mutters Redmond.
"What was that?" Gill asks Ava.
"I'm guessing that's where you are going, Professor?" she poses to Jumeau.
"Maybe not me personally, but yes. Xarn," he replies.

Gill and Carla are now looking a bit puzzled.

"Care to explain?" asks Gill.
"Yes, sorry Gill. I said I would get to this. Look, you'll hear more of this from Catherine, and I know you are so anxious to see her. But please bear in mind what she has gone through over these months, and also that there are responsibilities that she will have to take care of here."

Gill is listening intently, concentrating rather than responding. Christophe takes the hint.

"So, we're pretty sure that Catherine is in touch with a contact from another exoplanet. Not Kark, and it looks like it is habitable from what we know."
"Wait. What?" Gill interrupts. "You mean that another alien culture has access to the cornfield as well as the Karks? Then we *do* need to shut it down. We need to find a way to stop this or we'll be overrun by…"
"It's not like that," Kirkland chips in. "He means that we can use the wormhole connection to this exoplanet as a way to go off-world. To create our own interplanetary migration, and to potentially settle in some other solar system. It's crazy, but it's true. The

problem is, only the lucky few - like you guys - get the free ticket out of here."

There is a pregnant pause in the conversation as Phil's plain English sinks in. Gill goes over to the window, something obviously worrying him about Phil's take on things.

"Well, crudely, yes," Christophe comments. "But you said we need some actionable plan, Ava. So that's what I'm trying to get to. Put simply, I think that, following some commonly agreed rules of physics, the degree of entanglement between two entities will follow the same rules of probabilistic wave functions that Schrödinger worked out all those years ago. So, in Gill and Catherine's case, the two waves clearly have a great tendency to combine harmoniously so that they amplify. This will translate to having a greater sense of connection and a more powerful effect when combined. My first thought is some form of anti-gravity that Catherine experienced. We may be able to use this capacity to open the gate to travel to an exoplanet that can support life. Conversely, as we've heard from Gill, Nuvo and Novek clearly have a different relationship. Their wave functions seem to be at odds, and will cancel out in a lot of instances. For me, this means that the potential imbalance in power between them will weaken the partnership overall, and possibly lead to entrapment. Yes, Novek may display enormous strength, but my suspicion is that this will be at the expense of Nuvo, despite some obvious advantages Karks have over us in terms of functions, abilities, adaptation and so on."

The Professor is now motoring.

"In terms of how that will affect *us*, I imagine that putting an end to the Kark invasion might be possible if we can end the entanglement between Nuvo and Novek."
"You mean take out Nuvo?" Kirkland asks.
"Or Novek. Either way, end the entanglement. If Novek, the Karks that remain here will have at least lost their leader, and then we train our own troop of duallists to work with the settlements here on Earth to spot any potential Karks if they try to infiltrate our isolated 'New-Earth' communities," Jumeau responds.
"You've already got those?" asks Gill.

"Almost," Redmond chips in. "There are ten settlements in process. It's our best chance in terms of an on-world solution. But there are risks. Other governments will be doing the same, and we've already had reports that groups of vigilantes have been planning their own armed communes for months now."

"The usual suspects," Kirkland adds.

"This is where CAT should be going, Ava," Christophe advises. "Those good people down the corridor will need to be trained. These are the people who can potentially identify someone who is dualling, assuming the Karks are still super-positioning while here. Just like you spotted Garfield, Gill."

"I can't take any credit for that, Sir. That was your daughter, through and through," he replies.

"But you get the point," Christophe retorts. "If you are super-positioning and you observe someone else super-positioning, you collapse the wave function and they get trapped. That's one way to stop Karks from interstellar travel, and force them to remain on Earth. Once their human bodies naturally fall prey to disease, then the Karks will die out, naturally."

"Or we try to kill them in the cornfield?" asks Carla, bravely interjecting into Christophe's thinking.

The substantial frame of Christophe Jumeau, pacing the floor as he has been expounding his hypotheses, stops in its tracks.

"*As well*, Carla, *as well*. You guys that have special abilities in there need to be deployed to take out as many Karks as possible before they get too much hold in the field. Like we said, they'll probably be waiting there for the next wave of our duallists to show up, so we will need to be prepared."

"But isn't that just playing into the hands of the Karks?" questions Redmond. "Surely that's just what they want. If we keep the cornfield clear then all those Karks have no-one to kidnap and no routes down here. Or…?"

"But that's the problem. It's to do with the other side of the equation," Christophe replies. "In order to explore the possibilities of us looking off-world, we have to put the call out. It's what Catherine managed to do so well, and it's what we'll need Gill to do too if she's not there."

"You want me to put a call out in the field? Why can't you get Carla here to do that?" Gill asks.

"Well, it's more powerful I guess if both of you do it, but apart from that, we'll need you to make a special call."

"Wait, I don't understand," says Gill. "You mean, call out like Catherine did, yes?"

"Yes, but this one is really special. And it will be very particular to you."

Gill is struggling. And so too is Christophe, who can't seem to bring himself to give Gill hope when it might be in vain.

"It's Catherine. She's found Beth," Ava jumps in, unable to wait for the inevitable emotional smack that Gill needs to hear, and which he will need to use as motivation for getting back in the ring.

Gill can hardly take any more, his look of strained puzzlement there for all to witness.

"I need to get out of here," he announces.

He's exhausted, and this has sent his world spinning even further into outer space. Realising that the big detective is in some trouble, Ava approaches him, and lays a hand on his arm.

"Gill, look, I'm sorry, but it was the elephant in the room and it's only fair that you know. This is an enormous amount to take in. Take some time. Christophe, will you accompany Detective Gill over to the hospital to see your daughter?"

Christophe nods, assuming this is the best thing for Gill right now, and feeling rather awkward that he had to bundle yet more potentially explosive news into the conversation.

"One thing for you both," Ava announces, looking at Gill and Christophe. "Have a think about the radical alternative that CAT can offer, and how we might mitigate our risks by pushing on with trials. We have a bunch of guys here who can dual, just like you, Detective, but they don't know any more than that. We need to find a way to help them, to stop any further Karks, and to explore the links to

Xarn. You, Catherine and Carla here are the only ones who can do that. Take some time to come up with a plan. I'll give you twenty-four hours, and then we meet back here. My apologies for the brutal timeframes, but I need some answers," she concludes, clicking her way over to Christophe's window.

* * * *

CHAPTER 8: EXODII

"Fuck."

"Beg pardon, Sir?"

"This is really fucked up, Joe."

John Montgomery is angry.

"Yes. It is, Sir."

The President is in the main basement suite deep underground at the upstate Connecticut bunker, unmarked on any map. His eyes are transfixed on an enormous LCD screen, a conglomeration of at least sixteen ultra-high definition monitors that are joined seamlessly to create the impression of a cinematic and near three-dimensional view of any signal feed relayed directly to the hideout down the thick cabling running underground from one of only two second generation NG2-911-X fibre optic base stations in the country. Using the Public Safety Data Network, or PSDN, had been ruled out as a potential option for the bunker given some of the known data breaches in recent years, so Montgomery, in his focus on internal infrastructure developments, made a point of prioritising the construction of a quantum-encrypted private virtual network in which the intelligence community could have confidence.

Up on the screen, one of two remaining broadcasting feeds from CNN is relaying the footage caught on camera by local reporters in Washington which clearly shows how the President's airborne helicopter looked as if it was going to crash back down onto the White House lawn - the formidable skill and sheer presence-of-mind of military pilot D'André Williams the only divide between life and death of the country's political elite.

Underneath the video images runs the digital ticker-tape readout "Breaking…Washington: President and top aides seconds away from helicopter crash after attack on White House from armed rioters…".

Abe Hart and Joe Becker are in the room with Montgomery as Bibi Melnik and Maria Ortega consult with the chairman of the joint chiefs of staff, Lloyd Butler. Fifty metres above at the entrance to the bunker deep in the forest under the dense cover of pine trees and scrub, some sixty security personnel maintain their positions in a star-on-circle configuration in all directions. But you wouldn't know. Each command station in this setup is itself a hidden bunker, and elite army snipers are positioned in specially-made treehouses. Throughout the configuration lies a network of closed-circuit monitors, sensitised geodesic radars, radio frequency interceptors, geiger counters, seismic detectors, thermometers and pressure sensors. If anything moves, it will be a very public event.

"Bring up the GARI maps, Ellie," Hart requests to the control room. The screen fills with an image of the world from west to east, showing the incidence of GARI cases in blue, and deaths in red. It does not make for comfortable viewing.

"How come Japan still doesn't have any red?" Montgomery asks.
"I honestly don't know, Sir. If you look closely it's not that they are clear. It's specifically Hokkaido and Kyushu that seem to have something there that has prevented as many deaths. We've got Bill McFarlane and his team analysing that right now. I doubt it's anything other than how well those islands have isolated, but it's also why it's being targeted by the Chinese and Russians. If GARI isn't as prevalent there, then they are seeing it as a potential haven where they can start to settle their 'cleans'".

The section of the map in the far east surrounding Japan, even at this high resolution, is stained a deep red, like an open wound, the Korean peninsula the only exception. South towards China it is clear that the main cities are in meltdown, with India and Africa now haemorrhaging badly. In Europe, the scale factor of the image allows for some respite from the worrying stains, instead mixing blue, white and red in proportions roughly equal. Panning across and west to the eastern seaboard of North America, once again the intensity of scarlet devastation hits home hard, and so too across to the country to Los Angeles, San Francisco and up to Oregon, all seeping outward in overlapping circles, contaminating all but the sparse landscapes of Montana, Wyoming, Iowa and the Dakotas.

"With the joint settlement programme now signed off by the Canadian Premier, we also identified an area in Iowa in addition to North Manitoba, British Columbia and Alaska. It means that we will soon meet the target of ten settlements, all up and running within a matter of weeks," Becker states, perhaps in an attempt to shift the focus to something more positive.

"OK, Joe. You keep me posted on that directly. Have we the access routes sorted now?" the President asks.

"North Manitoba - yes. We'll use the same route for Alaska for the British Columbia site outside Fort Saint-John."

"And the other sites?"

"Central and South American bases are intensifying new construction work and security, and two of the Caribbean settlements have been approved in principle, but we'll have to negotiate with the Brits on the Turks and Caicos. The Barbados government is being stubborn, but we can work on them as the back up," Becker responds.

"Good news. We need some of that. Thank you, Joe."

Montgomery scans the map again, shaking his head.

"Antarctica?" he asks.

"We're already there, John. Several dozen new recruits, all tested and flown down with a year's worth of supplies."

"OK, and the situation in Europe?"

"It's patchy. They are behind the curve, but scared. Brussels has declared a universal lockdown with a guarantee of home delivery of rations by the military, but many aren't buying it. Like here, there are many dissidents and conspiracy theorists, all fired up by dark web operations and links into arms suppliers. They'll have their own worries. The UK has closed off its border with Northern Ireland due to the incidence in Ireland generally, and the only worry we have is Lachnagoil," Becker informs Montgomery.

"The launch site in Scotland?"

"Yes, it's fully functional, as is Faroe, but Abe and myself thought it best to increase security there as it's a bit exposed on that

North Atlantic, but it's still our number three. With Edwards and Vandenburg as the primaries, we are good to go."

'Canaveral is just too exposed, right?"

"Right."

'OK, thanks Joe. Thanks Abe. Call the others in - we need to get down to business."

As the major players in the U.S. cabinet gather around the table in the somewhat unusual surroundings, Montgomery starts the meeting by trying to put people at their ease.

"Well, thank goodness Doctor Strangelove isn't in the building, huh?" he muses, to a ripple of nervous laughter, and perhaps just one or two involuntary facial tics.

As the sounds fade to silence, Montgomery pauses and looks round the room, and then to the map.

"Thank you everyone for being here, and I hope your families are being well looked after while we get on with our duty of serving this great nation. It is appreciated. Later on we will be joined by Ava, Bill and more of the military and security chiefs, but for now, we have some important decisions to make. This is why I have had to call this meeting quickly. For all of you who have come through this evening's helicopter ride, let's be thankful."

The President takes a drink of water from the unusually heavy glass next to him on the table, and notices that on the bottom, infused into it, is an imprinted picture of Abraham Lincoln, somewhat disfigured by the water rippling above. The sixteenth U.S. president's eyes look disarmingly hypnotic.

"So, this is what we know so far, and please stop me if I get anything wrong. We are on the precipice, folks. The precipice of a giant cliff, and we need to find a way to find a pair of wings so we can jump with some hope of surviving. This *thing*, this GARI, is wiping out our people, everybody's people. Our world. And we can't seem to stop it. No sooner do we form a group of eminent scientists to come up with solutions than one or other gets infected and dies, and then we end up two steps backward. No sooner do we enforce a lockdown than ordinary folks break it in order to get food or stop from going crazy, or just because they don't believe the threat. Most of us are here thanks to our brave helicopter pilot, André. Otherwise the country might not have had a functioning government. As the rioting and looting continues, so too our forces are pressured away from anything strategic and pushed into keeping the country from imploding. They are doing a great job, but we are fighting our *own* people, while China and Russia are about to invade Japan and Korea, where we have a duty and a history of protecting our own interests and the interests of others. So far, our Sky-Twin programme has shown us just what the Chinese and Russians are doing to build up their military on their eastern borders. We cannot wait any longer to decide on Lloyd's proposal."

There is the rustle of shuffling, as the sound and smell of anxiety in the room intensifies.

"Our bases on the Japanese islands, on Guam, on Hawaii, Alaska, Australia and the Philippines, and of course the others down there, are all still functional at least. The problem, as I understand it, is one of tactic and deployment. Lloyd, would you care to talk us through?" he asks Chief of Staff Butler.
"Mr. President, Sir," replies Butler. "This is quite complex, but as you briefed me earlier, I will try to make this as simple as I can. The basic decision we have to take is whether or not to initiate tactical strikes on Khabarovsk or Hegang as clear indications of our intent. Our preference would be Khabarovsk to keep it down to a one-on-one. There seems to be a growing sense from our military intelligence that this could delay, if not prevent, an intrusion into Hokkaido in the first instance."

As Butler takes a breath, Abe Hart interjects.

"What's the downside, Lloyd?"
"Frankly, it's the escalation potential. The fact that Putin and Zhao are clearly planning to carve up Japan and Korea between them to create massive settlement areas, and have already put massive infrastructure in place to carry this out - there is no sense of bluff about this. Sky-Twin and our improved intel have shown that. So they aren't going to give it up, in my opinion."

"So they'll attack our bases first, I guess?" asks Montgomery.

"We assume so. They'll have options. But to minimise any future military action we wish to take down there, it makes sense to take out the short- and medium-range sites. And they can do that. Make no mistake. You know my views on this," Butler replies.

"Yes. So your advice is?" asks Montgomery.

"I say we go up a level."

A couple of coughs shatter the pause following Butler's remark. Ortega is stressed.

"We have to be very careful with this. Now is not the time to ratchet up international conflict when we have so much going on at home," she claims, and Bibi Melnik confirms her agreement.

"It's too late for that," replies Butler. "They did that six months ago when this was all starting out. Because they got it first, and knew it was worse than Covid, China suppressed the information and already decided that they were going to invade Korea. As the numbers grew and they started to look at the border with Russia, they knew they'd have to give out and divvy up Japan. I mean, yes, of course, those two will probably end up at each other's throats, but Japan will already be gone at that point. And if GARI doesn't kill every person on the planet, then they'll have the entire eastern coast facing Hawaii, South and Central America, and right up to Alaska. We simply can't let that happen."

"Hhhmm. Very interesting, Lloyd," Montgomery comes in. "Can you give us the best case scenario for a nuclear strike on the Chinese or Russian mainland? I mean, what's the fallout, if you don't mind me using that phrase?"

Butler shifts uneasily in his seat. He's a hawk. One of those military commanders appointed long before Montgomery and somehow able to separate from political partisanship, at least in theory. He's also in that camp that Montgomery has so infuriated by already having withdrawn much of the military from several strategic overseas bases. Even with the current D-zero potential from GARI, he still thinks like a military chief, and has to represent the views of all of the military commanders who give him counsel in his dealings with the President. But he knows that those around him today aren't going to be quick to hit the button, and need convincing that tactical nuclear strikes are required at this point in history.

"I see, Sir. Well, we would expect a limited retaliation. My sources say that they have plans in place. I mean, they will have thought this through, in detail. Those plans would be to launch tactical nuclear strikes on Guam, Hawaii and possibly even Vietnam."

"Jesus." Ortega's despair vents itself candidly.

"That's all we need," Becker comments.

"OK, let Lloyd carry on. Lloyd, what happens after that?" Montgomery cues Butler.

Butler hesitates, somewhat reluctant to play out the full implications of starting a nuclear interchange between and among the largest superpowers in the world.

"Well, it could be that this stops the rot. That's my take. After they see the devastation in those cities, and the fact that we can choose which others to strike at will, they'll get the message that, if they carry on amassing troops and moving on Japan, or Korea, that we'll be there to stop them. It's as simple as that."

"And the people in Hawaii, in Guam, in Vietnam? You are OK to make that sacrifice on this basis?" Hart asks Butler, to which Butler doesn't respond, instead contemplating the question more deeply. Before he can answer, Ortega has the follow up.

"And what makes you so sure that they won't take our pre-emptive strike as the green light for launching straight into Japan as well? A green light to take unilateral decisions to commandeer the entire south Pacific?" she urges.

"People," Montgomery intervenes as volume levels begin to increase. "Let's keep this discussion calm. Lloyd here has been asked, by me, to give me the advice of the chiefs of staff from our armed forces, and we need to listen to the arguments. Nothing is decided until we decide it. Now, let's understand the detail. Without that, we can't arrive at a sensible outcome. OK?" he asks rhetorically, and before anyone can raise any objections, gestures to Lloyd Butler to carry on his thoughts.

"I realise I might be in a minority here," he reflects. "I know that in theoretical exercises and military games we have looked at this scenario many times, and many times, we have decided not to act. Not to strike first. But we haven't had any military exercises where two interwoven layers of war have come together in such a way. These are unprecedented times not just because of GARI, but because of the complexity of the mesh that this makes with military action. I firmly believe that if we strike decisively and first, we will avert a major, all-out nuclear war, and I believe that because the Chinese, and for that matter the Russians, have just too much to lose by striking back. And if they do, they will fear that they will have started a war that they will not only lose, but will prevent them from populating the Japanese islands and Korean peninsula in order to protect the future of their peoples. They simply will not risk that. And you will already know that Prime Minister Akoto has taken a tough stance in order to signal his unwillingness to negotiate on any land deal around Hokkaido."

John Montgomery thanks Butler, hails one of the bunker staff to get more water for the table, and sits back in his chair.

"So, what would our next move be if, say, Beijing decided to attack Hawaii? You know, in order to prove longer-range capacity, to strike one of our states rather than an ally country or remote military base? What would we do? Maybe a million dead, infrastructure there wiped out, more or less unusable as a base any more. Like Pearl Harbour, but a thousand times worse," he questions Butler.

"Planning in this way, Sir, means that we have to be prepared for multiple outcomes, and this is certainly something that we would actively try to avoid. If we detected missiles heading to Hawaii at least we have the possibility to cancel them out," the senior military chief opines. "But as in any scenario, we have to prepare for any eventuality. We'd have to have both the fire power and the ground troops to follow up."

"What is the worst-case scenario for you, Commander? Please be frank and complete with your answer," asks Melnik.

"Ma'am. Well, that would probably be the potential for illogical, or at least, unplanned retaliation, possibly an over-reaction to an obvious tactical strike, where they decide to strike out harder. But I believe we could handle that."

"John, can I take a run at this?" Hart asks Montgomery, as chair of the group.

"Go ahead, Abe," the President responds.

"Well, for me, there are some non-military factors in here that play into this worst-case scenario. I mean, I'm Zhao, sitting in my palace in Beijing, watching an attack on Khabarovsk. Am I thinking 'Good, they've bombed our potential enemy' or 'It'll be us next'? If you don't know the answer to that question, then it means that things will be unpredictable if not chaotic. It's obvious that we're starting something that'll impact on the Chinese too, so we could have double trouble. That's just the start of it. Put on top of that the ideology of the Chinese and the history of Japan, and on top of that the fact that most of this will do nothing to prevent GARI from getting to the Chinese and Russians just like everyone else. I mean, the only use of a nuke in this scenario would be to kill the virus. Problem is, you also kill everything else, including our allies."

"Yes, I get that, Abe. OK, listen up everybody. This is complicated by - heck, brought about by - GARI. It seems to me that it's very difficult to reconcile a massive military initiative with the fact that many of our troops are dying from the virus as we speak. We know that there is nothing different about our military men and women; they are human like everyone else, and susceptible to this nightmare disease. We could get half-way into some conflict that we started, only to have very few troops on the ground to move in to defend Japan and Korea. And yes, that might be true for the other side too, but my feel is that we can't go down this route right now. We need two things; one, a significantly increased presence around Japan to show Beijing and Moscow that we aren't budging, and that we are supporting our Japanese friends, and two, an equal effort nationally to ensure civil order. Lloyd, I know you have been working with Ezra and Senator Fisk on this too, and we all understand the need for more resources. But we simply don't have any more time. My judgement is that we need to consolidate our troops on our own borders, internally to help our police forces maintain order and on the settlement routes with our allies. For this nation, or indeed any people, to survive the current crisis, we have to think differently, and that means ensuring the lockdown, using force if necessary, to get our own house in order. Once we have achieved that, we can start to think more about our international presence and any decisions around strike capacity, and any operations. For now, the tactic will be to transfer troops, battleships and aircraft carriers into the East China Sea and the Sea Of Japan. Lloyd, put as much in there as we can, but make sure we don't engage. Cuba taught us a lot. Let's use the experience wisely. I'll make an announcement to the country in about an hour."

—-

The night of a thousand clicks begins. All around the amphitheatre of the main dome in the Kark city, there is a cacophony of harsh guttural stops all vying for position amidst the rumble of the distant storms, adding a sense of urgency to proceedings. Every so often a screamingly high-pitched siren call pervades the circular space, no-one seemingly aware of its origin. The light is dim but for the flushing bodies of thousands of Karks, all hovering mid-air as if waiting to lift-off. Flashes of blue and yellow mix with green and purple, a mix of excitement, tension and restlessness all mixing to create a rainbow of colour to accompany the apparent aleatoric ensemble of atonal clucking.

On the main platform in the middle of the dome, raised up to allow all to see every movement on show, the imposing dark figure of Novek can be seen circuiting the edge of the platform, his large Karkian eye looking out at the assembled masses. In a display of showboating, his black body flushing to purple and then back again, this movement would seem to serve to whip up attention and urgency in the crowd and at the same time make the incessant clicking of the masses disappear, and within a minute or so a sense of nervous calm settles in the large arena. Only the distant rumble of dust storms remains.

Novek is accompanied by his elite guard; the generals and commanders that 'advise' him, although in reality most are intimidated by him and tell him what he wants to hear. But this evening is unlike others. Novek has been forced to hold this public address in order to avoid further unrest within the city. Rumour and gossip have been rife since the initial journey of Novek and his advance party to Earth, and given rise to talk about the future of Kark, and of its inhabitants. News has spread that only Novek's elite are eligible to travel to the new land. That only a few chosen ones with the capacity to dual will be able to survive the coming ice storms and decimation of the last of the fertile lands on the illuminated side of Kark. Such is the fear among the residents, that clashes with the city guards have become frequent and bloody.

As Novek finishes his final provocative circuit of the stage, the leader of the Imperial Council, Lord Kvonik addresses the vast crowd in Karkian.

"Welcome, Kark faithful. Thank you for your patience. We gather here to receive news from our majestic leader, the great Sultan Karosak Novek! But first, let me take the opportunity to reassure everyone here this day, that you are the most important part of Kark. We are here for *you*. And we know how difficult life has become under the dying suns. Our very existence requires us to make sacrifices, and the noble Lords and your imperial servants recognise how much you have supported the continuance of Kark, and the principles of sharing and trust that guide us in everything we do."

As Kvonik pauses for a gentle clicking of approval, Novek is impatient to get on, and in a gesture considered particularly rude in Karkian culture, positions himself by Kvonik's side to force him to acknowledge his presence, and in turn, his right to speak. At this, the crowd almost entirely in unison, flush amber, with some considerable clicking and ticking.

"Silence!" shouts Novek, his body flaming between purple and red. This alone is a sign of his increasing frustration with the slow pace and pedantic positioning by Kvonik, who he has found to be one of the barriers to the rapid progression of the elite dualling programme.

"Now you hear! You see! These noble lords wish you well. They are here for you, and will govern this place in accordance with our first principles," he clicks hurriedly, anxious to get to the point.

Lord Kvonik retreats back into the group of assembled nobles that circle in the centre of the stage while Novek struts convincingly around the edge, sometimes flushing a little grey with hints of yellow. He, too, has nervous energy coursing through him.

"They have also brought to my attention the matter of disobedience and the tyranny of the crowd. Of some of you, here, this evening, who question the mission to Krenek where the humans live in warmth and among many food sources. That some of you are concerned that you may not reach that land. That, somehow, only a few will go there. Well, let me tell you that this is a *lie*! A lie dreamt up by those who wish to collapse our efforts, and drive us back in time," he exclaims, shooting a poisoned glance at Kvonik and several of his fellow councillors, his eye beginning to turn first amber, and then red in a show of contempt.

"You all know that our passage to Krenek, our new land named in honour of the great people of the region of Krenek on the far plains of our world where the ice storms took so many lives, will not be easy. No. For there are many hurdles for us. Many battles to be fought and won before we can migrate together. That is why, as your leader, I have personally taken charge of the exodus. Why I alone have trained our Kark army in new techniques that will pave the way for *all* Karks in days to come. And so I say to you, do not question the motives of your leaders. Do not fear the isolation of Kark. For this place is still our home, and our world. And it will be for some time. There is no quick and easy answer to the ongoing problems of our suns, and of our lands. The solution is to be patient, and we will eventually find our way to the new pastures. To Krenek!" he exclaims and as his ventricles open and close furiously, he is somewhat disappointed that the crowd do not celebrate as they once did when he made a speech in the great dome.

As he looks around, Lord Kvonik makes a movement which suggests that Novek needs to carry on and offer something more concrete. Novek turns and faces the crowd again.

"Kark! Listen now! Hear this! And tell all the Karks you know who could not be here this evening. You will all be provided with a sequential. This will be allocated on a basis to be determined by the Imperial Council, and to be voted on by you. This will be your chance to have your say over who shall be allowed priority eligibility in our deliberations on the gateway to Krenek. I will leave this in the hands of the great Lord Kvonik and his councillors to organise so you can rest assured that every single Kark will be given a fair rite of passage to the new lands. Now, help us! Help yourselves, and help Kark by stopping the disobedience and disorder. For this may set our whole programme back so that our preparations for departure become at risk. Now, do you want to risk the future of Kark with your continued disobedience?" he asks the crowd, who don't seem to understand he is asking them directly.

"Well?! What say you, Karkian dwellers? Will you make noise now to show you will support the city, support Kark and support our brave and noble soldiers who are here to protect you and our great city?" Novek ends with the most ear-piercing high frequency which he then transmits in every direction as he hovers around the entire outside edge of the centre stage.

A growing sound of clicking, amidst the flashing of yellow and amber indicating intimidation and discomfort in equal amounts among the crowd, pervades the dome. Novek comes to rest in front of the crowd and once again begins to flash purple as he moves confidently from side to side. As the crowd become vocally humble, he turns to Kvonik.

"Make sure you get this done. Take your time and do it right. Make these people feel that they are involved in the process, and that everyone will have the chance to go to Krenek. Do you understand?"
"I understand that you wish to delay any further unrest, but setting up a selection process will only serve to buy you time when you are, again, away from Kark and, again, only taking your inner circle of guards with you. Why don't you take one or two civilians? Take them there, and show them what it is like. You can bring them back and then *they* can tell the crowds that everything will be OK. This is a better approach, is it not? After all, you have the human, and can open the channel at will, yes?" Kvonik asks.

Novek hesitates, flushing grey and yellow, which Kvonik notices.

"It is too dangerous for civilians. The Kark army I have trained because the battles will be tough. Worse would be to take civilians who don't make it back. Yes?" Novek challenges Kvonik.
"But you have all the advantages over the humans. You have already convinced us of that, and taken huge resources from Kark in order to pursue this. You must repay the trust that Kark has placed in you. I notice that you are not accompanied by Nuvo. He is much

admired by these people. You should have brought him with you to help the crowd understand."

"Quiet! Less of your insolence, old krinevik. Remember who discovered the gateway. Remember who started the Astraman project. And most of all, remember who is your leader!" Novek flushes between amber and red, and Kvonik realises that he has gone as far as he can.

"We will prepare the selection process as you ask. But for your own sake, and as your council, I advise you to bring Nuvo before the people when you return, and make sure the human is looked after well so he can continue to open the porthole when we need it."

Novek flushes bright yellow, at which Kvonik puzzles, himself flushing a deep blue. As Novek exits the stage and the crowds begin to disperse, Kvonik asks one of his council to enquire as to the whereabouts of Nuvo.

—-

A tear begins in the heart. The wave of emotion beating out around the body faster than the blood can carry, faster than an electric impulse, faster than thought. Strong enough to produce the equal and opposite reaction to hold it back, a struggle between two worlds. One of joy and the coming of age, the other of sadness and the coming into this age. The rivers run wild in Gill's heart as he witnesses new life. A life so uncertain that one might wish for a different world, a different time, a different reality. And so it is for him. But the tear comes, and as it rolls down his cheek, Catherine squeezes harder on his hand as their baby daughter emerges fully into the light.

The sense of atmospheric charge and time dilation pervades the small, six-bed ward in the Langley base hospital. An intense glow surrounds the two and creates an uncanny vision and odd calm for the staff, who are caught between the unsettling disturbance of light and motion in the space surrounding Catherine, and practicalities of ensuring a normal delivery as medical specialists.

Through the hazy light that forms the aura around the bed, the arrival seems to bring matters into acute relief.

"It's a girl!" exclaims midwife Jacqui Henderson, as she and her team work quickly and efficiently to separate mother from child and check the baby is healthy. "It's a beautiful baby girl, Catherine. Congratulations."

As Jacqui wraps the newborn baby girl in swaddling and prepares to hand her over, she asks Catherine if she would like to hold her first. Catherine nods and attempts a smile, her young body remarkably robust considering the labor of giving birth.

"Thank you, Sister," she says, coveting her daughter. She turns to Gill.

"I never thought it would be like this."

Gill kisses her forehead, and then his daughter.

"Neither did I. She has your eyes, Catherine."

Catherine smiles, and looks down at their precious gem. Midwife Henderson approaches the bed.

"And the name of our marvellous little girl?" she asks.

Catherine looks at Gill, who smiles broadly and nods.

"Alex Océane Jumeau," she announces.

A little while later, while the staff nurse tends to baby Alex, Christophe Jumeau invites Gill for a coffee while Catherine sleeps. The two men are basking in a moment of joy in between a desperate struggle to get a plan to Ava Redmond as to how on earth they are going to shoulder the problems of the world.

"She's truly beautiful, Gill. You must be very happy," Christophe remarks as they stand in the queue at the canteen.
"They both are. I never thought I'd see Catherine again, and coming back to this has been the best thing that has happened to me in a long time. A shock. It's mind-blowing. I wish I could somehow enjoy it more."

"I understand. Must be tough bringing new life into this world at the best of times, but right now, it's a different type of challenge."

"Your daughter is so strong, Christophe. I could see it in the field, and I can see it here. What happened after Garfield?" Gill asks.

"I could hardly credit my own sanity back then. I mean, a few of us got the picture. Who Garfield really was, why he did those things, and how he, or should I say Nuvo, fought so hard to get that ticket home. But what a cost. Just a handful of people who lived through that - that retain a consciousness of it - know that we somehow split the universe, or at least went back and chose a different path. And now to see Montgomery struggling to cope with events surrounding us; well, it just makes it so ironic. But like I said to Ava, we are sure better off with John in office than Garfield. This country would have crumbled if it weren't for him," Jumeau asserts.

"That seems so long ago," Gill muses.

"Fixing A Hole' by the Beatles is playing through the tannoy speakers in canteen B on the Langley base compound. As the men are served their coffees and make their way over to the window table away from others, they are aware that they are still breaking the social distancing rules. But as Christophe pointed out to one of the guards when asked, the two men are family. And that's not a lie.

"So, I looked at some of the information you have shared on Kark. I got an astronomer friend to dig into that and come up with any ideas around its location. If I'm right, it looks like it could be in Centaurus, a nearby galaxy, maybe the North-Eastern sector. There's a planetary system there around a star called HR4523, which has a rocky planet at some distance from its sun, and probably at the edge of the habitable zone. That star is like ours, but it's less hot, so if the planet was viable at some point, it will have become increasingly cold over time. Of course, this is just conjecture, but it's as good a guess as we've got right now," the Professor informs Gill.

"Interesting. I guess knowing where it is helps focus on further research, right?" Gill responds.

"Yeh, I guess. It's maybe more to get a sense if there are particular issues there, and also for us, things like how far we can dual. This is important right now, as you know."

"So, how far is this planet from us, then?"

"About thirty light years. Nuvo must have been some duallist to travel that far. Unless he could pick up activity that, say, you or Catherine or even Beth were exhibiting. There may be some spacetime proximity that collapses those light years, and I guess it has to be the wormhole connections. Like I said, maybe it's the wormholes that happen to be entangled."

"You've lost me, Professor," says Gill.

"Ah, don't worry, I'm just musing. Perhaps none of this will matter. Maybe we should focus on the things you need to know, assuming you still want to help? I wouldn't blame you if you just wanted to go to one of the settlements with the family and live as best you can while they look for a vaccine."

Gill looks at the Professor with a deep intensity, before answering.

"I don't have a choice, Christophe. I'm too far into this to opt for the quiet life," he remarks, and Christophe smiles wryly at Gill's humour.

"So you're going to go back?"

"Once the others are ready, yes. Carla seems strong, so we may have a chance. Catherine says that Mal Baines came to the clearing. I could hardly believe that."

"And apparently moves quickly, like Catherine and Carla," Jumeau says. "You think that Nuvo is keeping the connection open somehow? Novek is bringing more to the field?" asks Christophe.

"Most likely. I would expect there to be more there by now. So we'll need some sort of miracle, or for Nuvo to wake up."

"How do you mean?" asks Christophe.

"The experience he had here changed him. Gave him some human insights. Made him consider things. I saw how Novek treated him. I saw how ordinary Karks and even the Kark army live in fear of Novek and how powerful he is. But Novek's weakness is Nuvo, and I am going back as much to save Nuvo as to stop Karks claiming our space."

"You want to save Nuvo? Why? If you kill Nuvo you kill the entanglement and Novek's power is diminished. You'll trap Novek at the point of Nuvo's demise. That means he'll be on Kark and unable to come here, or he'll be here and we can trace him. Either way, it's better than keeping Nuvo alive, surely?"

Gill looks around the room, hunches slightly and lowers his voice.

"Christophe, look. Nuvo is the key. I didn't get it at first, but now I see. Nuvo is not only a duallist. He carried me to the Kark wormhole. He used some form of cloaking mechanism which meant that I *could dual*, even after being trapped there. I don't know how he does this, but no-one else can do that on Kark, otherwise there really would be hundreds of thousands of Karks in that field. No, there are about two or three hundred, maybe a few more, who dual. And one that can cloak, and that's Nuvo. Novek doesn't intend to go back to Kark. He is leading the invasion here, and won't let anyone else control that. He might send Nuvo back to Kark once he's through with him at the field, and if Novek is on Earth and Nuvo on Kark and the entanglement still intact then of course they could potentially join the wormholes and use the clearing to continue the invasion, *if* one of us is there and creates the opening. But it would be hard, if what I picked up is right. I mean, Nuvo could only cloak me. So to cloak half a million Karks one-by-one to Earth is going to take a very long time. Too long."

"You are saying that Novek might break the ties with Kark? Why would he do that? It doesn't make sense," claims Jumeau.

"Novek is losing power there. Nuvo told me as much. Nuvo is the true leader of the Karkian people. Not Novek. I could feel it. And once Novek is certain that he's established an advance colony on Earth capable of reproducing here, he'll want to start afresh, without all the baggage he has to cope with back there. This is his blank canvas, his promised land. He'll either try to imprison Nuvo, or get rid of him altogether."

The Professor takes a sip from the disposable coffee cup, and winces. It's terrible coffee.

"You haven't told Ava or Phil about this? The cloaking?"

"No," replies Gill. "I couldn't be sure, and there could be other explanations as to how he managed to get me to the field, but to be honest I can't think of any. We need him. There are so many things I have to do when I go back into the field. It's crazy. But if I can get to Nuvo, assuming he's still there, then I need to find out how he cloaks. That's what we need the most if we are to establish a viable crossing to Xarn."

"Catherine has filled you in on the detail?"

"Yes. I'm waiting for the next revelation. You got any more up your sleeve?" Gill quips.

"Yeh, sorry about that. I should have told you straight away. But you were in shock, and I didn't want to send you over the edge. You're going to be the great hope. I don't want to put any more on those shoulders," Christophe says supportively.

"It's cool. Don't worry. But if Redmond gets wind of the cloaking deal too soon, she'll jump all over it and suffocate us. I need to explore that. If Nuvo is no longer in the field, or I can't reach him, it's a non-starter, so we'd need to keep it under wraps for now. Got it?"

"Sure. Cloaking could be a game-changer for us. But just like the Karks, we'd need to scale it up for it to be meaningful."

"Maybe," Gill replies. "But if there are so few of us left after GARI, then wouldn't it be better to have one person that can cloak rather than none?" Gill asks.

"I hadn't thought about it like that. You said 'one person'? Is that you?" the professor asks.

"Maybe. Or Nuvo."

"Wow. Now you *are* losing me. You think he might switch?" asks Christophe, somewhat confounded.

"I have to give it a shot. I just need to find him first."

"Uh-huh. OK. And Catherine knows you're heading off soon? Once we give Ava a heads up?"

"Yeh." Gill looks down sheepishly at the aromatically-challenged coffee in front of him. "Well, I'm going to get back to Catherine, Professor. Let's catch up in your office later."

And with that, the two men head off along separate corridors from the canteen to consider their plans for the coming encounters.

—-

"Did you see Beth?" Catherine asks.

"I felt something. Heard music. Maybe her presence. Like she wanted to get into the field, but couldn't," Gill replies.

"Ah, she has her own place, you know. It's a theatre. Really cool."

Gill smiles, finding it warming that his little sister created her favourite theatre as a wormhole.

"Knowing her, it will be the Academy in Inglewood. We went down there when we were, like, twelve or something and she was completely blown away by how cool it was - all gothic and old school."

"Yeh, it was amazing. Surreal place. I've never been," she replies. "To the Inglewood one, I mean."

"Catherine, listen…I…I need to see her. I need to let her know that my mom and dad are OK, and that we'll all be reunited one day soon. I must try to tune in and get to that far side."

"I understand." Catherine pauses while Gill reflects on Catherine's update on her visit to Shirley Gill. "Can I ask you something?"

"Sure."

"Do you think you can match Novek in there? I mean, truly overcome him? And don't tell me what you think I want to hear. Just level with me, right?"

"Right," replies Gill. "Honestly, I don't know. But I don't have an option. I feel stronger with each minute I'm here, and with you. We have Carla, and Mal, and the others. I won't be alone there."

"Right. But these guys are just new to the space. No-one can expect them to go head-to-head with the Karks. They're just ordinary guys, being asked to risk their lives in some faraway field. Carla's not even American."

"Neither are you. And look what you've done," says Gill.

"Yes, but she's not in love with you."

Gill smiles, and kisses Catherine before she can say anything else.

"Now, this is true. My God, it's so good to be with you."

The two embrace for the countless time that day, unable to keep their hands off each other, and each touch creating a spark and dilation of time that allows them to steal the clock and enjoy the moment in its entirety.

"Now, you have to rest. Alex will need you soon, and Miss Redmond will be cross if I'm late for that meeting," he says.

"You watch that one, Detective Gill. She's got her eye on you - I can tell," Catherine jokes. "But before you go, I want to say something."

"Yes?"

"I became strong in the field because of us. Not just because I was going there a lot. The key to that place is in your head. If I imagined you beside me when I was there, I could do more. It gave me strength. Some part of you never left there, and I guess what I'm saying is that maybe some part of me is always there too. So you have to use that."

"I felt the strongest when I saw you there. I think that's how I managed to escape. The weight at the edge, it crushes you."

"Yeh, but only if you let it. I got through to Beth partly with her help, but also because I refused to let the weight get me down."

"You can fly in there, right? How do you do that?" Gill asks her.

"I just felt really light. Almost like one of my childhood dreams where I could soar above the Montreal skyline and look down on the city lights. There must be something about anti-matter and reversing gravity. I mean, like, realising that your actual body - this body -," she says as she runs her hand over his forearm, "means nothing in there if you can interact with alternative dimensions that release you from yourself."

"You mean the mind can create that power in there?" he wonders.

"Something like that I guess. I know that time dilation means that we *should* be bound by some massive bump in Higgs. You know, highly condensed matter in wormholes weighs us down and all that. My dad thinks that we overcome this when entangled pairs reunite - a sort of fusion energy that propels you to access to higher dimensions. I don't know. So much can happen in there, and yet it all stays the same. I'm still working it out."

Gill and Catherine sit for a moment, pondering. Finally, Gill breaks the silence.

"I'll think of you," he says.

—-

That evening, with Catherine still on base. Gill, for the first time in a long time, fires up the Oldsmobile. It sounds fantastic, and with a few beefy revs of the overhead ninety-degree V8 engine that catches the interest of the crew-cut smokers outside in the parking lot of the research lab, he heads to the main gate before hitting the freeway over to Oakton, "I See Monsters' by Ryan Adams up first on the mixtape.

After dinner with Christophe and Mary Jumeau, he asks Mary if he can sleep in Catherine's room, and without hesitation she agrees. Upstairs, he takes a little time to look around and understand the sense of his partner's space at home. There is the smell of her perfume, and of fresh linen. Pictures of a younger Catherine, and some of the prizes she won at school. Of Wendy and Catherine on a night out in Boston. Of Catherine with her cousins in the vineyard near Rouen. And of her with her parents, looking happy and relaxed in some restaurant. On the hook beside her large mirror is Gill's basketball cap. On her side-table there is a scribbled note with the name of the auto shop where she got the car refurbished. It makes him smile. Next to it, is a mug with some remaining green tea, the teabag still in. It's a white mug with purple and red hearts intertwined, above the word 'Gill'.

As he falls asleep, he stops himself from heading to the cornfield, instead breathing deeply and preparing for what will be a momentous day, in one way or another.

* * * *

CHAPTER 9: THE FIELD

The sun beats down majestically across a sea of gold, gently undulating and whispering in the wind. A fabulously blue expanse above, flawed only by the deepening hues on the horizon where the edges of the field face the beyond. Here lies a world as the perfect painting, only the eagle eye able to spot its imperfections. The secrets within are many, and the superficial beauty persists only in kind, deferring to what lies beneath and beyond its magnificent reeds.

Gill's heart beats a slow rhythm. Before him, lined up all around the far side of the clearing, hover perhaps fifty or so Kark guards, ready to fight. The flushing amber and yellow bodies catch the glare of the sun, creating a mesmeric display of flickering, dazzling flashes which make it difficult to see. The clicking has stopped. The assembled troops waiting for their noble leader, Karosak Novek.

Knowing that his fellow duallists are waiting to emerge from the reeds gives Gill a sense of advantage, albeit untested against what could be a formidable enemy. But he must try to negotiate.

As the reeds begin to part directly ahead, he can sense Nuvo's presence. And so too that of Novek. And sure enough, the Karkian twins present themselves. Novek floats out into the middle of clearing to address Gill.

"You cannot hope to survive this," he states.
"Nor can you."

Novek flushes yellow and purple and back again, his contempt for Gill obvious.

"Look around you. Your little field is no longer yours to behold. You are just as weak here as you are on Kark. There will be nothing left of your fledglings once we have concluded here."

"There is just one route for you. And that's my route. Look behind me."

Novek peers behind Gill to a wall of golden reeds, save one small gap from where Gill has stepped out.

"You and I will fight for this space, and if you win, you can take that route to Earth. This would be fair, yes?" proposes Gill.

"Really, Detective. That is very childish of you. Look behind me. You see the great Nuvo, famous Kark astraman, poisoned by your feeble thinking after so much time among your kind. Look closer. Look how weak he is. Look how the guards have to support him. And now understand that I know that you hold some kind of sympathy for this wretched being. That you need him. You need him to understand how we Karks can do what we do. Well, I shall like you to know that in this place, and after this…'meeting'…there is no need for the great Nuvo. And if I kill Nuvo? What will you do then? Mmm? What will you do once the disease attacks every last one of your people until there is only you and the girl left? Mmm? What will you do to stop your mother and your father, her mother and her father, from dying like dogs in a ditch, helplessly gasping for air as they float off into the unknown? What…"

"Enough!" Gill shouts, seeing red. "Fight now, or be quiet. Prove yourself."

Novek transforms into Wesley Wilson-Green, a slightly-built Londoner who is about half Gill's height.

"Oh dear, look at me. I will never be able to take on the mighty Detective, will I?" and with this, Wes clasps his hands together tightly until an intense light begins to shine through the skin, turning the fists bright orange. With lightning speed, he throws a ball of light at Gill which smacks him right on the chest, sending him flying back into the reeds.

"So you think that all those people you have back there are just going to stand around while I beat you to death? Is that your plan?" asks Novek. "Guards, prepare Nuvo," he continues, and as Gill wipes himself down, he can see Nuvo now has two Kark spears pointed at his head.

"Now I will ask you again, Detective," Novek explains. "You can invite your fellow duallists out here to fight with honour, or you can keep them shivering and quaking back there and Nuvo dies. He dies here, and he dies everywhere. No more Nuvo."

"You need Nuvo more than I need Nuvo. Without him you can't get out of here," Gill counters.

"Shall we find out? Do you really think I need this weak piece of Kark plasma to accomplish my mission? You are not too clever, Denton Gill. This is a one-way trip, you should have realised."

Novek turns briefly and gives a signal to his guards. As Nuvo wrestles to try to break free, another guard comes and the two hold him down, while the third guard raises his spear to Nuvo's head ready to lance. He quickly pulls his arm back, ready to thrust.

"Wait!" screams Gill. He can't let this happen, for reasons of strategy as well as humanity.

Gill approaches Novek so the two are only a couple of metres apart. He notices how young Wesley's features are, and laments his death at the hands of Novek. He swivels round and, using his inner voice, screams to the duallists he has trained for this event, to come out into the clearing. Upon the call, around twenty or so men and women quickly appear from the reeds in a broad circle, dark gaps in the reeds where they emerged. There is a mix of expressions, most of which might be unfamiliar to the ordinary Kark, but to Nuvo in particular appear as fear and anxiety. The only difference with humans is that they don't show their emotions through discolouration of the body, and in this instance it is a small mercy.

"Let him go and we will battle like soldiers, with honour. All of us," Gill proposes.

"Very well." A further signal from Karosak Novek, and the Kark guard draws back and lowers his weapon.

No sooner has Novek spoken than the smaller form he occupies jumps up and smashes his fist directly into Gill's face, forcing the larger man to stumble back. Wes is quick and Gill not so. As he regains his posture, Gill sees the Kark guards now charging across the clearing, and turns to Carla and Mal, shouting at them to strike.

He quickly grabs Wes by the leg in a football-style tackle and sends him to the ground. With a huge leap up in the air, Gill focuses all his downward energy and with huge force slams into the ground, missing Wes by inches as the younger, ragged-haired college kid dodges his large opponent and scuttles away. As Wes turns, he throws another light-rock at Gill, which narrowly misses his head, instead hurtling high and behind him into the reeds.

Carla and Mal are both doubled-up, gathering their energies. In unison, they rise up and eject balls of intense light that hurtle into two of the oncoming Karks, causing them to deform and collapse. They appear dead. Carla then calls to all the duallists on her side to do the same and most are able to focus energy to a greater or lesser extent. It is obvious that few have the capacity to kill the Kark guards though, and as Gill sees this, and Wes scurrying away to take protection behind some of his guards, he takes up the pursuit. He must stop Novek in his tracks. To do so will potentially stop the other Karks from breaching the reeds.

As he rushes one of the guards and tries to wrestle it to the ground, he slips off the slimy and elusive body, and the guard rushes off towards the reeds. Engagement must be through the light bombs that he and the other duallists can muster. As another guard rushes towards him, hitting Gill hard with its limb formed into a hammer shape, he hits the ground again. Size obviously does not matter in this arena. He is taking a bruising. The guard now shapes his limb into a spear and raises it high above his head. The spear begins to come down swiftly, Gill rolling away only just in time for the spear to pierce the ground deeply just inches from his head. A close miss. Adrenalin pulses sharply inside as he makes out Nuvo at the hands of a dark assailant. As Gill's chemistry transforms, he remembers what Catherine said. With an almighty effort of concentration and channeling of the vacuum fluctuations around him, he releases a huge gravitational wave in an attempt to slow time and avert an unparalleled disaster unfolding in front of him.

Standing directly above and bearing down on the helpless Kark astronaut, Novek has reverted to his dark Kark form, intermittently flushing bright crimson and turning his flaming red eye slowly towards Gill. But time is on Gill's side. Curling up a blindingly white ball of shining mass in his hands, he hurls it directly at Novek, who tries to claw his way to achieve enough movement to avoid a direct hit. He just about succeeds as the pulsing light-rock grazes his torso sending the mighty Sultan to the ground, a cloud of black gas expelling from his upper ventricles. Gill moves over to finish the job. Struggling against the heavy blanket of condensed mass descending all around him, the resilient and battle-hardened Novek regains some mastery of the space, and manages to re-establish himself in the air, quickly releasing a cloud which obscures his form from view. Gill arrives only in time to grab hopelessly at the vapour trail left behind. He maniacally searches in the Karkian fog that Novek and his guards have left in the space, but in vain.

Behind him, Gill can hear screaming. As he strains to see what is happening, his eyes widen in fear. It's Emilia, who is being dragged through the corn reeds from where she arrived.

"No!' cries Gill, and attempts to run over to stop her captor from succeeding, but now Gill is the victim of time, and she disappears. Further away he can see an older man, the tech guy Don from Wisconsin, being taken by two guards, again back into the reeds. Things are not going according to plan.

"Carla! Mal" he shouts. They look over.

"Fall back! Close the gaps and get out!" he shouts, turning to see if he can spot Novek.

As many as twenty or so of the Kark guards have successfully breached the reeds, and that's twenty too many, so now is the time for Gill to step up. He can feel Catherine's presence, and wonders if she has shown up, despite their agreement that she wouldn't. He looks around, but can't see her. Yet he feels the power surging through him.

Gill starts to head towards the remaining guards and to where he last saw Novek. Incandescent with rage, one by one he smashes the guards with this fists, which glow white hot. As one guard forms his limb into a spear and aims it directly, Gill launches a hot rock at lightning fast speed which eviscerates the Kark totally. Gill is getting the hang of it.

As he works through Kark after Kark, soon dozens of the alien guards lie in fragments around him, any remaining flushing or evaporation dying out. But there is no sign of Novek.

Frantically, Gill takes one leap, then another, and on the third, he starts to float up about twenty-five feet above the ground, seeing further across the clearing. There, from where he emerged, Gill sees a flash of purple, and immediately musters all his mental energy to scythe through the air to where an injured Novek is dragging a young man back into the reeds. Faster. Faster. Faster. Gill is furiously trying to reach the young man's legs as he disappears into the opening in the reeds.

"Aaaaggghgh!" comes the scream, and behind it the high-pitched clucking of Novek which seems to shatter the air.

Gill swoops down and desperately grabs at the shoe of the young man in one last gasp attempt to save him from the fate of his Kark captor and certain death. As he grabs the shoe and digs in as hard as he can to the foot underneath, the shoe loosens with the pull and comes off in Gill's hand, making him fall backwards. Clambering onto his haunches to stop the reeds from closing, the last dark slit of the return passage closes in front of him. Dejected and exhausted, he falls to the ground. Looking across to his left, he sees a dozen or so Kark guards who look to be heading back to where they emerged into the clearing. As suddenly as it started, the running battle has come to an end.

As he scans the clearing, there are signs of blood, remains of Karkian flesh, torn limbs, and some pieces of clothing that must have been lost in the skirmish. There is no sign of Carla, nor Mal, and no gaps in the reeds now left open. A strange sense of unknowing sweeps over Gill, and he is petrified that some of the duallists that he briefed this morning have lost their lives.

"Catherine?!" he calls in his head. But there is no response. There are others in the field, though. He can feel them. Suddenly he knows he needs to see if Nuvo is still here. To communicate with him now that Novek has fled to Earth. His flying prowess has been lost somewhere in the dog fight, so he will need to try to find his way to the far fence on foot. In the distance he can make out the sound of thunder, just like before, so he decides to use this as his signal, and steadily makes his way through, every so often mustering enough energy to bounce up and hang for a short time to get a view ahead. There is more to come today. And yet already he is feeling the burden of duty beginning to bear down on him as he approaches the perimeter fence.

—-

The alarms on Darkrooms eleven, thirteen and nineteen are all red, and the piercing, overlapping audio of the three separate sirens are sounding a cacophony of danger.

"Sir!" anxiously calls one of the burly soldiers guarding number thirteen. "Come quickly!"

Hank Waters and two other guards race towards the far pods. As they arrive, the CCTV cameras relaying the inside of all three pods are steamed up, as if they were sauna baths. The doors to each are beginning to buckle and the latches beginning to melt.

"Quick - get up there and let them out," instructs Waters, believing that the duallists inside are in danger.

He isn't wrong. As the guards on each of the pods reach up to open the doors, the first screams in agony, the latch burning through his hand. Simultaneously, all the pod doors crash open and several of the duallists emerge, coughing and spluttering.

"Get Garry over to the medics, right now," commands Waters, as two of the guards hurry the injured guard away.

The security chief then approaches one of the duallists he recognises; Don, a tech specialist from Wisconsin.

"It's Don, right?" asks Waters.
"Yes."
"What happened to you guys? Are you OK?"
"We had to fight," says Don. "We were told to come back."

As this sinks in, a young man in the crowd of duallists begins to cough and Waters can see he is injured.

"Is Detective Gill still in there?"
"Who?" asks Don.
"Gill. You know. The big guy that was training you earlier. You know. The guy you followed in there?"

"Oh, yes. Sorry. Yes, he is still in there," Don replies.

"Listen up, buddy," Waters draws near to Don and lowers his voice. "I think it's best if we get all you guys over to the medics at the hospital for some checks. You know, just to make sure you're alright. Seems like you and your buddies are a bit shaken up."

Don looks around at the other duallists, some twenty-odd who are displaying some obvious signs of lack of orientation, and then he scans the rest of the space, counting the armed guards at the pods and at the entrance to the customised research space inside the hangar.

"Yes, that will be best," he replies.

As the group are escorted up the corridor and towards the exit, one of the guards sees the injured young man is limping. Of slight build, and dressed plainly in a Cavs hoodie and a pair of faded Levi's, he looks frail.

The guard tries to make conversation to help.

"You OK, buddy? What's your name?"
"Kevon. Kevon Clark. I'll be OK," comes the response.
"Looks like you lost a shoe in there, huh, Kevin?"

The young man looks down.

"I think…I was lucky," he replies, and the guard smiles.

—-

"Dad?"
"Yes, dear?"
"Do you think Alex will be able to dual?"
"I would imagine. I mean, I don't see why not."
"But who would she be entangled with?"
"Ah, now that is the question. If we knew that, we'd be able to predict a lot more about duallists."
"Hhmm. It's crazy to think that there is someone out there right now who is…" Catherine tails off.

"…her twin?" offers Jumeau senior.

"I guess."

"Look, honey, if we get the chance to delve into this, I'll be delighted to get back into experimentation, but right now, we've just got to celebrate this little bundle of joy. Your mother says she looks just like you did."

Catherine laughs.

"Yeh, well, she would do, wouldn't she!"

A quiet, stifled little sigh spills out of the crib next to Catherine's bed.

"I feel like I wanna go home, Dad," she says.

"I know. I do too. But you've seen what's going on. We'll need to wait until this thing is over before we can hope to return. We have to be ready for a reality where we can't. You understand that, right?"

"Yes," she replies. "Everything seems to be falling apart. I'm so afraid for Alex. She's so innocent."

"Of course. The children are the losers in all this. Starved of any life. That's why we need to get you two to one of the settlements," Christophe offers.

"And you and Mom, of course."

Catherine's father pauses.

"Listen, we can talk about all this later. Right now, we need to make sure Gill is OK, and find out what happened at the clearing."

"Oh, he's OK," Catherine asserts.

"How do you know?"

"I just do. Don't ask," she smiles at her father, who gives her that look that dads give their children when they know that they've been naughty.

"So, Gill talked to me about Nuvo. About the 'cloaking'. Do you know what that is? I mean, how it works?" asks Catherine.

"Not really, no. Apart from the fact that Gill seems sure that it is only Nuvo that can do that, it's kind of thrown a lot of things up in the air."

Catherine sits further up in bed.

"It has to be related to his time here. I mean, he must have been the first Kark to take on human form. Like, he was Garfield, and then turned into a Montgomery, right?"

"It's some form of amalgamation of two particle descriptor sets, with a complete memorisation of the structure of both. The nearest thing I can liken it to is teleportation. It appears that Nuvo can dual as one entity masking the presence of another. So all the Karks you saw in the field will be those who dual on their own, but of course cloaking Gill allowed them to open the join between the two wormholes. Once that was open, as long as the Karks can keep it open, they have free rein to occupy the field. Gill can update us as to how many there are and what Nuvo is doing," Christophe proffers.

"Novek just used Nuvo and Gill as mules, Dad. They were needed to open that hole in the fence for sure, but my question is really about Nuvo and what he is doing. I mean, the reason we helped him was in part to reverse the damage he had caused, but in all that we realised that he wasn't the devil that we imagined him to be. There is a soul there. Maybe some of John Montgomery is still inside him. Maybe that's why he can provide cover for ordinary humans to dual. That's not very scientific, I know, but fragments or patterns of particle sets must persist over time I think. Anyway, if Nuvo's the only one, I just wish we had him on our side. He could help us get Beth."

"Sweetheart, that's a great thought. But it's not likely that any Kark would willingly help us here to dual. They have proclaimed themselves an invasion force by kidnapping and killing innocent people just to function without spacesuits or other technology here. Nuvo answers to Novek, and that is all we need to know right now. Our focus must be on getting you and Alex and Gill, and Mal and the others firstly to the settlements here, and if necessary we look at Xarn. But that will come in time. I know Gill will want to try to connect to Beth as you did," he says.

Catherine looks up at her dad, with a sombre face.

"Oh, Dad, it might be too much. We're asking so much of him. I saw how strong he can be. But he's only just beginning to adjust. I sure hope Mal and Carla have his back."

As she finishes the thought, Catherine's face begins to darken and she starts to shake, falling backwards as if fainting.

"What, honey? What?" asks her dad, as he grabs her arms and stops her slumping back in bed.

Seeing his daughter is in trouble, Christophe shouts to the staff nurse to come across. Baby Alex wakes up and starts to cry. With Catherine looking grey and nauseous, the nurse picks the baby up and starts to cuddle her.

"Catherine!"
"Mmmmm…"
"Catherine, what's wrong?" shouts her dad, trying to get Catherine to snap out of what looks to be some sort of seizure.
"No. No! Can't be…" Catherine is muttering.
"'Can't be what, Catherine?" her dad asks.

After a few moments, Catherine begins to come to, still looking unwell, but recovering slowly. The staff nurse comes over and asks Jumeau Senior to leave to give Catherine some time to come round, offering her a glass of water.

"It'll be fine," the nurse tells Christophe. "It's perfectly normal for things like this to happen post-partum."

Reluctantly, the Professor heads towards the Nurses station near the entrance to the ward.

"Here's my biocell. Please call me immediately when she has come round fully," he suggests to the duty Matron, who nods and puts Christophe's eco-graphene ID card next to the others under her desk.

As Jumeau exits general ward B and out into the main hospital corridor, Hank Waters and a big group of the duallists come filing down towards him, two-abreast, with guards in front and behind. Further away, he spots Phil Kirkland running to catch up with them.

"Just taking our brave troops up to ER for checkups, Professor," informs Waters.

In a hushed tone, Jumeau asks "Hank, have you checked that these guys are, you know, all 'present and correct'?"

Waters looks at the Professor with a reassuring smile.

"They're all showing signs of trauma, Professor. But we'll be vigilant, don't worry. We'll get the medics to check them out from head to toe. Anything unusual we'll separate out, take 'em down to block C. OK?"

"Oh, OK, Hank. Where's Gill?"

"He hasn't come out yet. But Phil has been checking in."

"Yeh, he's just coming up now," says Christophe as he points towards the back of the group.

"Professor!" Kirkland shouts from about twenty yards, approaching quickly.

"Phil?"

"Professor, come with me, please."

"What is it, Phil," Jumeau asks.

"We need to get the debrief from Carla and Mal. There are more of the group coming out of their pods. Gill is still in there."

As the conversation filters in to the small crowd of duallists under the supervision of Hank Waters and his guards, Don, Kevon and Emilia all look to Kirkland. Hank Waters thinks he hears someone tutting in disapproval.

"Everyone OK?" he asks, and silently most of the group nod.

"Jeez, these guys seem pretty shook up, Hank," observes Kirkland.

The atmosphere seems tense, which Kirkland and the Professor put down to potential post-trauma. It was always going to be risky putting a bunch of novices in to bat against an unknown team.

"Yep. Dazed and confused, you might say. Sounds like it was a bit messy in there. You can debrief once I get 'em checked out up at the emergency ward, OK?" Waters replies.

Kirkland hesitates, weighing up the priorities.

"OK, Hank. Take good care of them and buzz me when you're done."

"Will do, chief," Waters responds, and waves to the group to re-engage with the journey up to ER. "We'll need the others up here too, once you're ready."

Kirkland nods. "Come this way, Professor," Phil urges, ushering Jumeau to follow him at pace back to the research facility.

—-

The first sense that something is wrong comes through a hissing sound. Intuitively, Gill knows that this isn't right. Somewhere in the atmosphere comes a familiar smell, one that he remembers from Kark. He hunkers down instantly. Just up ahead at the edge of the field he can hear familiar guttural clucking, yet he is still unable to decipher its meaning.

Gill is weak, and figures it's not a good idea to try to confront any more Kark guards, let alone do battle with them, so he has to be very careful. The reeds all around him sway gently in the breeze and make a constant swishing sound, within which his slow movement blends, offering some disguise and cover. He creeps, slowly and with increasing sloth, towards the tear in the fence ripped not so long ago, but perhaps a very long time ago. It's hard to tell.

Using just the tips of his fingers to part the reeds in front of him, Gill peers out through a small gap. Two dark forms occlude the fissure, then disappear through the other side of the fence. Strange. As the hole joining the two worlds of Earth and Kark becomes visible, so too does Nuvo. Beleaguered and in obvious distress, Gill can see that he has been forced back to ensure the gap in the fence is kept open. One Kark soldier remains guard over him, acting as his captor rather than his comrade. It is an unedifying sight, even for Gill.

Looking more closely, Gill sees that Nuvo is actually bound to the fence with what appears to be barbed wire ends. They circle his torso in an overlapping criss cross, somehow chaining him to the fence pole behind him. Small green clouds of vapour form at each of his main ventricles, seeming to diminish in volume at each iteration. Nuvo doesn't have long.

It's different in this part of the field. It's always more dangerous at the edge, but it's also where possibilities magnify and the ridiculous shouldn't raise an eyebrow. Gill's inner detective powers compensate for his rather encumbered movement. There are more Karks on their way. This is the main channel for the invasion and it must be closed down. But how can he do this without killing Nuvo, the one being in this universe that can help Gill bring his loved ones to safety on Xarn? The one Kark who has lived long enough on Earth to understand the human condition in some way, and the one Kark that has shown Gill some modicum of respect in all his time there. Gill must decide what to do, but he is hesitating.

When the sound of a click is slowed right down to perhaps a tenth of its speed, it becomes warped and fractured, the distortion at reduced speed affecting the pitch so that it sounds sad. A soft stream of this sound is pounding in Gill's chest. In some strange connection that he has with Nuvo, Gill feels his own life force starting to ebb as he crouches still just feet away from his Kark foes. The shock hits hard, and Gill's willpower to act becomes force majeure. As if a tightly-knit raging ball of anger sets his internal organs on fire, he takes one leap into the air, hanging for a second to prepare his limbs which become heavy like hammers and he plunges down directly onto the guard standing over Nuvo, splitting the torso and killing it outright. As he stands over Nuvo, who can barely raise his head to see what has happened, Gill grabs the barbed wire cutting into Nuvo's body.

Nuvo struggles, thinking that Gill is going in for the kill. Nuvo's eye burns a bright orange, and Gill realises that this noble warrior still has some fight in him. Good.

"Wait," Gill tells him. Nuvo is staring at Gill in fear. "I can help."

Gill's hands start to bleed as he unsuccessfully tries to get the sharp metal from hurting Nuvo further. A low-pitched hiss comes from Nuvo. It's a sound Gill heard moments ago from Novek. Nuvo is in big trouble. What to do?

"This is going to hurt," Gill tells Nuvo. "But it will free you from these chains."

Gill forms a fist with his right hand, which starts to glow first red, then white like a soldering iron. He pushes it gently into the barbed wire, breaking the chain but burning Nuvo's milky flesh underneath. More hissing, this time louder, and surely broadcasting Nuvo's distress all around, and back through into the Karkian temple, still full of extra-terrestrial duallists.

"Ssshhhh!" Gill exclaims. "Keep it down."

As Gill burns through both strands of barbed wire and gently pulls it away from Nuvo, the acrid smell of burning Kark and human flesh begins to drift through the gap in fence. More evidence which will endanger them both.

"Can you move?" Gill asks.
"No," Nuvo replies.
"Well, you're well enough to speak to me in English, so you're well enough to get out of here. I'm going to carry you to a safer place, over there," Gill says as he points back into the reeds. "OK?"

Nuvo flushes yellow, which is good enough for Gill, and, with some difficulty, he grabs the smaller Nuvo and lifts him up into a fireman's lift, taking great care not to let him slip his grasp. As he makes his way back from the fence, he can feel Nuvo struggling.

"Take it easy. Don't fight it."

Gill looks back to the fence.

"Will that close on its own, or do we need to close it?" Gill asks Nuvo, pointing at the rip in the wormhole. But Nuvo doesn't respond, and Gill needs to get Nuvo to a place where he can recover. It's a tough decision, one of several today that are like forks in the road.
"Fuck," Gill mutters, and carries on through the reeds moving further and further away from the perimeter. After about a minute, he notices Nuvo is much lighter, and that he is regaining strength. He

looks up, and sees a bird high in the sky, something that he has never seen here before. He squints hard to try to get a longer focus. Could be an eagle, at altitude. But anything new in the field is of concern, beautiful as it might be.

Gill needs Catherine. Now. Gently resting Nuvo on the ground, Gill stops for a second. He is breathing hard, even though the space does not demand it. He has again lost control, and it is bugging him.

"Come on!" he pushes out between his gritted teeth, trying to contain his self-loathing.
"I'm here, Gill."

Gill looks up. Is that Catherine?

"Give me strength, Catherine," he asks the voice.
"Calm down. It's all in your mind. You have command here. Look at me…way up here. I'm here because of you. Come and join me."

As Gill looks up, the bird has disappeared out of view. The sublime sound of Catherine has somehow lifted him. He reaches down and picks up the drowsy Nuvo, rapidly slipping into unconsciousness. Straining every sinew in his body, he imagines himself up with Catherine, and begins to elevate, hovering several feet in the air, enough to see above the reeds. In the far distance, he can make out a break in the reeds. The clearing. He must get more height. Inch by inch, he pushes up. Up.

"Up!" he screams, forgetting about his cover. 'Up!"

As he rises up some ten feet above the reeds, a sudden and shocking whizzing sound passes his left ear. Before he can adjust and turn to see where it came from, the spear in front of him breaks up into a cloud of gas.

"What the…"

Another spear just above his head.

"Shit." Gill turns horizontally, and begins to force his way forward giving less of himself and Nuvo as targets for the Kark guards, now chasing through the field. As Gill flies just above the reeds for as long as he can, the clearing approaches. No more spears. For now.

Finally, at the opening, and rapidly scanning all around him, he turns to Nuvo.

"Nuvo! Nuvo!"

A quiet click comes back.

"Nuvo, listen to me. We need to get you to safety. We can help you. We can get you to a doctor, but only if you form as a human. You need to change back. Do you understand? It's your only chance. Do you understand?"

Nuvo looks up at the big detective. His eye is now a pale blue, and half open.

"Come on, Nuvo! You can do this. Think about Garfield. You've done this many times. You can do it once more. Just focus. But do it *now*."

Gill thinks he is losing the battle. Nuvo seems to be far away. The hissing has subsided and Nuvo seems quite still in his arms. As Nuvo's torso begins to glow from pale green to yellow, Gill sees some hope.

"Step away. Leave me," Nuvo asks.
"I'm not leaving you here," Gill replies.
"No. Stand back. For a second."

Gill rests Nuvo on the ground, and moves back a couple of steps. He anxiously looks around. Still no Kark guards, but they are coming, he knows it. They have seconds left.
Nuvo's body begins to dissolve, becoming gas. Gill can't make out if this is Nuvo's moment of death, or resurrection. Then a shape begins to clarify. It's a human form, Gill knows it. And sure enough,

before him, in the clearing, Ellis Garfield takes shape. As the body becomes solid, and starts to move, Gill can't hide his elation.

"Yes!" he exclaims. But no sooner can he hear his own words, than the rustling in the reeds starts to grow loud.

"Come on! Quickly!" Gill commands.
"Ugghh…" Garfield mutters, as he stumbles along behind Gill.

As Gill reaches the corn stalks he frantically tries to find his entrance point. Panicking, he grabs Garfield and both men hunker down to try to hide. If they are caught now, they will both surely be killed. As he scans all around, still nothing.

"Catherine, show me the way," he calls from inside his mind.

The two wait, in silence. On the far side of the clearing, Gill can make out a pair of Kark guards emerging, flushing amber and limbs formed into spears. They scan the space and one spots the crouching men, possibly sensing that Garfield is one of their own.

"Any time now would be good."

As the Karks speed their way across to the men with purpose and vigour, Gill's heart misses several beats. Half way across, Gill has had enough of waiting, and grabs Garfield.

"Come on, buddy, we got to get you out of here, one way or the other."

He tries to bundle energy into a light-rock, as he has done before, but it's a weak attempt. He throws it towards the centre of the clearing, aiming for the first Kark guard, but it is relatively weak and slow, missing the guard, and now drawing attention to where the rock was thrown.

"Dammit," mutters Gill.

The guard raises up his spear, extending its limb far up into the air, and, pointing it directly at Gill, fires a thunderbolt so fast Gill can only see it for a split second as it heads straight for him. As it reaches within a foot of his forehead, a pair of claws grabs it and carries it into the air.

As Gill looks up, a golden eagle has caught the spear and flies off. Over in the clearing, the second guard starts to run towards the two men. He is coming fast and forms his limb into a giant axe, raising that up high while making an ear-piercing clucking shriek which slams into Gill's head causing him to cover his ears and screw up his face in pain.

Just as the axe is about to fall, the guard is speared right through the body, causing a sizeable hole that starts to fill with black gas. Mortally wounded, the guard loses its ability to hover, and falls to the ground, its slimy torso deforming in front of Gill. No sooner can Gill contemplate what is going on, than a rustling sound comes from behind him. It's Ellis Garfield, clawing at an opening in the reeds.

"Wait!" shouts Gill, not knowing if Garfield is trying to escape or survive, or both. A slam dunk for the Karks would be for Garfield to get away, and Nuvo to be in some far flung corner of the Earth. But the reality is somewhat different.

"Come on! Quickly!" Garfield responds. And through a small opening in the reeds, where Gill can spot some feathers on the ground, he clambers to join Garfield as a ball of intense light just misses his left foot as the fissure closes.

—

Back at Langley, the bodies of Denton Gill and Ellis Garfield lie slumped across the table and floor, respectively, in Darkroom One.

"I don't believe it," exclaims Phil Kirkland.

"Oh, I do," replies Christophe Jumeau, as he turns to Carla Piccioni and Mal Baines, who look to be somewhere close to Catatonia.

* * * *

CHAPTER 10: FRAYED

"Ed. Shauna. Two bodies."

"Uh-huh?"

"Female - fifties or early sixties - a 'Mrs. Wilson-Green'. Single wound to the head, looks like the weapon was a poker from her own fireplace. Second body is a younger man, could be the son. He's clean, no wounds. Some frothing at the mouth though."

"GARI?"

"No. There is no evidence of that from an initial test. You can relax, Ed. We'll know more once the forensics and autopsy come back."

"OK, keep me posted."

"Yes, Sir. We've got the place dusted down and scanned for bloods, so you can move around freely."

"Thanks, Gavin."

"One thing, Sir."

"Yes?"

"The neighbour over there has reported that two of her daughters are missing. Don't know if it's connected, but I believe Davis is on his way down to speak to them."

"OK. Keep me posted."

Detective Inspector Ed Ganz and Detective Shauna Harrison enter the house on Morgan Street in London's East End. After a brief reconnoitre around the house, Harrison comes down the stairs.

"Sir?" she says. "I think you might want to look at this."

Ganz follows his colleague to an upstairs bedroom. An odd haze pervades around the room, causing both police officers to wave a hand to see clearly. Harrison opens the window, letting fresh air in. All around them, clothes are strewn across the floor, the bed and hanging out of the chest of drawers in the corner. It's as if the room has been ransacked. It's puzzling. Enough to make Ganz put on his protective gloves and pick up a couple of sweaters on the bed. As he lifts them, some drops of a slimy substance drip onto the duvet.

"Jeez," Harrison remarks. "That's gross."

"Yeh. Let's bag it in case Gavin missed it."

"It looks like someone had a party in here."

"What makes you say that?" Ganz asks.

"Well, sir, it's just that you get the feeling there were a lot of people in here at some point. Do you sense that too?"

"Yes," Ganz says. "This is most likely the son's room, right? So he was having a party up here, Mum came up to tell them to shut up, then one of the them decides to go down and take her out with a steel poker? Makes no sense. Even if they were getting up to no good here, you don't kill your host's mum. That's just bad form."

"Do you think the son killed his own mother?" Shauna asks.

"No idea," Ganz replies. "None of this makes much sense so far."

As the two Scotland Yard officers descend the stairway and into the hall, Ganz looks again at Wesley Wilson-Green, and, approaching the body, notices something strange.

"What is it, Sir?" Harrison asks.

"It's that slime again. His mouth is full of it."

—-

"Is that Professor Jumeau?" asks the voice anxiously.

"Yes, speaking. What is it?"

"It's your daughter, Sir. She's left the ward against our advice. She wouldn't listen to us. It's far too early for her to get up and about. I thought I'd let you know."

"Is she with the baby?" he asks.

"No. Baby is safe with us, Professor, but she headed off down to the exit so I'm not sure where she might be headed. She's just this minute gone, though, so you might want to come over."

Jumeau Senior grabs Phil Kirkland by the arm.

"Sorry Phil, I've got to go."

"What? You can't go. What are we going to do with these two?" Kirkland asks, pointing up at the CCTV screen outside Darkroom One.

"I don't know. Keep them there if you can. We'll need Gill to signal he's OK. I'm sorry I have to go. It's Catherine…" Christophe trails off.

"Wha…?" Kirkland replies, turning to the remaining duallists. "OK, Carla, Mal, you guys need to be careful. Go and find Hank, he's up at ER. You'll need to get checked out. I'll join you up there once we get these two sorted."

Carla and Mal stare at Phil.

"Go on! Do as I say!" Kirkland is clearly agitated, and his booming voice jolts the two young duallists into action as they scurry off. "Danny! Carl! Get over here!" he shouts to his men guarding the entrance to Corridor H1.

—-

Don Townsend looks across to Kevon Clark, and nods. The ER nurse up ahead is taking in the first of the duallists accompanying Hank Waters and his crew. Hank's phone goes off.

"Yeh?"

"Hank. Phil. Look, we've got a situation here. I can't explain, but I think you should come down here." Kirkland is sounding anxious.

"OK, Phil. Easy there. The guys here are just getting checked out. It's all calm. I'll be there shortly."

"OK, Hank. Is anyone saying anything yet? Did you get a handle on what happened in the wormhole?" asks Kirkland.

"Apparently some of the guys didn't even go in. A couple of the younger guys seem a bit messed up, but apart from that, it looks like they'll all check out fine," Waters replies. "You got Carla and the big fella…uh, Mal?"

"They're on their way to you now. You'll pass them. But hurry, Hank. I need you here before I let these guys out."

"Sure thing. Leaving now," Waters replies. "Sharpe, Buzov. Come with me."

Waters' departure leaves just two Langley military guarding around twenty people, most of whom are in an orderly queue waiting to see one of the ER triage nurses. The guards are relaxed, having seen most of the faces before, and in full knowledge of their important sacrifice. One of them - a newer recruit named Angelo - is making small talk with one of the girls.

A high-pitched scream rings out, shattering the calm. Angelo is lying on the ground, blood pouring from his ear. In an instant, the slightly-built Kevon Clark has rounded on the other guard and has clubbed him over the head leaving him unconscious on the floor.

Several of the group race out of the emergency ward while the others remain, stunned and petrified. The girl talking with Angelo kneels down and shouts for help. At least they are in ER.

"Put out the alarm…" Angelo whispers.

"The nurse is doing that now," she replies, smiling at him as she takes out a tissue from her pocket and begins to wipe his forehead.

Forming a tight circle and making sure they are not being followed, Kevon, Don, Emilia and the rest of the Kark-human chimeras swiftly exit the hospital building and gather in one of the ambulances. Don takes the wheel and fires up the engine and the flashing lights, leaving the siren muted. The large van speeds across the base towards the main exit. Kevon grabs the ambulance jackets, placing one around Don, and both assemble so that they appear official.

One of the duty sentries raises his hand, as the ambulance approaches and slows.

"Window down…" the young officer beckons.

"Officer, we have an emergency. Several members of the public have been injured in the research lab over at the north quadrant. We don't have the facilities to treat them here so we have to get them over to Sentara in Norfolk. It's urgent," Kevon tells the guard.

"Can we check inside, please?" asks the young guard.

"Sure, go ahead, but please be quick," Kevon comes back, taking a look in the large side mirror for signs of military police or sounds of sirens.

The guard opens the doors at the back of the large ambulance. Seven or eight weary-looking civilians, all wrapped in standard issue ambulance blankets, greet the guard.

"Hi there. You folks OK?" asks the guard.

A couple start nodding, others look down. For a moment the guard hesitates, not knowing if this is a good sign, or a bad sign.

"We're OK, officer. We've been told we need to get to the general hospital for treatment," Emilia tells him. She smiles, and the guard's first thought is how pretty she is. He smiles back at her, broadly.
"OK, Miss. You take care. All of you take care."

As the guard goes to open the huge security gates, Kevon is again looking around, checking all the time. As the gates open fully, he waves to the guard, nodding and mouthing 'thanks' as the ambulance passes onto the ring road towards the freeway.

—-

As Catherine stutters and shuffles down the hospital corridor she gasps for breath. Coming out over the compound towards the research hangar, the light wind helps with the nausea and she manages to deal with the dull ache within from the birth. She can feel something is terribly wrong, but can't figure out if it's Gill, or something else. The sense of shock and terror she felt in the general ward was overwhelming, forcing her to investigate.

Reaching the side entrance where corridors H1 to H3 all meet, she is trying to remember her code for the security exits so she can open the door. She needn't have bothered, as the door is slightly ajar. It's still some way to go to get to the pods, but she is determined to soldier on. Up ahead on H1, she sees a body slumped over a trolley. Speeding up to see who it is, she takes a deep breath, then stands aghast, for a moment unable to breathe. It's Carla.

"Carla!" No response. "Carla! Wake up!" Still no response. Catherine feels Carla's neck for a pulse. It's there. It's weak but it's

there. Thank God. She checks Carla's pockets to see if she has a
biocell. Nothing.

"Help!" Catherine shouts, as loud as she can. "Someone! Help!"

Suddenly Catherine realises that she is alone in this dark
corridor, and that Carla has been attacked in some way. She didn't
see anyone on her journey here, and is now deeply worried that
Carla's assailant could still be here. She decides that quiet is the
better option, and grabs one of the fire extinguishers off the wall, in
case she needs to protect herself. She creeps forward, her senses in
turmoil, the goal to reach H9 and the pods; to make it to Gill. Even
though she is buoyed by the knowledge that he is back from the
field, she still treads forward with an uncharacteristically hesitant
gate.
Thud, thud, thud. Pounding heels charge towards her. She can
make out a large figure, only the outline visible as the overhead
lights shine in her face. As she brings her hand up to dodge the glare,
she can see that this is a huge man, and as he gets closer and closer,
Catherine's heart beats out of her chest. She raises the fire
extinguisher above her head and musters the breath to shout at her
oncoming attacker.

"Stop or I'll throw this!" she screams at the top of her voice,
and tries to make her own shadow as big as she can make it.
"Catherine!" comes the response. "It's me! Dad!"

—

"Put your hands in the air! Do it *now*!" Phil Kirkland shouts.

Ellis Garfield is descending the small step ladder from
Darkroom One, one arm draped over Denton Gill.

"Don't shoot!" Gill cries. "Don't Shoot! He's hurt!"
"Back up, Gill. That's a nasty piece of work right there. Let the
guards take him, and step away. Do it now." Kirkland's old military
training and high-level security mindset is taking the stage.
"Dammit, man. He's badly hurt and needs help. Come and get
him. But put the guns down - *please*!" urges Gill.

As Kirkland and the guards grab Ellis Garfield, Gill tries to gather himself, but he too is weak, and he sinks down to lie against the steps.

"What the fuck is going on, Gill?" Kirkland barks.

Gill is breathing heavily and doesn't have time for Kirkland right now.

"Think about it, Phil. That's Nuvo. I'll tell you all about it, but first you need to get him to the hospital. He's in bad shape and will need to recover. Whatever you do, don't let him slip away. He's too important."

"But he's the fucking enemy!" Phil retorts, angry that Gill has brought a Kark into the secure NASA base. "What the hell are you doing bringing him here?"

"I had no choice. And besides, he's better here than anywhere else, believe me," Gill replies. "And Phil…"

"What?"

"He's not going to be a problem. Take my word for it. Yes, guard him, but *protect* him. Right?"

Phil Kirkland looks bemused. But sees that Gill has clearly gone through some sort of ordeal, so backs off.

"OK, Gill, it's your call. But this…*guy*…ain't going nowhere. I'll have six guards outside the detainment room over at Block C. Come over when you're ready. We got to get Ava and Maria here. Heck, Abe Hart too if we can. This is huge."

—-

"And in tonight's bulletin, multiple shootings of looters by police in Norfolk, Charlottesville, Blacksburg, Greensboro, Durham, Huntington, and a major hold up along route eighty-one outside Knoxville. Riots are also causing major disruption upstate and into D.C. However, Norfolk Mayor David Gonzalez has told RVCB that the public should rest assured that the police are dealing with these as they arise and that most are isolated events within the inner city limits or on the freeways. Chief of Police, Dionne Ross has tonight instigated a further curfew for nine p.m. She is advising all residents in Virginia and on the border with West Virginia and North Carolina to stay indoors and keep the FM channels open any way they can. Here at RVCB, we are keeping our broadcasts open across Richmond and the county while we still can, and we'll be coming live into your homes to keep you good folks up to date with all the information and news of the day. Any time we are off-air, use the FM channels to get that live audio feed. That's the backstop if you need it - RVCR will be on air 24/7 with news and the usual mix of great music. But for now, from me, Johnny Hardt with a 'd', I'm handing over to Sue Hobson who'll take us through the evening with some hot tunes from the world of jazz and soul. Sue…"

As the television screen glitches slightly, and Johnny's face comes a bit unstuck, forming a kind of jagged parody of the well-known anchor of Richmond's local news station, the patchwork of live newsfeeds from different parts of the state remain on screen and it is clear that major incidents are, or have been, taking place throughout. It's disturbing, more for the vain attempts by Johnny and the team to hang on to any sense of normality during the bulletin.

"My goodness," Mary Jumeau comments.
"It's pretty bad, that's for sure," husband Christophe replies.

The couple are preparing the large rustic table in the expansive kitchen for supper. The main gathering room these days for the family, the table has four places set. The house on Hannah Farm Road is set back in its own grounds, although security is fairly lightweight with the electronic entrance gates left open most of the time, and the garden meeting the surrounding scrub and farmland gradually and without any demarcation of a border. Christophe took advantage of the gun laws a while back, and has a small arms cabinet in the basement to augment the rifle rack in the garage, occupied by the Winchester 70 he bought over in Wilmington, and two Mauser 98's that the landlord keeps there. While the esteemed Professor is no crack shot, and a real pacifist at heart, recent events made him bite the bullet and get enough firepower to frighten off any chance visitors feeling lucky enough to try gaining entry.

Catherine is upstairs in her room, fidgeting. Having insisted on taking her premature baby Alex home to Oakton, against the express wishes of the medical staff at Langley, she has just got her off to sleep and is taking time to figure out what happens next. The strange pictures floating around in her head don't help.

She reaches for the biocell on the bedside table and tells it to play her 'Feelgood' playlist. 'Under The Milky Way' by The Church starts up. She thinks of Gill, and about what he might be thinking. He's due back soon, once the debrief with Phil and Ava is over. She smiles at the thought of her entire family being under one roof, here, tonight. Marty Piper's voice kicks into the chorus and out of her bedroom skylight she can see a clear sky, hundreds of stars glinting in the dark, even in the small rectangle framed by her window pane.

One of them could illuminate Xarn, she thinks, and from elation Catherine turns to more pensive reflection. Gill's family are completely torn apart, and for him the search continues for Beth. How she - they - will somehow manage to connect and explore Xarn will be one of the top subjects at dinner, after everyone goggles over Alex for as long as they can. At least Gill will be with his daughter, and people who love him. It's about time her guy got a break, she thinks, as she grabs her favourite green sweater, pulls it on, and reaches for the hairbrush.

—-

"Kark," Ellis Garfield says.

"And this is an exoplanet some thirty or so light years from here?"

"Yes."

"OK. Before we begin the tape, Ellis…or should I say Nuvo… can you just confirm that you grant us permission to make this recording? I mean, we'll do it anyway, but it would be better if you go along with things," Ava Redmond asks.

"I suppose. Yes," Nuvo responds.

Ava seems to be scribbling.

"Gill, help me out here, but am I being dipsy? You're here, and Nuvo's here, so, I mean, are you not observing him? Does this not mean that he is trapped?"

Gill looks to Garfield, who raises his eyebrow imperceptibly, then across at Ava.

"Right now, neither of us are dualling. At least, I'm not. I always understood that entrapment happens when you are dualling, and when the other person is dualling. If you're not in super-position, getting trapped doesn't come into it."

"OK, I wish I hadn't asked," Redmond quips, before turning back to Nuvo. "Don't worry, Nuvo, this will be classified and for use by the CIA and NSA in the first instance. Bear in mind, the purpose is not to haul you over the coals for the prehistory with Montgomery. Heck, we couldn't prove any of that *anyway*. No, this interview is about two things. Number one, what you know about the Kark invasion currently underway in the U.S. and elsewhere, and number two, what Gill here refers to as your ability to hide others while you do your super-positioning. Dualling. So, if we are all ready?"

Gill, Kirkland and Waters all nod towards Redmond, who starts the digital recorder. Without any rest, or even the chance to freshen up, Gill and Garfield look like a pair of bedraggled drunks after a night in the cells.

"You appear in front of us as Mister Ellis Garfield, former Vice President of the United States of America, and now the human face of an alien being named Nuvo, hailing from the planet of Kark, which we believe is found in the solar system of a known star, HR4523, also identified as HD102365. Is this correct?"

"Yes."

"And it is also true to say that, to all intents and purposes, the presence of the body of Ellis Garfield here is an illusion, or better a shell used for the purposes of surviving our atmosphere and managing in our environment in a more functional, and less obtrusive or obvious way. Is this correct?"

"Yes."

"I need to formally caution you that you are currently under arrest within the jurisdiction of the Unites States government, but understand that you have voluntarily agreed to help us with our enquiries, and are not doing so under duress. Is this correct?"

"Yes."

"Good, then I would like to begin by introducing the rest of the panel…"

Ava Redmond goes through the formal protocols for NSA and CIA detention and interrogation of potential foreign intelligence agents or informants, or in fact any suspect identified as being a potential threat to the security of the nation. It's standard stuff, but still heavy duty, and after a series of questions around Novek and the Kark plan to invade, to which Nuvo can only partially answer most, Gill is anxious to move things on to the intricacies of cloaking and what this could mean for Earth-based or off-world settlements.

Ava lets Gill take up the reins.

"Nuvo, when I was on Kark, I couldn't dual. We discussed this, and I think you said that this was because I was so far from here - from Catherine - that the entanglement would be too weak for the connection to allow me to dual, right?" he asks.

Garfield sits up in the chair.

"Do you guys have cigarettes?" he asks.

The assembled group look at each other. Ava is the only one who smokes.

"Here,' she says, "knock yourself out."

Garfield fires up a Kent lite, and takes a deep lungful.

"It's one of the advantages of this not being my body. I really like the effect of this substance. I always did," Garfield says, exhaling in a triumphant billowing that seems to relax his large frame, and somehow make his angular features more accessible. "In answer to your question, that was my best guess."
"Then how did you manage to dual to Earth?" asks Gill.
"Now that, I am not sure of. I mean, I built up the ability on various occasions, but I think I must have locked into a frequency here, or what you would call a wormhole. I remember following instinct and before I knew it I was in the middle of the Antarctic,

near one of your bases there. It might have been something they were doing down there that I picked up. I remember thinking that at the time."

Ava quickly scribbles something in her notebook, before Gill picks up on the thread.

"So it is possible for you to dual quite far distances? That's what I am driving at? I mean, it's thirty light years to Kark, and you managed it, but I couldn't. So there must be something different about the way you can dual. And if you put that together with your ability to cloak non-duallists - you know, ordinary Joes - then this feels pretty special to me," Gill remarks, and turns to Redmond, letting Nuvo hear what he says.
"Ava, I believe that Nuvo might be strategically very important to us if he is prepared to help."
"Well, we need to find out what the 'pro quo' is then, don't we?" Ava replies.
Gill turns to Garfield, and raises his eyebrows. "Your call, Nuvo," he says.

Garfield takes another puff on his cigarette, and places it in the ashtray on the table.

"Look, Detective Gill, you have been kind to me. You saved me from dying in the field. I am obliged to repay you. But I am just one person…one Kark. I've never tried to do this 'cloaking' other than with you. When I do, it is…I get tired. It is not an easy thing to do. You must understand this. There is a higher dimension which I believe you humans only perceive in the dimensions below, so there are certain things you cannot see. Or maybe it would be better to say that in this higher dimension, many more possibilities exist. These dimensions are, what is the word…orthogonal to yours, at a very particular angle. Using the deformations possible within higher dimensions - five more than those you commonly see - then I can hide a codified version of you. But it takes a lot of energy to convolute space in this way. If you have one or two very important people that you need to transport somewhere using this method then I will agree to help you, but it can't be my 'job' as you call it. I mean, I need to return to my home. I have to tell you that I do not like your planet. I never did, and I do not like your planet with Novek here. This is why I will not stay."

"Got it, Nuvo. I understand," Gill says, as his eyes ask Ava for a little more time, to which she nods.

"There are many things we can't see, you're right. We don't want to abuse your trust in the way Novek has done. We are honourable people, just trying to save our planet from a pandemic, and some of your guys. You know about the pandemic and what it's doing, right?" he asks Nuvo.

"Yes. I am sorry about this."

"It's not your doing. And as a precaution we need to make sure you don't succumb to the virus," Gill replies.

"I don't think we will," says Nuvo. "My senses tell me that Karks will not be affected."

"But Ellis Garfield, those guys who escaped off the base, what's he called, Don? And Emilia? They are all susceptible just like anyone else, right?"

"I'm not sure. I think we might pass some kind of immunity, but I can't be certain."

Ava looks round at Phil Kirkland.

"Phil, get Bill McFarlane or one of his aides on the line. We might have something for him here."

Gill picks up again.

"That aside, Ava, if Nuvo here can stay healthy - hell, if we can all stay healthy - then we have a mechanism to potentially get more folks into the settlements. Maybe even the President if needed. You see?"

"Oh yeh, I get it, Gill. But until we get some proof and some testing done, you'll forgive me for not giving a green light to *Ellis Garfield* taking John Montgomery under his wing for a spot of interplanetary travel just yet?"

Despite the intensity of the current predicament, Redmond still manages to fulfil her professional duty, and Gill, although a bit narked at her quick fire rebuttal, nonetheless admires her. A little more nuanced negotiation will be required.

"Nuvo, Ava, everyone, we have very little time for planning, and Phil I know you will provide official updates on the back of this meeting, and these recordings. But let me put this in a nutshell. Nuvo, in return for helping us, I personally guarantee you that I will not only track down Novek, but I'll help you open the connection to the Kark temple so you can go home. That's the deal, and it's the best one you're going to get, so what do you say?"

Ellis Garfield looks at Gill, then Ava. He takes a last drag from his cigarette, and takes a second to mull over what Gill has proposed.

"I am unsure how many of your people I can help. I must go back to Kark soon. Novek will know I am here, and he will try to kill me either here or in the cornfield. You realise this, yes?" Garfield says.
"Yes," Gill responds.
"And you will promise that the girl will fight with us so that we will overcome Karosak Novek?"
"I can't guarantee that, Nuvo, and you know that," Gill tells him.

Garfield shuffles in his seat, looks at Phil Kirkland and Hank Waters, almost as if he is thinking about trying to escape, but slumps down in the chair, still showing the signs of his discomfort and pain from the battering in the field.

"Then you must also promise that, if I am taken here by Sultan Novek, you will kill me, how you say...out of mercy...and break the ties with the dark side so he can never return to Kark."

Gill feels entirely uncomfortable. Nuvo is a soldier, pilot and astronaut, and even in Kark culture, he abides by a code of conduct akin to the Samurai or Ronin. And Gill knows that if he makes this promise now, he will need to keep it. There is a lot at stake.
He stares intently at the face of Ellis Garfield and, seeing the soul of Nuvo inside, nods gently.

"OK, Nuvo, looks like we have a deal," Redmond concludes, and moves on to tell Nuvo about CAT and where he'll be staying at Langley, managing to sound enough like a holiday resort hostess to give the impression that Nuvo's stay will be as luxurious as it gets as a prisoner of the federal government.

—-

Just off interstate one-forty on route seventy-four, Kevon gets out of the ambulance and shuffles across to the reception at the Rodeway. It's still open despite some break-ins to the Fairfield and Red Roof motels down the road. A young woman is watching the news on the television. Her name badge is at a forty-five degree angle and smudged with some sort of yellow sauce, possibly mustard.

"Howdy," Kevon greets her as he saunters in, turning his head to read her badge. "Crissy?"
"That's right. Hi!" she says, taking the chewing gum out of her mouth and sticking it on the side of the ashtray under the counter. "Please stay behind the marker there, Sir." She points to the big red cross on the floor about a foot inside the reception and a good ten feet from her desk. "How can I help you?" she enquires in an impossibly cheery tone entirely at odds with the state of the world.
"Uh, yeh, uh, I phoned ahead about thirty minutes ago? Need a couple of rooms for me and my buddies there?" he says.

The girl looks over to the ambulance.

"Oh, you got some sick people in there?" she asks.

Kevon gives a forced laugh.

"Hell, no, we just picked that old piece of junk up from the wreckers. It's our travel wagon, if you get my meaning?" he tells her and gives her a little wink. It's quite cack-handed as conversation openers go, but the girl seems impressed with the cocky youth with the messy hair and big smile. It's working for her.
"Oh, I see. Well, how many of you are there?"

"There's six of us, Ma'am. But we ain't got too much money on us, so we thought we could take a couple of rooms if that's not a problem for ya?"

"Hhhmm," she drawls. "Let me see, now."

She flicks through the book, and Kevon can clearly see there are dozens of vacancies.

"I'll put you in seven and eight, just over there. That way you'll have no distance to walk for breakfast in the morning. You'll have to stagger though - only four people allowed in the diner at a time and strict distancing will apply. That OK?"

"That's fine, Miss. And, uh, we're all travelling tomorrow from Wilmington? It's not far from here, right? Just off this road?" he asks.

"I'd say give yourselves *lots* of time, especially with some of the traffic buzzin' by these days. People takin' off to get away from the cities. That what you folks doin'?" she asks him.

"You bet. We're heading north. You wanna come?" he asks her.

The young girl blushes, lowers her head and starts to laugh.

"I mean it. Come with us. What have you got to lose except be stuck here while people with disease come by and infect you?"

Crissy stops laughing and focuses intently on Kevon, who she is still finding very attractive.

"Well, I can't just take off. I mean, I got my shifts to work, and my boyfriend would be mad at me…" she trails off, realising that, despite his affable approach, she's still talking to a stranger and it's not the era of flower power.

"I understand. Well, suit yourself, but the offer is there. We're all virus-free - got the tests to prove it. We'll be getting up early, so if you want to go on a bit of a ride with us, come say hello before we go."

Crissy smiles again, and nods.

"Yeh, I will. Gee, thanks!"

As she gets the keys ready for Kevon, she can see a couple of girls getting out the back of the ambulance, and two tall, rather burly guys following. They look cool to her, so she makes her mind up to think about the offer carefully.

Later, in room seven, all the Karks gather, clicking and clucking at first, then speaking English. Kevon is clearly the one in charge.

"Enough now. Listen. You understand the plan. This must be done carefully, and according to my exact instructions. Don, you will lead in with Emilia, as a couple. The rest of us will be behind you, going for the same flight, American one-six-six. It's one of only two departures tomorrow, so we'll need to be very careful. Use your abilities only if needed, until we get on the plane. I will be in command. If any of you fail to board, go into Wilmington and try to find a different shell. That way you will be safe if you hide within the community. Wait a couple of days and take the next one-six-six - they run every three days. We will make contact via the human wormhole in the field - I will make my way there and announce it is open for you. You will know what to do. If we all make it to the settlement, we will position to the field and allow more soldiers to enter. I will take charge of Nuvo and the opening. Remember, you are able to mimic the human behaviour without detection, as these bodies are young and healthy and still finding their way. The minds are not made yet, so we can easily improvise. Be as natural as you can - there is no need to be afraid. Do we understand?"

The group nods as one.

"Will the girl be joining us?" asks Don.
"One way or the other, yes," Kevon replies.

—-

"Fuck yeh!"
"Pull over here, Dwain."

The large, magnolia and brown Crusader Lite RV rattles and shakes to a stop just outside Rocky Point, a little further down the road on route one-forty.

"Hey, buddy! You need a ride?" Carlito Palomar shouts out the window.

"Hey. Where you guys headed?" asks Mal Baines.

"To the very end of the Earth, my friend. Or Canada, whichever comes first, dig?" Carlito answers. "What happened to you? You look kinda 'all shook up', amigo!"

"I got into a fight, further back there," Mal says.

"Hey, we all gotta look after ourselves, buddy. No doubt. You look like you can handle yourself too. You give those bastards something to think about?"

Mal looks back along the freeway. It's getting dark and he's very obvious out here, hitching along one of the major routes in the state.

"Canada sounds great. Are you headed up near Boston on the way? I can cook," he says.

Dwain Stubbs looks at Carlito, and they both start to laugh.

"Boston? Who the hell wants to go to Boston, man? That place is infested. Hell no," Carlito responds, looking over to Dwain. "But hey, Dwain, the man can *cook*. Well I'll be. Let me tell you, good buddy. Where we goin', that skill will be very welcome. You know how to cook bears?"

The two double up in laughter again, clearly high on weed or more.

"Is it just the two of you heading up?" asks Mal.

"Hell, no, man! We got some chicas in the back, couple more hombres, and we are virus-free. Virus-free, you hear. Are you virus-free, amigo?" Carlito asks.

"Virus? Oh yes, I am completely virus-free. Completely."

"Well, he dang sounds sure, Carlos!" Stubbs giggles.

Stubbs points his biocell at Mal and after about two seconds, the screen flashes green. Carlos Palomar nods at Stubbs.

"Well, if you are completely, completely virus-free, then I say you just damn ought to be part of our escape plan. What's your name, amigo?"

"Mal. Malcolm."

"Dude, I don't call anyone 'Malcolm'. Shame on your mother for such a badass name. The only Malcolm I heard of is Malcolm X, so 'am gonna call you Mal X. 'Mallicks'. That's it. 'Mallicks' it is. You hop on up at the back there, Mallicks. We got ya. No need to buckle up, cos we are now our own bosses, and from now on we do what we do to survive. We done got everything we need in that big old Winnebago back there. You name it. We got it. We are the new settlers, buddy. Canada here we come!"

Before Mal can thank the Cheech and Chong lookalikes, the RV starts to creak into action, and he has to run round the side to one of the main doors. A young woman, about mid-twenties with dark frizzy hair and what sounds like a French accent shouts to him to jump up before it's too late.

Inside, Sonia introduces him to the others, and Mal takes in the huge array of arms, tins of food, cleaning products, toilet rolls, sacks of rice and pasta as well as what looks like huge pots and pans; the sizes you could probably only find in industrial kitchens. There's hardly any room to move, so Mal takes a seat and begins his journey to one of many unofficial settlements in the hinterland north.

—

'Mr. President, Sir."

"Yes?"

"I've got Langley on the phone. It's Colonel Redmond."

"Very good, put her on."

Up on the screen, an internal news flash in green text rolls across slowly.

'Rogue AA 166 ILM-YVR as of 07:21….Pilot reports hijacking…No demands…no government personnel on board… possible unofficial settler insurgents…'

"John, are you looking at your screen?" Ava asks.

"Yeh. You're going to tell me these aren't just any insurgents, right?"

"Right. We've had fallout here. Up to ten alien life forms are believed to have escaped from the labs here. I'm sorry, Sir, it was a gamble and we have won some ground and lost some ground."

"Ava, don't give me the bullshit. Tell me why they've hijacked a plane and where they are going."

'Yes, Sir. Well, our best advice here is that they will try Dulles and then on to reunite in London where we think there is a small vanguard, or ditch the plane and head towards one of our settlements. Most likely Thompson or Kodiak, but I can't be sure."

"Can we shoot it down?" Montgomery asks.

"Well, if we can scramble jets, yes, but where from? Eustis, Andrews, Pope, Arnold, Shaw… all report infected or dead with massively reduced personnel. And of course we've got about forty civilians on that flight."

"Malmstrom? Ellsworth?" Abe Hart asks.

"Reports are very similar, Abe. You saw General Trent's briefing, right? We need to talk to Edwards and Fairchild."

Abe Hart nods to himself, silently confirming.

"Any intel on possible plans to crash?" Montgomery asks Ava.

"We can't be certain, Sir. There's no intel to support that. My best guess? I can't see it. They are here to invade, not to kill themselves."

"OK, get onto military ATC and Joe's people. They'll track it. Get the info to me and Joe as soon as. OK?"

"Yes, Sir. I'm on it, Sir," she says. "Could I just update you…"

But Montgomery has hung up.

"Maria, where are we with the settlements? Where is this flight likely to head?"

"Likely Thompson, like Ava said. It's headed north right now, so unlikely to turn down to Florida."

"And what is the status of those?"

"Thompson is pretty advanced. Hawaii the least so, given the situation building to the South there," Maria updates.

"Abe, what's the deal with these 'Karks' that have broken into Langley and London? Is this a big threat right now?"

"Sir, I never thought I'd talk to you about this in quite this detail, but right now we are fighting our own people. We can't handle fighting other people. If you put this threat alongside the Chinese and the Russians, personally I'd take my chances with these aliens. I mean, from what we know they can't breathe our atmosphere, have to use human bodies to function properly and are here in such small numbers that from a military perspective and in this very moment, I couldn't advise prioritising a fight against them. *And* security is no longer compromised at Langley. But what we can do, is keep them under surveillance and try to get Ava's recruits on her CAT program to see if they can track 'em down. In the meantime, the settlement programme and the situation in Japan and Korea must be priority. At least that's how I see it, Sir."

"OK, thanks Abe," Montgomery replies. "Joe?"

"I'm with Abe," Joe Becker replies.

"But what if they infiltrate one of the settlements?" asks Bibi Melnik.

"That's good, Bibi. What I was thinking too. Gentlemen? Maria? Any thoughts?"

"Sir, if I may?" asks Maria. Montgomery nods.

"I think Bibi's point is a good one too. We can recruit extra security, and Langley has identified those that broke out of the base, so we should be able to ID them."

"But they take on human form, right?" asks Montgomery.

"Right," Abe Hart says.

"So, how do we know they can't ditch one body and take another?" asks the President.

There is a muted silence around the large room.

"We need Ava here," says Hart.

"I tend to agree," Montgomery reflects.

"Is she still training those guys? You know, the, uh, 'duallists'?"

"Yes, sir. There are, I believe, around twenty or so at Langley. And then there is the Detective and Professor Jumeau's daughter. You might remember them - they are very skilled in super-positioning and spacetime travel, and are central to the CAT program. They are the ones who will potentially lead some of the selected settlers to off-world colonies as well as on-world. That'll be in addition to Nelson's mission," Abe Hart reports.

"Where are we with that? What's the hold up?"

"It's just down to the number of staff at the launch site, Sir. With so many ill, or already dead, we are looking at an 'unplugged' version of the shuttle launch. It's just a skeleton crew there, but I know Nelson and the team are ready to go. We just need to get everything in place and that's not easy."

"ETA to Mars?"

"Well, I'd have to check, Sir, but best guess would be three to four days. If everything goes to plan."

"OK, I want to be appraised of progress - and I mean *any* progress - as soon as you get wind. Got it?"

Abe Hart signals his willingness, and looks anxiously down at the circular from Olakunde on the Centronus project. The launch date has been changed several times, and the latest prediction is plus five days.

* * * *

CHAPTER 11: EVOLUTIONS

"Well, that was just what I needed. Incredible to taste some real cooking again. Wonderful wild venison. Thank you Mary. Thank you Christophe."

"It's our pleasure, Gill, and welcome to our small family," Mary replies.

"Here, let me help you with the plates," Gill offers, but Mary steadfastly refuses and insists that everyone retires through to the lounge, where Christophe pours himself and Gill large brandies, Catherine sticking to water.

"It feels great to be here with you guys," Gill remarks.

"Well, you have both had so much going on, I guess we have to make the most of these moments," Christophe replies. "But of course, we have to talk about CAT and our plans. I fear this can't wait until morning."

"Gill, Dad doesn't want me to dual unless it's absolutely necessary - that I need to be with Alex. I think he has a point," Catherine begins.

"Of course, and I agree. This is the last thing you should be doing right now," Gill reassures her, pausing for a second. "Hey, how do we know if we can trust the others? I mean, is there any way we can tell if someone is a Kark underneath?" Gill asks.

"It's a good question," Jumeau senior responds. "I would take it that only those who broke out of the base are Karks. Wouldn't make much sense for them to remain in plain sight unless they planned on a takeover of the base, which would seem a little over-ambitious, even for them. Mind you, if they did, most Karks are strictly speaking dualling while on Earth, and they may be less likely to directly interact with their environment over time if occupying a human form. Theoretically this could mean that they are both insulated from any decoherence and harder to detect."

Catherine follows up. "If they don't intend going back to Kark, I can't imagine it would be terminal for them to be observed. All it would mean is that they lose the ability to dual here on Earth. And if their entangled twins get through the cornfield, or change in some way that would cause the entrapment to cease, then that could all change. It's like electron spin - if you observe an entangled electron and force it into a particular state, it doesn't mean that it can't become entangled again."

"At the level of complexity and mass of a human body though, I find it hard to believe that you or Gill, for example, could ever be entangled with another person. The odds of that are ridiculous," muses the Professor, before Gill interrupts the thought experiment, a sanguine smile on show.

"Sounds like the most important thing is to ID these guys. My gut tells me Nuvo would be best at that. Once we have that ability, we can hold them, or take them out, whatever makes most sense," Gill concludes.

"I agree, Gill. But I think therein lies a problem. His agreement to help is wonderful news, but from what you've told us he will still feel very loyal to those soldiers, even if they are under the command of Novek. We need to get the military guys appraised of how we would recommend handling this, or it could get extremely messy," Christophe suggests.

Gill and Catherine nod in silence, contemplating the way forward.

"Guys, I need to tell you something," says Gill, carrying on his thought immediately, turning directly to Christophe. "I want to use Nuvo to get you, Mary and Alex to Xarn. It makes the most sense to me right now. The settlements here are places they are earmarking for young couples and families. They are specifically targeting those groups because they have the greatest capacity to reproduce and grow communities. If I were leading this country, I would one hundred percent follow this strategy. But these settlements won't be holiday camps. Security will have to be tight, and with food and water rationed to an extent, it will be tough, especially the principal northern ones where it will feel like winter much of the year. As much as I'd like to think that we could all get a ticket to St. Lucia or somewhere down there, and live a life of luxury, I just don't see it happening. I have another agenda too. I am going to bring my parents to Nuvo. I know this might sound very selfish, but they have gone so many years without seeing Beth, and I know that they would give anything to see out their time with her. It's the one thing I can try to do to make up for all the hurt I've caused them."

Catherine moves as if to reassure Gill that he should not be thinking in those terms, but she refrains, instead letting him continue his thoughts.

"So, anyway, I don't have much time to do this, but I do know that I have to go to Portland and get them. It's just something I have to do. But first I need to know more about Beth and Xarn, and how we get everybody there safely. I'm guessing you have both been thinking this too, right?"

Christophe takes a sip of his brandy, and gestures to Catherine to see if she wants to respond. She takes him up.

"It's not the easiest place to live, Gill. Even Beth will tell you that. She said it was like going back in time. No technology, no big cities. Just villages and maybe one or two provincial towns, but by and large medieval. It's a completely different world, and I'm not sure any of us are ready for something like that. I want Alex to grow up like any other kid, and I want her to do that here, not on some planet where people live like savages and where wild animals attack settlements and prey on the weak. Don't you think trying to get us into one of the larger settlements *here* is a better option? Going to Xarn seems, like, very *final*."

Another silence ensues. Gill takes a swig of his drink, and swills the brandy round the glass, deep in thought.

Catherine saves the most obvious question to last.

"Gill, I know you now. Is there a reason we can't use Nuvo to bring Beth back *here*? Wouldn't it be better for your mom and dad to see Beth at home, in Oregon, if you could make that happen?" she asks.

Gill gets up and goes over to the large French windows. They look over about an acre of beautiful gardens that reach out into the countryside that surrounds the large Oakton house. The uplights and solar-powered lanterns illuminate what is becoming unruly and overgrown, nature having its way in the absence of the attendance of the local gardener, and the inevitable tendency towards increasing disorder is winning in the void that the pandemic has brought to the land.

"When I first realised that Nuvo could carry me into a wormhole - potentially anywhere - even if I couldn't dual, I had a chance to reflect on what this amazing ability would allow me - you, us, others - to do. It blew my mind. I mean, back then I didn't know anything about what was happening here. The pandemic, the international conflict, arms race; all those things in such a short space of time. I came back to a completely different world. Everything has changed. Don't think that things will ever get back to normal. Our world - this Earth - is not going to be a good place to be, and soon there might be no-one left in it. That's the new reality. The new normal is that there is no normal, because there is likely no *us*. It's hard to explain, but as I got to know Nuvo, and the situation on Kark, I could see it - *feel it* - in them. They are afraid. Every day is a challenge, and they need to get off that planet 'cos it's killing them. They can't survive. And that's what is happening here. Being away makes you see more when you come back. And this…"

Gill points out the window to the garden.

"What you see out there…is breaking down. It's already a free for all. You can see it. The weeds are beginning to take hold, and any sort of definition will gradually disintegrate. Even your immaculate borders are overgrown. How long since your gardener guy last visited? It's what's happening everywhere."

Gill moves over to where Christophe and Mary have put up their photographs of Catherine as a baby right up to graduation, proud parents and childhood friends by her side. The most recent of Catherine and Wendy Xiu and Malcolm Baines, happy and carefree celebrating their selection into Walter Melrose's postgrad scheme at

Harvard. Gill squints in and takes a good look. Christophe and Catherine are transfixed, awaiting a conclusion.

"You see these?" Gill asks rhetorically. "These look like amazing memories. But any kid growing up from now on won't have these. They'll have to wise up way before their time. Live with the reality that most of their loved ones will die prematurely, or worse that they'll be left to fend for themselves when they have no hope of survival. Sorry to be so blunt, but that's the prospect. I overheard Ava talking to one of her senior government guys yesterday. They're not expecting a vaccine any time soon. In fact, most of the guys that are supposed to be developing the vaccine are either ill or dying. Most of the military and air force bases have huge numbers in hospital. Langley is a bit of an exception. The point is, any hope that the world will somehow be back to what it was within the next twenty or thirty years is just fantasy. Even with the settlements up and running, they'll be targeted by foraging tribes of the virus-free, all looking for some sense of organisation, structure, supplies, reasonable living standards. And the locations of these settlements *will* get out, make no mistake. If the prevalence of GARI is similar elsewhere - that it's truly a pandemic - then all this is going to be true wherever you look. International borders might not be relevant any more. Governments will have a very different role, probably to govern over the settlements and ensure security as much as they can. There may be abandoned nuclear missile sites all across the globe. Or worse, that some militant far-right falange of frat boys, farmers and ex-forces get control of one of those. I could go on…but I won't. You get my point. Catherine, I don't want to bring up our daughter in this world. She'll grow up scared. We already hunt wild animals. Always have done. We've always protected ourselves from them too. We always will. Going back to an earlier form of existence - one that's more basic and focused around villages and communities - is that such a bad thing? Sure, there are dangers, but I'd say way less than here. So going to Xarn - to start a new life - gets my vote. And Nuvo can help us achieve it."

Catherine and her dad seem to sink into their seats in introspective mood.

"We can't make a decision without Beth," Catherine announces after several seconds.

"May I…?" Christophe interjects. Gill nods. "The way I come at this is from a practical point of view. Looking at what makes most sense."

The Professor gets up and goes over the where Catherine is sitting., placing his hand on her shoulder.

"This little girl is all Mary and I have had for a long time. Thirty years in fact. She's very precious. I know that you understand that. But now, we have a granddaughter, and hopefully a son-in-law…"

Catherine smiles, holding the thought. Christophe doesn't give her too much idling time though.

"So you see, the last thing I'd want to do is break any of that up. But I fear that it is inevitable, unless we stay here."
"Here?" asks Gill.
"Yes, here. Oakton, or Langley. I couldn't justify leaving Phil and Ava to the CAT programme. It's too important for that, and they rely on me to take this forward as best we can. Catherine is key to that, and so are you. We must complete this programme before we attempt any migration to Xarn. I mean, *yes*, you and Nuvo could meet with Beth to find out more, so we can test the water, as it were. No need to jump in too soon, in my view," Christophe replies.
"And the virus? The disintegration of law and order? You think we can all remain immune from those?" Gill retorts, feeling more uneasy at the prospect of missing an opportunity to get his parents and extended family together in a place he considers to be a better hope for a future life.
"Not indefinitely, no. But we have a bunch of young people back at the base who didn't choose to be part of the war against Kark, nor become astronauts who travel to distant exoplanets to try to carve out a new existence. They're just ordinary people, like you and Catherine, who have this strange ability and who have their own families too. I can't abandon them, and I won't. They are the future for a lot of different reasons. Even if I could, I wouldn't go to Xarn

knowing that I have left men and women here in grave danger. I just can't do that."

Catherine is beginning to get upset, and feels the need to chip in.

"It's OK, Dad. Gill and I both get that. And you're right. We need to make sure that the programme succeeds. Gill is only thinking about how to reunite his family. You know that."

Jumeau senior acknowledges his daughter's thoughts, allowing her to continue.

"Gill, you need to get your mom's house. For sure. You can dual there, right? Put them on a plane or drive them back, whatever, but you can do this in a couple of days. Dad and me will work with the new duallists, and with Phil and Ava to prepare things for when you return," explains Catherine.

Gill is beginning to visibly stress. "If there are Karks still in the field, I don't know about dualling just yet. I need to sort out some things. I need time with Nuvo so he understands what we'll be doing."

"We just need to prioritise. It is important to speak to Nuvo, but it's also important that he recovers and both he and Garfield are well enough to go back into the clearing. You can take a flight over to Portland if they are still flying that route - might not take that long," Catherine replies.

"On those Karks, Gill," asks her dad. "You said that there were dozens, even hundreds of Karks in the field, right?"

Gill nods.

"Well, where did they all go? I mean, if only a few took our guys and went to Langley, there must either be a lot of Karks in that field, or they grabbed some of our guys but went elsewhere, no?" Christophe asks.

"Good point, Dad," Catherine reflects.

Gill tries to reply to Christophe's question. "I only saw a few of our guys getting taken. I told Carla, Mal and the others to retreat back and, well, as far as I know they did and weren't harmed. I can't be certain, though. We managed to take a lot of the Karks out, though. Like, a *lot*. Twenty, thirty. Maybe more. And then when I saw Nuvo at the fence, he was keeping that open as much for Kark soldiers to retreat back as to let them in. Once all the portholes closed in the reeds, they will have known that they either had to go back, or risk getting trapped in the field. I suspect some are still there, though, in limbo. That's a worry."

"It is if you are going back in there. But there's no rush. Not yet. Going to Oregon and getting your parents will give us a little time to work things through," Christophe proposes.

"Ava and Phil won't be happy," Gill states.

"I heard Phil say that Ava is due to travel to that war bunker up in New England somewhere, so that will buy us a day or so. I'll deal with Phil. Tell him you're ill and Mary is looking after you, something along those lines."

"And Nuvo?" asks Gill.

"Hhhmm. That's where I come unstuck a little," the Professor contemplates.

"Dad? How about I talk to Nuvo? I mean, yes, it will be strange looking at Ellis Garfield again, but I can contribute here. I won't be dualling and we'll just be talking…."

"They won't let you talk to Nuvo, Catherine," Gill states. "It's nothing about you, it's just protocol. They'll keep him isolated, and only let your dad do any further interrogations," Gill butts in, rather clumsily, which leaves Catherine feeling somehow inadequate.

"He's right, honey. Nothing to do with you, and everything to do with process and security. You'll obviously need to talk to him too, Gill. Or maybe you can give me a list of questions and I can make a start while you are away," states Catherine's dad.

Catherine has the beginning of a smile coming on, but suppresses it. "OK, Dad, but it'll be quite a long list."

"OK," the Professor replies, as he and Gill respond to Catherine's gentle humour.

The group are interrupted by Mary, who reports that Alex is crying, whereby Catherine and Gill both swiftly get up.

"It's OK, honey," she says to Gill. "I'll get this one."

As the two men finish their drinks and contemplate what's to come, Christophe has a final question for Gill.

"Does she know that you'll have to track down Novek?"

Gill looks sheepishly at his glass, realising that the Professor either knows, or has worked out, that this must be part of Gill's deal with Nuvo.

"Not yet," he replies.
"And you'll most likely have to use Nuvo as bait for him. Right?"

Gill doesn't respond, but doesn't deny it.

"I'll bear that in mind," Christophe responds.

—-

Sonia Deschamps and Mal Baines are peeling potatoes. The rest of the group of new settlers from around Georgia and South Carolina are outside by the campfire. Mal can hear the sound of an acoustic guitar and someone on harmonica. An extraordinarily ropey rendition of Springsteen's 'Born In The USA' floats into the Winnebago , causing Sonia to laugh.

"My God, they are bad!" she jokes.

Mal laughs hesitantly, finding it hard to engage with Sonia's chit chat.

"So what's your story, Mallicks? You are from Virginia? West Virginia?"
"No, I…my home is in Boston."
"Ah, Boston!" Sonia says, pronouncing the city with the accent in the wrong place. "What's it like there?"
"Uh…" Mal is finding it difficult to focus. Something inside his head is stopping him from functioning properly. He drops the potato he is peeling.

"Ooops!" Sonia reaches down to pick up the potato in an effort not to waste anything or allow it to get dirty. "Are you alright?" she asks.

"Yeh. I…" Inside Mal's head, a silent code circulates, clicking a series of messages that somehow stop him from thinking straight. As he looks at Sonia, he finds himself weighing up her suitability as a host for an occupying Kark. Struggling against it, he attempts to re-engage. "Sorry. I…maybe I'll do this later," he tells her.

"Yes. This is OK. It is not a problem. You go. Go! Enjoy the music, yes?" she says, shooing him away in a humorous way.

As Mal moves away, he is aware that Sonia is, for the first time, a little intimidated by his presence. And still he is assessing how good she would be as a younger, lively shell. As he descends the small staircase from the RV to the outside world, his visual field becomes distorted by radiating heat energy coming from the fire, and also the group of people surrounding it. He is detecting heat visually as if he were wearing night vision or heat-tracing glasses. As he looks up at the sky, everything becomes super-sharp, his focal acuity seemingly limitless.

Suddenly, an intensity of high-frequency clicks and glitches makes him wince and buckle over and collapse. The others haven't seen him yet, and he struggles back to his feet slowly, his head splitting.

"Jeez…" he mutters, as he struggles to regain control of his body.

"They are perfect," the clicking spells out, and he easily interprets. "Create a cloud tonight. Go to the field, and allow our soldiers access to these shells."

——-

As Gill queues at Dulles for the one Portland flight that day, he anxiously scans the airport terminal. Others are doing the same, but for different reasons. If it weren't for the overwhelming army and police presence, it could probably pass for a large accident and emergency unit as much as an airport. With only a few passengers dotted around, all wearing face masks, some even with surgical caps, gloves and rubber boots on, Gill looks decidedly out of place.

The thought strikes him that Karks in human form could be anywhere here, and nowhere at the same time. Two invisible enemies to deal with on a routine journey across America. For someone who has seen as much as he has in his years, the large detective is unusually nervous.

As the flight reaches altitude, Gill looks around the main passenger space, empty seats in the corporate blue and red checks forming the internal panorama. Five or six rows up there is an older couple holding each other's hands and visibly tense. Over to the left is a mother and her two young boys. The carefree youngsters play with some model aircraft that the stewardesses have given out on entry, while the mother seems stressed and focusing on the very practical elements of a domestic flight, including repeatedly taking out the entire contents of her travel bag and reorganising before packing anew.

When you are in the air at thirty thousand feet during a pandemic, there's not much you can do but accept that the pilots are virus-free and not about to collapse and crash the plane. After all Gill's been through, this would be pretty ironic. After a deep breath, he takes out his biocell and his ear buds. He scans through a bunch of tracks until he comes across Winton Marsalis' version of 'Caravan'. He smiles. He's going home.

Later, as Gill takes the two-oh-five past Montavilla and Lents, the freeway is pretty empty, save a patrol car that speeds past on the opposite side, sirens blazing. And then, all of a sudden, several gunshots whizz over the car, causing him to duck. Two more shots, this time hitting the concrete barrier to his right. More sirens, this time in the distance. As he looks over to the criss-cross streets of Lents, he can see a couple of shops on fire. A sudden screaming toot from the horn of a rapidly approaching TransAm behind causes him to swerve as it races past his Kia Optima. There are clearly bullet holes in the front of the car, and as it accelerates a huge cloud of smoke forces its way in Gill's direction, obscuring the view. He curses the lack of acceleration on his hire drive as he floors the gas and the car lurches forward as if belching after a huge meal.

A while later, Gill takes the turn-off for Lewisburg and Corvallis, and eventually reaches his parents' modest plot in Newport.

"Denton!" cries Shirley Gill, as she rushes out to hug her son. "Oh, Denton," she says as she holds on tightly.

The two hug it out silently for a further minute or so. Eventually, Shirley breaks off, a tear still clinging to her eye.

"Come and say hello to your father," she invites him.

Joe Gill is out back on the airy porch outside the kitchen.

"Gill!" he says, and Gill's first thought is a joyous one; his father recognises him. "How are you, son? I've heard that you've hit a spot of bother over there?"
"You could say, that, Dad."
"Honey, would you like a coke, or a beer?" asks Shirley.

Gill asks for a coke and Shirley returns with drinks for everyone. After explaining the situation and Gill's plans to get the two to safety over in Langley, Shirley is silent.

"You OK, Mom?" asks Gill.
"I guess. I appreciate your concern for us here, son. But this is home for us. And with Connie just down the road, we are doing just fine. I can't imagine leaving here. And if we do, can you imagine what will happen? All these looters and robbers will just break in and take everything. All our things are here, honey," Shirley says.
"Mom, do you realise how bad things are out there? When was the last time you were in Eugene or Portland?"

Shirley Gill is trying to remember.

"It's a while, right? Well as I drove up here I got shot at. You know, like, real bullets? It's the same across the state - Albany will be the same. Right across America. You must have seen the news, or talked to neighbours, right?" Gill prompts.
"Well, to be honest, dear, we sort of stopped watching the news. Since they brought Joe back from the Care Home due to the dangers there, he doesn't like to hear all that. Neither do I. When it all dies down, we'll still be here, though."

"No, Mom. It's not like that, you have to trust me on this. I have seen so much of what is going on, and believe me, living out here you are lucky, but like you said, it's only a matter of time before those city folks won't have enough food or meds and they'll travel up here. You and Dad wouldn't stand a chance. I'm sorry to be so blunt. It's just a fact that you'll be safer if you come back with me, even for just a short while. The house will still be here, but you'll not be in danger. Do you understand?"

"That's so thoughtful of you, son," Shirley says, pausing a moment and looking at her husband, who is looking out over the back garden and not participating in the discussion.

"And…?" Gill urges.

Shirley turns to her son, looking him directly in the eye.

"Do you know why your father looks out on the garden like this? It's because he remembers Beth hiding in the bushes down the bottom there. Hiding from him, then jumping out to surprise him. He looks down there because his one hope is to see his little girl again, and he figures that's where she's going to appear. I don't want to take that away from him, son."

Gill goes over to his Dad, and hunkers down in front of him.

"Hi, Dad," he says. "It's beautiful today, isn't it? I remember us playing in the garden. You always told us that we were very good at hide and seek. That we'd be great magicians, or crooks, one of the two."

Joe Gill raises a smile in among the premature creases that line his face. The animation makes Gill reciprocate, and he squeezes his dad's hand.

"Dad, I know that leaving here will be hard, but for a short time, you, me and Mom need to visit where I work, and we need to see if we can be together through the current storm."

Joe Gill looks at his son, puzzled.

"You can't see it yet, Dad. It's just over the horizon. But it's coming, sure as the winter cold. Let me take you and Mom over to my place, just for little while. We can hang out, have some meals together, and, hey Dad, I want to introduce you to my girlfriend. Her name is Catherine."

"Yes, she was here," Joe replies. "Your mother said she was a nice girl, son."

"She is, Dad. She's the best, and, well, I didn't know how to tell you both…" Gill looks over at his mother, who has suddenly sat upright in her chair.

"Didn't tell us what? Denton Gill, you gone and got married without telling your folks? Why…"

"No, Mom, it's not that. It's better than that. Before I was… before I got lost, Catherine and I…we were very close. What I mean is…"

'She's with child!" Shirley exclaims, and an overdue smile finally arrives on Gill's face.

After Shirley's joyous shock subsides, she brings out some beers, and all three celebrate in a small and inconspicuous way, on their back porch. Gill's announcement is a game-changer, and that night, Shirley Gill packs two travel-beaten brown leather suitcases for herself and Joe, and phones Connie to invite her to come and say goodbye to Joe in the morning. Gill's planning is almost perfect, and after a slight delay and some tears from Joe and Connie, the Gills head back down to the airport, hoping that the security is still in place, and that the return flight to Dulles hasn't been cancelled.

—-

"Dad!" Catherine whispers.

Christophe Jumeau grabs the old Glock 43 from the case, choosing the micro-compact SIG for Catherine. He slides the 365 Nitron along the kitchen floor, and the two Jumeaus brace themselves.

Outside, the figure is silhouetted against the driveway spots making it difficult to see who is out there. As the pair move silently across the kitchen space, Christophe signals to Catherine that he's going to take the front door. Catherine nods and moves over to the kitchen door. The two can just about see each other in the dark, the downstairs only lit by the moonlight and the fraction of photons penetrating the glass.

Another movement, this time the figure is closer, and seems to be striding towards the front door. Catherine's eyes widen as her adrenalin levels rise. Jumeau senior nods, and with as quick a movement as the burly academic can muster, he flings open the large front door.

"*Stop right there!*" he shouts in a huge bellowing voice. Certainly enough to scare the local cats.

A solitary figure, and one that is obviously slight, stands before him. In the light, Christophe squints to see who it is, as his finger begins to squeeze the trigger.

"Mr. Jumeau?" comes the voice. It's female, and doesn't sound nearly as dangerous as he was expecting.
"Dad!! It's Wendy!!!" Catherine screams as loud as she can from her vantage point looking sideways from the kitchen window.
"Wendy?? What the…"
"Mr. Jumeau, it's me, Wendy Xiu. Are you OK?"

Catherine comes running through.

"Wendy! My God, what are you doing here?" cries Catherine, as she lowers her gun and runs between her father and their solitary guest.

The two women hug, and Christophe shouts to Mary upstairs that everything is alright. After a few minutes of hugging and general easing of tensions, the Jumeaus and Wendy assemble around the kitchen table. It's two a.m.

"I'm so sorry for barging in like this, and so late. I got a ride down. It was awful. You just don't know who has the virus and who doesn't. So scary. Anyway, I walked from town. These things are great…" she says, pointing to her biocell.
"What brings you here, Wendy? Are your parents OK? Are they safe?" asks Mary, as she places a pot of hot green tea on the table.

"I had to come and see you guys. Yes, my folks are holding up. But I haven't heard from Mal since he came down here last Thursday, and I couldn't make contact with you guys. Like, I tried so many times to call you, but I just got a 'no connection' error, so I started to panic. Do you know where Mal is?" she asks.

"Oh God, Wendy, I'm so sorry. They changed our cells to the security network, and they must have limited our access. I didn't realise," Catherine replies, avoiding for a second the elephant in the room.

Her dad steps in.

"Mal is OK, Wendy. But something happened on his return from dualling. There is a search going on for him as we speak. He's probably in the vicinity of the base, but we can't be certain. Have you heard any more, Catherine?"

"No, except that Carla reported that he went a bit crazy when they both came back from the battle with the Karks."

"Battle? You put Mal in to fight those things? He's just an academic!" Wendy states, obviously anxious and increasingly concerned that there is no definitive word on her future husband.

"Hey, Wendy, we didn't know what would happen there," says Catherine. "But Mal is going be fine; he just needs to make contact with us. Listen, this is classified, but some Karks escaped from Langley. That's the bad news. But Mal wasn't in that group, Wendy. He might have had a really strong reaction to what he witnessed in there, but Gill saw him and Carla and they both came back, unhurt. Look, stay here. Stay with us. We will be the first to get any news on Mal - my dad has seen to that."

Christophe nods.

"Wendy, he's a strong boy. He can take care of himself. He'll be in touch. But we need him to do that on his own terms. We can't force it this end. Let's go to the base in the morning, and we'll check again. He can't be far away."

The Jumeaus continue to try to ease Wendy's pain, and momentarily this comes when baby Alex wakes up and Wendy has the chance to see her for the first time. Exhausted, Wendy eventually gives in to slumber, and Catherine makes a note to call in to Langley first thing to increase the effort to find Mal.

—-

Kevon Clark disembarks from one-six-six, one of few people doing so. The rest of his group descend the staircase, looking around. Behind them are twelve innocent passengers tied down in their seats, four of whom are dead. Having cut all communications and outward radio transmissions, the last two hours of the flight were invisible to any air traffic controls, and Captain Dwight Kovic from Des Moines, Idaho, did everything to save his passengers and crew by dutifully landing on the tiny provincial runway. With his skillset, Kovic was an obvious target for the group, and the clean cut pilot is now a new shell for one of Novek's guards.

As Kevon walks across the tarmac at the isolated airport north of Glasgow, Montana, he momentarily stops in his tracks. He looks around to Don and Emilia.

"Did you hear that?" he asks them.
"Yes," Don replies.
"It's him."
"What are you going to do?"
"He's got Nuvo, I can sense it. It's time to take care of things once and for all."
"Are there more of us in there?" asks Emilia.
"A few. Not many," Kevon replies.
"So, we'll come with you?" she asks, hesitantly.
"Not this time. You and the others need to find new shells, and head North. They'll be looking for you as you are now."
"Manitoba?" asks Don.
"Yes. This is where we part company. You have to have access there to as many partners as possible in the reproduction phase. Your biology, biochemistry, physiology; they're all exactly like humans with the advantage that you will be virus-free. This is the key. They have enough to worry about with the virus that you will be approved for settlement status, especially if you take shells from nearby. Avoid brain scans, or any lie-detector tests if you possibly can. Those might show up some anomalies, but like I told you, act normally and improvise. You are ninety-nine point nine percent undetectable."

Don and Emilia nod, and wave the others to come and join them as they approach the small terminus, no more than what appears to be a bus shelter.

"You are not going to bring the others?" asks Don.

"We have cells in England, France and soon Germany. Those brave soldiers will start their own programmes. Some of them will join me in the field if they hear the sound. I'll bring the rest from the Kark temple, and any remaining in the humans' field. But my group will go to Alaska. I will run a check on that settlement, and join you in Manitoba later if possible. It will not be long till I put out a call, but do not travel to the field until you get that. It will be dangerous for you until the humans and Nuvo are dead. Are you clear?"

Don and Emilia nod.

"Good. I'll leave it to you to tell the others. Remember that your role is to infiltrate, reproduce, maintain cover. This is a long game now. This planet will be ours in good time. Now, you must get transport and make your way north. Remember the temperature difference there. You will need better clothes."

And with that, the skinny, floppy-haired youth with the big teeth and bigger smile, jogs over to the shelter.

——-

"Did you hear that?" asks Mal.
"Hear what?" Carlos replies.
"That call. The guy shouting. Did you hear?"
"I heard nothing, amigo. Nada. In fact, the only thing I can hear is the crickets and the only thing I can see are those firebugs."

Mal feels queasy, and it shows.

"My friend, you look like you seen a ghost. You need a little cooling down? You wanna go and see Sonia? I think she likes you, dude. Go on. Go see the nurse, amigo!" Carlos tells him, letting out a sleazy chuckle as he lights up.

Mal makes his way over to the RV. There are a couple of the others inside, so he ducks around the back and lies flat under the clear sky, responding to the call.

—-

In the long dormitory, the lights are dimmed and the small group of women are lying quietly, most awake and listening closely. Carla has already got up, and is the only one putting her clothes on.

"What are you doing?" whispers a young polish woman named Marta.
"I'm getting dressed."
"Where are you going?"
"I'm not going anywhere. I'm staying right here," Carla comes back. "I just don't want to be cold. Are you joining me?"

As each one of the five women gets dressed and gathers at the dormitory door, outside they can hear their male counterparts. As they open the door, Carla ushers the men in, telling them to be quiet. Soon, the dormitory is full and everybody chooses a bed, preparing to dual.

—-

Ellis Garfield stands behind Gill, on Gill's strict instructions. A massive blast of superconducting fluctuations has just resonated throughout the field, and for a moment, the reeds lie flat, the vast entirety of the quantum vacuum visible as far as the eye can see. Gill scans the horizon. Nothing obvious, but at the moment he broadcast that wave, two or three darker dots seem to appear and then disappear. Very possibly Karks.

"You sure we should be here alone?" asks Garfield.
"No," answers Gill. "But it's too dangerous to let any more of our guys get captured. That's the point."

As the reeds begin to unfurl and regain their height, Gill sees the sharp bolt of lightning on the far left side of the field up ahead.

He can't ignore it this time. He must discover if, as Catherine believes, that is Beth again. His senses feel on fire, and with so much to focus on, it's difficult for him to calibrate positive and negative energies, especially with a Kark standing so close.

"I don't like this," Garfield complains.
"Ssshhhh…"

Gill begins to feel a change in atmospherics, his super-sensitivity in this place - *his* place - allowing him advanced notice of an imminent arrival. As the air thickens, and newly-formed condensed matter generates in the reeds facing him, he knows that Novek is approaching. And as intimidating as that is, it's part of the plan.

"Stay close, Nuvo," he orders Garfield. "He'll need you alive to open the fence again. Stay away from him, even if I am in trouble. Follow the plan. If you see anything happen to me, use the porthole back to Langley."

Garfield can't speak, instead creeping closer to Gill.

"What's that?" Gill asks, as a high-pitched whizzing sound seems to fill the air.
No sooner has Gill begun to raise his head to squint into the sun as a white-hot arrow shoots past his left shoulder, slamming into corn reeds behind him. Others are following, hard on its heels.

Whisshh. Whisshh. Sshhhtoop.

"Ahhghhh!" Garfield yells as he hits the ground as quickly as the arrow pierces his shoulder.
"Fuck," Gill exclaims, as he drags the injured Nuvo over to the edge of the reeds. He quickly grabs the arrow and, in an act of seeming cruelty, whips the arrowhead out quickly. Garfield screams in pain, Nuvo's human response to pain hard to listen to.

As a couple more arrows whizz past into the reeds, Gill can smell burning. He'll not have much time before he needs to move.

He gently places his hand inside Garfield's jacket and presses on his wound, focusing some energy into his fingertips.

"This might hurt," he tells Garfield, as heat energy begins to seal the wound from the arrow, his fingers acting to stitch up the skin. In this place where matter warps and time dilates, it is a particularly visceral action, and maybe it isn't real. But Gill needs Nuvo in one piece, wherever they are.

"Sorry. Had to be done. Stay here. Stay low," Gill tells him.

With a plethora of nature's performance-enhancing chemicals surging through his body, anger is building inside the owner of the field. He cannot - *will* not - let them run amok. To do so will jeopardise everything he and Catherine have gone through to get to where they are now.

Gill is hunched over Garfield, wound tight like a ball of elastic, the potential energy increasing exponentially and about to be released. Heightened vision, hearing, touch come to the fore, and Gill leaps up, taking to the skies. This time there is no more jumping, bouncing or leaping. Hang time is infinite. He shoots hundreds of feet into the endless bright blue above, and scans the field. Ten or so of the Kark-humans are striding towards the clearing, some holding hammers, some bows, and yet others with what look like rifles.

Without hesitation he shoots downwards with the speed of a military jet, spraying the field in front of the Karks as a flamethrower, setting the reeds on fire. Blazing stalks quickly carry the flames and Gill hears screams. Looking back he can make out several Kark forms burning.

A sudden flash of lightning and thunderous sound of cracking from the far side of the field pervades and perturbs the air so much, he loses his balance and falls, much like an aircraft would do in extreme turbulence. Righting himself at about fifty feet, he orientates himself towards the clearing. A small figure is rushing across the flattened centre circle towards Nuvo at the edge. Gill knows it's Novek, who's approaching at speed.

As Gill descends and swoops in towards the fast-moving Kevon Clark, Gill flies directly into his path, causing the two to tumble and roll several times back and away from Garfield's prostrate body.

"Get up!" cries Gill, initially to Garfield, who starts to gather himself and get back on his feet. But so too does the diminutive Kevon.

"I'm getting tired of you, Detective. It's time for you to leave." And with that Novek launches a light-rock directly at Gill. It hits him straight in the stomach, causing him to bend over double and howl in pain.

Garfield quickly approaches Gill, grabbing him by the arm and retreating away from the powerful Novek.

"Wait!" cries Gill. "I'm not going anywhere."

Gill is holding his stomach, using his healing hands to repair his injury. But it's not quick enough. The figure of Kevon Clark approaches, taking control. Transforming to Novek in a flash, and taking on the now familiar black and purple form, he forms his limb into a spear, and raises it, ready for the kill.

The jagged spear appears above Gill's head, and as it lifts to its apex, the sun is blocked from his view, leaving only the silhouette of the large Kark Sultan as Gill's final vision. The spear begins to descend.

"No."

The very edge of the opal spearhead, where the metal will meet Gill's skull begins to slow down. Slower. Slower. Slower. Stop. The blade halts a fraction of an inch above Gill's temple. Time has come to rest. Freeze frame. The air is still. Novek may be conscious but unable to move. Likewise, everything in the field. Even the crackling of the reeds as they burned behind comes to a stop. Silence.

Gill carefully moves his head to avoid being grazed by the blade. Rolling over to one side, he first crouches, then gets to his feet. He is in a three-dimensional still photograph, able to move freely among the characters. At first he is elated, and reflects on what made this work. Right now, he doesn't know. Condensed matter in a quantum vacuum could behave in a number of exotic ways, but the intense effect of the force he used has rooted everything to the spot. Even the wind has disappeared.

But how long will this last? His adrenalin is returning, as is awareness of his surroundings, and his vision. Over to his right, Carla and the rest of the duallists are in limbo, all carrying various tools and blunt instruments. It's an impossible scenario, and one in which he must kill Novek first, to dissuade the rest of the Karks from attempting to infiltrate further by kidnapping more of the human duallists.

"Damn!" he exclaims, realising that Carla and the others have come to help out of loyalty and bravery, yet have potentially left themselves open to capture.

As he approaches Novek, Gill registers that the dark Kark leader is conscious, his eye glistening behind a disturbing stare.

"I make no apology for what I am about to do. You have left me no choice," Gill proclaims, as he forms his fist into a white-hot rock of light. He draws back his arm, about to deal Novek a catastrophic blow to the head.

Click.

Before he can start his forward punching motion, Gill is battered by an almighty blow to his ribcage. Reacting in agony with a howl of agony, he falls to his knees. He can sense that movement is returning to the space. It's a frightening moment, and one in which Gill is once again vulnerable.

Above him stands Mal Baines. He is preparing a savagely violent death blow to Gill's head. All Gill can hear is high-pitched clicking and clucking madly patterned in the painful spectrum of sound frequencies. He can hardly bear it.

No sooner does this madness reach a crescendo than Gill sees the large frame of Mal hitting the ground beside him. Gill looks around quickly. Novek is coming to, but Nuvo has disappeared. Was that Nuvo?

Gill checks the porthole where he and Nuvo entered the clearing. It's open. As he turns back to deal with Novek, the Karkian form is racing off, hovering away at speed into the reeds on the far side of the clearing.

"Shit."

Gill takes chase. This time, weakened by the body blows, he can't fly. He runs as fast as he can, trying to spot Novek's trail.

"Gill!" cries Carla from behind him. "Gill!"
"Go back! Close the reeds!" he shouts back. "Don't leave the reeds open!" He screams at the top of his voice, hoping that she'll hear.

As he frantically searches the far side of the clearing, Gill's efforts seem in vain. Novek and the Karks have disappeared. The only way to find out if they are still in the field is to rise above the clearing. Breathing hard and summoning what little he has left, he tries to spring up and into the sky. But the legs will not respond. He drops to his knees, dejected. Having lost Nuvo, the only saving grace is that more Karks did not get through. But he can't count that as a success. This plan has failed.

—-

Carla orders the rest of the duallists to return, which they duly do, seeing her as the one with the most command in the wormhole. Before she leaves, Carla gives one last long scan of the space. Focusing round, Gill is kneeling across from her on the far side of the clearing. He looks hurt, so instinctively she takes a step towards him, before stopping in her tracks.

In the sky above her, and through the glare against the sun, she hears a rush. A large bird hovers over her, some fifty or so feet above. It swoops down and over to Gill, and Carla can see it lift Gill up and off over the reeds into the distance. There is an air of eerie calm about this, and Carla senses the bird is familiar. Powerful, yet peaceful.

Carla is now alone, among the quiet in the clearing. The wind brushes her face, and she realises how beautiful a place this can be. But not today. As the remains of the acrid smoke reach her nose, she checks for fires or flames behind her. Nothing. Just the breeze. She turns and walks slowly back into the reeds.

—-

As Gill's eyes begin to focus to the distance, he is immediately struck by the tranquility all around. He is high in the sky, held only by the claws of a giant bird. He shouldn't feel safe, but he does. Up here, Gill can see practically everything. To his left up ahead, that lightning on the glitchy horizon continues to flicker and twitch. To his right, he spots some tiny figures, scrambling through the reeds. He knows one of them is Nuvo. It's unclear if Nuvo is leading the group, or the group are marching him over towards the fence.

"First thing is to get Nuvo," comes Catherine's soft voice.
"Is that you?" Gill asks.
"Yes. Don't ask."
"But, how can you…"
"Anti-gravity. But we can do this later. Right now, we're going to find out what's going on there. Hang on."

The huge golden eagle swings down and quickly over the Karks, now clearly marching Nuvo against his will over to the join between Kark and Earth. As they land, the eagle ruffles all of its feathers, transforming beautifully to a radiant and smiling Catherine.

"How did you…?" Gill stutters.
"It's just an appearance, you'll see," Catherine replies.
"You really shouldn't be here," Gill remarks.
"You think, huh…?"
"But you sure got the hang of this place," smiles Gill.

Catherine offers a broad smile, and Gill is captivated by her beauty.

Click-ik-ik. Click-ik.

"Quick!" Gill whispers. "Over there!"

They look around to the wavering reeds about twenty feet away, clearly signalling the arrival of the Karks. Catherine scurries away into the reeds while Gill braces himself.

The Karkian form of Nuvo immediately spots Gill, and his large eye blinks repeatedly, which Gill wishes he could interpret somehow. Nuvo's body simultaneously flushes bight yellow, a warning sign to the guards behind him, who move forward, raising their limbs into sharp spears and pointing them straight ahead at Gill.

Gill raises a slight smile for Nuvo, trying to indicate that things will be OK. In the same instant, Gill launches a series of waves which pulse though the air in front of the guards, just enough to cause a rippling effect that distorts the visual field. In this moment, the huge golden eagle claws savagely at the limbs of two guards, ripping the spears from the body and causing a frenzy of clucking and gutteral noises which Gill takes to be Kark screams. The first two guards fall to the ground, releasing small clouds of pink vapour, each one's ventricles flapping frantically while the bodies begin to convulse.

As the eagle flies up and discards the spears, Gill hurls a large light-rock at the next two in the squad. It's only strong enough to stop the guards in their tracks, and they quickly regroup and lunge towards him. As they do so, Nuvo turns and faces the guards, this time forming his own limb into a wide pitchfork and spearing the two guards in the lower torso, rendering them incapacitated. The remaining guards, realising their plight, turn and flee back into the reeds.

Gill begins to give chase.

"Wait! Gill!" cries Nuvo. "Leave them, they won't come back unless I call them."

"But…" says Gill, as he stops and turns back to Nuvo.

"Please let these guards go. Given the choice, they will opt to leave. I know it," Nuvo asserts.

As Catherine reappears, she turns to Nuvo.

"Can we trust that you won't take the path back to Kark? I might do that…if I were you," Catherine asks Nuvo.

"I only want these guards to have safe passage back to my homeland. They will be treated fairly on their return, and will tell others of what Novek tried to do here," Nuvo responds. "I have agreed to help you, and I will. But you must promise me that we will return here soon, so that I may also go home."

Catherine looks to Gill.

"It's already decided," he tells her.

Gill and Nuvo help the injured guards over to the boundary, where Nuvo and Gill manage to force open the rip in the fence. It takes an almighty effort, and soon with Nuvo's high frequency callout to the last of the two guards, they too return and, with a few clicks of encouragement from Nuvo, take flight through the gap.
Shuddering suddenly, Nuvo signals that other Karks may be approaching from the Kark side, and all three work quickly to mend the wire fence, avoiding the barbs.
Repairs completed, Gill stands back while flashes of brilliant white light and violent stretches and bends of the black sky above the fence threaten to burst and rip open.

"Will that hold?" he asks Nuvo.
"I don't know, but from the other side we could only get through the fence itself."
"Guys. We don't have time for this. I need to get out of here, and so do you, Nuvo," Catherine asserts.

Gill gives Catherine a quizzical look.

"What?" she retorts. "You've got Beth waiting to see you, remember? She's over that side. I suggest you hurry up."

Gill smiles at her.

"So you don't want Nuvo to come with me?" he asks her.
"It's too early. Go see her. Talk to her. Find out what *she* wants. Nuvo is on our team, now. Right Nuvo?"

Nuvo flushes green, then a deep purple.

"Now, go on. But Gill," she says.

"Yeh?"

"Don't be too long. Things are getting really ropey back there, and we *all* need you back."

The prospect of seeing Beth sparks such emotion in Gill he could burst, yet the elation is tempered by parting from his true love. For a second, it is overwhelming.

He and Catherine embrace, fighting the impulse to linger on together.

"This is our place. You'll know when I am back," Gill says.

Catherine nods, and radiates a smile before carrying Nuvo off back to the clearing.

—-

* * * *

CHAPTER 12: KODIAK

"All set?"

"Yes, Sir. Air Force Six is on the runway now, Sir."

Mitch Nicolescu and four heavily armed military guards are deep in the basement of the President's war bunker, accompanied by Al Mason, Joe Becker and Maria Ortega.

"You know you don't have to do this, John?" Becker informs Montgomery.

"I know, Joe. But we've spent a lot of money, energy and resources to get these places operational and secure. They need this."

"We've got the itinerary pretty slimmed down, Mr. President," Maria Ortega chips in. "We'll be back in under sixty hours if we stick to it."

"OK. Give me a couple of minutes with Ava, will you. I'll be right there."

The members of the entourage retire to the adjoining breakout area next to the main control room, leaving Montgomery and Redmond visible through the large window.

"Thanks for making the journey, Ava. I expected to have longer with you, but last night I realised that I have to show these communities we mean business, and that they are our future, for now."

"Glad I made it in time, Sir. And for what it's worth, I think it's a brave and bold decision that will help everyone involved."

"Thank you, Ava. I appreciate that. You'll understand I need to give them some longer-term outlook."

"Yes, Mr. President, I understand, Sir."

"So, what's your advice? What would you say to these guys?"

Ava pauses, looking over at the huge screen dominating the far wall of the Ops room.. There's a rolling four-way split video showing scenes from Moscow, Beijing, New York and Los Angeles.

The parallels are frightening. Running gun battles between masked rioters and police and army convoys spill onto screen from downtown areas in each city, with many iconic buildings ablaze. In Times Square, the enormous LCD displays used to show adverts and public information films are damaged from gunfire and other projectiles, causing most videos to be fractured into incomprehensible pieces. Below them, lifeless bodies lie on the ground while others can be seen running through the square carrying anything from piles of clothes, to hessian sacks of vegetables and partial animal carcasses. In Moscow's Red Square, hundreds of masked rioters dressed in black have overcome a police water-canon truck and its crew, who can be seen being battered with sticks. Each scene is shocking in its own right, and Ava feels the simultaneous revulsion and sadness that any human would feel. But she has to focus, and help her President, the man she knows has come back from the dead, only to be forced to manage the worst catastrophe the world has faced since the Black Death.

"I'd be honest, Sir. I'd tell them that if this had happened a year ago, we'd be in big trouble, but that we've put together a gargantuan programme of innovation in quick order which has led to some amazing discoveries that mean we stand a fighting chance of getting through this thing," she replies.

"That's good. I like that. But I need more. I need some detail. Give me your appraisal of our best shot among these special projects we have funded."

"Well, in my opinion, Sir, we are spread-betting to allow us maximum security. Centronus One launches in a few days. I'd tell them that we're likely to have a sister settlement on Mars within two weeks - keep it short so you get buy-in. I'd tell them that our guys are up there orbiting us right now and building the light-sail that can take up to twenty passengers over there on a regular basis," Redmond suggests.

"Hhmm. Those small numbers might panic them, but yes, worth a shot. And CAT? Those security breaches are a real problem, huh…"

Redmond moves away from the screen and clicks her way over to John Montgomery, eye-balling him with intent.

"The younger settlers are more likely to believe that there *is* another way, another future. You could relay the news that some very capable people have credible experimental evidence that a working portal in space and time is within our control. Actually *functioning* and providing a new form of travel. And that it gives us the prospect of superfast emigration. I'd say to Mars. Nearer the better."

"OK, Ava, maybe you should give the speech," Montgomery replies, and the two share a smile. Montgomery is fond of Redmond, and rates her beyond many others. But right now, he needs to be careful that his judgement is not clouded with personal preference.

"Level with me. How much of that is true and how much do I need to pare back against that optimism?" he asks.

"I've seen things, Sir, that frankly supersede Area 54. I know that this reality is just one among many, and that maybe a year ago I might not have believed I'd be talking to you, right here, right now."

Montgomery nods.

"Hhmm. I have that residual memory about Ellis. Somewhere. It still makes little sense to me, but yes, when we come to a fork in the road, we need to decide."

"Sometimes we don't decide, John. Sometimes others decide for us. We just need to trust that they are on our side."

Montgomery stands a little more upright, buttoning his jacket.

"OK. Good. I'm going to use this visit to announce that we will be putting more funding into all these projects, including CAT. But you know what would be the best proof that CAT is working for us?"

"Sir? Ava asks, puzzled.

"Get one of your 'duallists' to dual to Kodiak. Set it up. We'll introduce him or her to the audience there, and show a live stream of their double back in Langley. We can do that, right? I mean, that's probably simple for one of your guys?"

"Not *that* easy, Sir. And such a demonstration might make it clear that others could potentially use this technique too. Russians. Chinese. You know. Also, don't mention aliens - that would be bad," she says with a smile.

Montgomery lets out a small chuckling sound, trying to contain his amusement as Ava strides on with her thoughts.

"Besides, most duallists are still inexperienced and rely on clear pathways and signs from those in the other location. Some are more advanced, but those guys are pushing forward on the exoplanet discovery. I'd not want to divert them from that for the sake of a PR opportunity." As she hears herself saying this, Ava is aware that Montgomery has noted her apparent cynicism. "I mean, I understand that it would be incredibly powerful and inspiring to show them dualling in action…" she follows up at speed.

Montgomery smiles.

"You're on form, today, Ava. But I get it. OK, no live action then, but give me *something*. I need to show some form of progress on this as it's the real big hope."

Ava is desperate to take out a cigarette and light up. Instead, she about turns and clicks her way across to the big screen. Live fire can be seen coming from all around Los Angeles City Hall.

"Tell them the truth. Tell them that you survived an assassination attempt back in April thanks to the first duallist, who intervened in the nick of time. Let them know that there are many more with these abilities, and that they will provide a protection force for the new settlements. No-one can tell this story the way you will, John, and I know this will have many parallels that will give them the reassurance and hope that you need them to have," Ava tells him.

Montgomery nods, and signals to Nicolescu that he is coming.

"Thanks, Ava. Keep going with CAT. I know it's got legs. I can feel it. And thanks for your advice. Appreciate your input."

—

The black Ford E350 trundles past the sign for Sterling on the highway down to Homer along the rugged coastline of southern

Alaska. At the gas station restroom back at Copperville, Kevon Clark forced the trucker next to him into one of the cubicles, shedding his human shell and engulfing the terrified and unsuspecting American, infusing himself into the body and taking charge of Billy Hancock.

At the embarkation point at Homer, a small group of passengers line up for security checks. It's less formal and rigorous than up at Anchorage, and most folks seem to be getting through quickly.

"ID please," asks the rosy-cheeked security officer.

Hancock shows his ID, driver's licence, health card and firearms licence.

After scanning for temperature, the guard plugs Hancock's health card into the scanning machine, waiting patiently for a green, or red, light. A few beads of sweat make their way onto the large trucker's forehead. Eventually, the officer looks up.

"You going round trip?"
"Yes, Sir. Got ten sacks of assorted seeds, four cornflour, four wheat, and ten crates of tinned food. All stamped," Hancock replies.
"OK. Guns?"
"Just the hunting rifle. Kodiak bears."
"Not many attacks, but better safe than sorry. You got your security slip?"
"Only what they gave me. Here…" he offers the guard the border control pass he found in the truck, used to get in and out of the Canadian border control quickly.
"Hhhmmm, this ain't a settlement security slip. They didn't give you one of those?"
"Guess not. It was crazy in Seattle. I just followed what my boss told me, Mister. Didn't ask no questions."

The security guard looks at Hancock up and down. In need of a shave, the driver is dressed in a light overcoat, the bottom buttons on his red checked shirt undone revealing a significant middle-aged spread above the standard issue blue jeans turned up at the ankle where they hit his boots. If there were ever a stereotype of a truck driver, this guy fits the bill pretty nicely. The clincher is in the face, however. Hancock's natural look is open, slightly goofy, as if he is confused most of the time.

"Alright. The system is still new down there. I see you guys got a lot of trouble in Seattle."

"For sure. Folks running scared. I ain't looking forward to going back," Hancock tells him.

"I don't blame you, fella. OK, carry on."

After all the vehicles embark, the ferry engines start up and the rusting lump of floating metal makes its way out to sea. An hour or so later, into the gulf of Alaska, Hancock can see the large island of Kodiak up ahead.

—-

"My fellow Americans…"

There is an audible murmuring among the large crowd gathered in the car park outside Kodiak public library, the opening line in the President's speech reminiscent of his famous forebears. Some four thousand people, practically all of the population currently on land, are in attendance, the remainder out at sea fishing, or manning utilities in and around the island.

John Montgomery is on a makeshift stage, some twenty or so feet across, erected at short notice for the President's visit. He stands behind a lectern hastily purloined from the local high school, and a public address system that crackles intermittently and occasionally screeches with feedback due to a loose connection and the biting wind that streams across the open space.

"Thank you for coming out in the cold today, and to all of you who, like me, have journeyed here to participate in the Kodiak programme, I say 'you will not be disappointed in the hospitality that these fine folks show visitors, nor be short of anything you need here.'"

As a modest ripple of applause waves across the crowd, Mitch Nicolescu scours the scene from side-stage, spotting the individuals in his team of ex-SEALS dotted around the location. As this is bear country and carrying hunting rifles or private arms is normalised, Mitch is especially anxious. That's why he has insisted that the crowd be vetted, one-by-one, throughout the day to ensure maximum safety.

On the roof of the library, several snipers scan the crowd continuously. Further spotters lie over at Rezanov Drive and the Brewing House on Lower Mill Bay. Among the crowd, thirty-five government agents mingle in civilian clothing, while around the perimeter of the car park, a line of military guards keep a close watch for any unusual activity.

Montgomery looks around, and over to the Marina area down towards the sea.

"You have a wonderful home here. This is the perfect place for us all to do our duty. To ensure that the future of the United States of America is secure, stable, and productive. I am delighted to be with you today, not only to show my personal support, but also to officially announce that the Kodiak programme will be the primary site for our sustainable future…"

Montgomery leaves a pause, and the crowd duly clap, slowly at first but then growing in volume. The islanders' future is not only a new focus for investment and growth, but it is also at the frontier of their nation's survival.

"Today, under these crisp blue skies, I want to tell you about what your country is doing to keep ahead of GARID-7, and also the troubles that you must all have seen coming out of some of our cities. Feel reassured that our police, and our military, have maintained control despite some difficult circumstances. Now, you might feel distant from the hurly burly of New York, or Detroit, or Los Angeles. Heck, even Anchorage, right?"

There is an audible chuckle round the crowd. Kodiak people have to go to Anchorage, but don't have much time for some of the city folks there.

"Well, let me take this opportunity to update you on some exciting, and I *mean* exciting, things that we are doing to ensure that

America, and its people, continue to thrive in a world where, in future, very few things are going to stay the same. Folks, we need to embrace change in this time. Many of you are here because you have been invited through the New Earth initiative, and others will be the hosts for this programme designed to create a brand new type of community. One where American values, respect for your neighbour, prosperity and growth across all areas of life, will be the key to a wonderful new world, post-GARI and post-conflict."

Montgomery pauses, as another ripple of applause circulates round the crowd.

In the earpieces of Joe Becker and Maria Ortega, Mitch Nicolescu can be heard advising 'Brown bear northeast one-twenty, approximately one hundred yards'. The pair look around and, sure enough, behind them, just visible is one of Kodiak's bears, ambling nonchalantly down the slope behind the grounds of the library. One of the snipers is the next to come over the airwaves. 'Got it. In range,' comes the voice.

Maria shuffles rather uncomfortably in her library chair, the hard wood bottom even colder out here in the car park. She's hoping her President will make this quick.

The film crew down on Lower Mill Bay Road, usually pre-occupied with stories about bears, don't bat an eyelid at the sight of the Kodiak brown clumsily struggling with some shoots from a tree up and to the left of Montgomery. Zooming in, they have a perfect view of the handsome, camera-friendly John Montgomery and his striking features. Soon Montgomery's face fills the screen as the camera pans in to focus on his expressions and detailed features.

The irony is that their footage will never be seen. Neither will any reports from today, as the government secures the communication channels, internet provider substations, private virtual networks, and all biocell-based communications, intercepting and modifying messages in, and out of, Kodiak island.

—-

As the President's speech is piped through on Kodiak radio, Billy Hancock is listening intently through a small FM receiver.

"Blah, Blah, Blah…" he finds himself saying, in between involuntary clicking sounds.

The Ford van is parked up just before the Near Island Bridge and Billy has rented a boat for the day. As he strolls across the bridge, closed off to vehicles for the President's visit, he looks out to sea, then back to Kodiak city. Alone, and struggling with the cumbersome shell that walks awkwardly and in marked contrast to the nimble Kevon Clark, Billy has a sweat on, even in the cold.

"Stupid," he mutters to himself. "Stupid, stupid, stupid."

——-

"Four major settlements are now in operation across mainland America," Montgomery reports to the crowd. "Kodiak represents the new vanguard. The places where our children will feel safe, have a productive life, where new industries will emerge, and where we can feel secure at night. Know also that your fellow countrymen are settling in new campuses in Iowa, Florida and in Canada too. My pledge to you, here, is that these settlements will be our new frontier, our new beginning. I have instructed the military to ensure that each one of these settlements is impenetrable to external threats. That those who wish any harm to our settlement programme will be dealt with swiftly, fairly and decisively. I can announce today that, from next week, our military and navy will be fully mobile here in Southern Alaska and in the Bering, so that you folks can feel reassured and relaxed. My request…" Montgomery announces, "is that each and every one of you marks this moment. That you take time to consider what is at stake here, and what your individual responsibility is. Just like with the distancing measures that everyone has had to take with GARI, so too must we now, as a virus-free settlement, ensure the sanctity, the impregnability, and the…"

Maria Ortega, feeling somewhat uncomfortable in her freezing cold chair and lack of sufficient clothing for the current circumstances, has shifted in her chair, causing the metal legs to make an equally uncomfortable screeching sound which is picked up on Montgomery's microphone, and pierces through the public address system causing an almighty burst of unwanted frequencies to hit the crowd.

As Montgomery, Joe Becker, Mitch Nicolescu and several guards instinctively react, looking over to Maria, the chief of Homeland Security awkwardly struggles with her balance, her legs having gone numb in the cold air.

Nicolescu is the first to move across the stage, initially focusing on Ortega, realising something seems wrong.

As the shot rings out, much like many shots on Kodiak Island, in the still moment around the sound wave, people seem bemused rather than alarmed. Someone scaring off the Kodiak bear with a warning shot. One of the boat engines in the marina, puttering into motion. A car tyre bursting further down into town. But something is very wrong.

As the second shot rings out, adrenalin rushes through the crowd like one of the giant waves off Mill Bay.

Nicolescu shouts into his close microphone.

"Shooter! Shooter! Man down!" he shouts. "South West. Forty-five degrees, rooftop."

A series of further shots ring out across and above the crowd, causing panic. Up on stage two bodies lie prostrate, and four of the armed guards swiftly form a makeshift ring around both as the crowd begins to disperse in all directions.

"All spotters, report!" shouts Nicolescu.

After an initial silence, two voices come through on the earpiece.

"Possible suspect terminated at Big Ray's."
"No sighting. Repeat, no sighting," comes the latter voice.

As the gravity of the situation hits home, Nicolescu is struggling. This has happened to him before, and he was determined that, as the new Head of Security for the White House, this would not happen again on his watch.

In that moment, a further shot.

"What the…take the goddamn shooter out, now!!" Nicolescu screams down the microphone.

Nicolescu shoots a glance back at the stage, shouting to the most senior guard.

"Bradley, what is the status of the President?!"
"Sir, the President is down, Sir."

—-

Click.

# # #

ABOUT THE AUTHOR

Thank you for reading this book. I really hope you enjoyed it. Do please connect with me online if you like what you read.

Tipton Froy was born in Scotland quite a long time ago. He has studied natural sciences, sociology, psychology, music and languages, and traveled extensively. His writing reflects a quest to figure out the meaning of life.

—

The original book in this series, DUAL, is available at these locations:

https://www.amazon.co.uk/Dual-Tipton-Froy-ebook/dp/B088ZV4L33

https://www.smashwords.com/profile/view/TiptonFroy

Connect:

Mail: tipton.froy@gmail.com
Twitter: https://twitter.com/TiptonFroy
Smashwords: https://www.smashwords.com/profile/view/TiptonFroy
Amazon: https://www.amazon.co.uk/Dual-Tipton-Froy-ebook/dp/B088ZV4L33

www.ingramcontent.com/pod-product-compliance
Lightning Source LLC
Chambersburg PA
CBHW051426170626
46809CB00006B/2342

* 9 7 8 0 9 5 7 5 5 8 8 6 1 *